MAJESTIC

By Ken Warner

For Juno,
the best dog in the world.
We will love you and miss you
always.

"I don't know!"

"You're lying. I can feel it."

Malia reached into Melinda's mind; she could sense her fear growing closer to panic. She truly hadn't known that Malia would be able to do this. Reaching into her memories, Malia found a recent conversation Melinda had had with Lucifer.

"You're making them stronger? Why?" the hybrid asked her boss.

"There is something I need them to do for me."

"But you have us! What do you need them for?"

"They can do things that you cannot."

"But you haven't tested their DNA on us yet! It might work on the hybrids."

"I will not take that risk. You are half-human."

The memory ended there. His last comment confused Malia—their DNA *had* given a human their powers. Why wouldn't he want to give it to the hybrids?

"He wouldn't tell you! And that made you jealous! He has some special purpose for us—something you can't *do, and he won't even tell you about it!"*

"NO! He values us far more than he ever will the two of you! We are superior in every way!"

Malia heard someone else entering the room. She removed herself from Melinda's mind.

"What is going on in here?"

It was Lucifer.

"Nothing, it's... she's fine... I..." Melinda stammered.

"Put her under."

Malia felt the drugs hit her system like a sledgehammer. She fought it—she tried to remove the compound from her bloodstream like she had before. But there was too much; it was like a tidal wave overwhelming her. She sank into darkness.

Malia woke up again, this time lying on the floor of the hangar bay. Sitting up, she took in her surroundings. Wendy Bell was lying flat on her back nearby. Two saucers were floating in the far end of the bay. This was strange—they'd annihilated one of Lucifer's ships with a nuclear grenade. Where had the second one come from?

Through the windows at the closer end, Malia spotted Lucifer watching her.

"Wake up, Ms. Bell," came Lucifer's voice over the speakers.

Wendy stirred and sat up. Malia gasped—the last time she'd seen her, she looked like she was probably seventeen or eighteen years old, tops. Now, she could pass for someone in her mid-thirties.

"Wendy?" said Malia, getting to her feet. "You look... older."

"Huh? What do you mean? I'm eighteen..."

"What's going on with her," Malia demanded of Lucifer.

"It would seem your DNA has accelerated her aging. I would like you to try to stop it."

"*What*? How am I supposed to do that?"

This explained why he didn't want to give their DNA to the hybrids—it might accelerate their aging, too.

"We know that you possess augmented healing powers," Lucifer drawled. "It's the sole power your DNA has conferred upon me. You used that ability to counteract the sedative, which is why we've had to increase your dosage so much."

"What do you mean, 'sole power'?" Malia asked.

"Unfortunately, your DNA has not given me your telekinesis or telepathy. But, of course, it's much more than telepathy, isn't it? You used it to penetrate Melinda's mind. It has become apparent to me that this is how you managed to counteract your brother's sedation—I'd wondered about that before.

"In any event, I would like you to try using that same approach to stop Ms. Bell's rapid aging."

Malia remembered hearing that her mom's original twins, born in ancient Egypt, had experienced rapid aging. It had taken decades to find a way to alter their genes and counteract the effect—ultimately producing her and Jaden. And Malia realized she knew one of the geneticists who'd worked on that project.

"Bomani was the one who edited our genes to eliminate the rapid aging," she said out loud to Lucifer. "Wouldn't this be more his specialty?"

"Yes, well, he did include the alteration he made to your genes in the DNA we used to augment Ms. Bell. As you can see, it didn't work as expected. She is fully human; that sequence must rely on your Othali genes. And in any event, he is no longer here to work on this problem. You are."

"But I can't change her *genes*," said Malia. "And I—"

Malia felt intense pain wrack her body—it was emanating from the back of her neck. She fell to the floor, writhing and screaming. The pain stopped as abruptly as it had started.

"Try," Lucifer said with a smirk.

Malia regained her feet. She reached out to Wendy with her mind; she could feel her fear and confusion.

"Whoa—what are you doing to me?" said Wendy, scrambling to her feet and backing away from Malia.

"*Relax*," Malia said in her mind. "*I'm not going to hurt you, I promise.*"

"What the hell—how are you inside my head? Are you like... telepathic or something?"

"*You are, too, don't you remember? It's the only reason I'm able to communicate with you this way.*"

"*What are you talking about?*"

"*Lucifer gave you some of my DNA. He brought us both here to test your powers—don't you remember?*"

"*I've never seen you before in my life!*"

Malia gave up the effort—Lucifer had clearly suppressed her memories. Instead, she went to work probing Wendy's consciousness; despite her physical appearance, her thoughts felt like those of a younger person. Malia found it difficult to pinpoint how she could tell—but Jaden's mind had felt more youthful, and Melinda's older. Wendy's was closer to Jaden's, although she now looked older than Melinda.

Malia tried to sense Wendy's cells. She could feel the blood coursing through her veins and the residual sedative in her system. But she had no sense of the DNA inside of her cells.

Malia returned to Wendy's mind instead. She tried to access her memories of the last time they'd met in this chamber but found the area dark and murky. Malia imagined shining a bright light on the scene. Slowly, images surfaced—Wendy facing off against her and trying to lift her off the ground. And feelings—the pain Lucifer had inflicted as punishment for Wendy's initial failures.

"Whoa!" Wendy said out loud. "I do remember being here before!"

Malia was torn from Wendy's mind by the agony suddenly ripping through her body. She fell to the floor again, screaming on the top of her lungs.

Moments later, the pain subsided.

"I do not recall asking you to retrieve her suppressed memories," Lucifer's voice drawled over the speakers.

"I can't access her genes!" Malia shouted, getting back to her feet, her breathing heavy. "Beyond her mind, I can heal injuries and control chemicals in her blood, but that's it! I can't even sense my *own* genes—there's no way I can get to hers!"

"Hmm. Very well," said Lucifer. "Sleep now. We'll have one more experiment today."

Malia felt herself growing drowsy. She tried counteracting the sedative they were giving her, but like before, it was overwhelming. Darkness engulfed her.

When Malia woke up again, she was in the hangar bay—again,

or still, she had no way of knowing. Jaden was here this time, still unconscious, also in his spacesuit. Wendy was gone; a young Black woman was lying on the floor.

Malia kneeled by Jaden's side and shook him by the shoulder. He stirred and opened his eyes.

"What are we doing in here?" he asked, getting to his feet.

"You'll see in a moment," Lucifer's voice drawled over the speakers. Malia turned to see him smirking at them through the windows at the rear of the room. "Rise and shine, Ms. Knox."

The woman on the floor woke with a start. Scrambling to her feet, she took in her surroundings and backed away from Malia and Jaden.

"Ms. Kwan, you will attempt to communicate with Ms. Knox telepathically," Lucifer commanded. "She is a normal human; we have not altered her DNA."

"That's not gonna work; we can't talk to humans that way," Jaden observed.

"It might," Malia told him. "I was able to get inside Melinda's mind earlier."

"Are you serious?"

"Enough chit chat," said Lucifer.

Malia turned toward Ms. Knox. The woman backed farther away, eyeing Malia in terror.

"I'm not going to hurt you," Malia assured her.

"*Can you hear me?*" she called out in her mind. Ms. Knox showed no signs of having heard her. Malia concentrated as hard as she could. *"My name is Malia. Do you hear my voice in your mind?"*

The woman couldn't hear her.

"This is no use," Malia said out loud. "It's not—"

Pain exploded inside of her, and Malia fell to the floor. She screamed as her entire body seized up. By the time the agony had subsided, she found Jaden kneeling beside her, trying to console her.

"You're a bastard!" she shouted at Lucifer, getting to her feet and moving toward him. "This has never worked on a full human before! You want the impossible!"

"Nonsense," he drawled. "The hormone treatment we've given you may well enable you to bridge this gap. You're simply not trying hard enough.

"Mr. Kwan. Your turn."

"Yeah, okay," he said, eyeing Lucifer skeptically.

Jaden moved toward Ms. Knox, who promptly backed away, searching for someplace to hide.

"Hey, relax—nobody's going to hurt you," Malia could hear him say telepathically. *"Well, except that shithead out there. He's gonna keep hurting all of us..."*

"Jaden! That's not helpful!" Malia told him.

"So, can you hear me?" he asked the woman. "Yeah, this ain't working," he added out loud to Lucifer.

Jaden fell to the floor, screaming and shaking as if he were having some sort of seizure.

"Jaden!" Malia screamed, running to him and dropping to her

knees beside him. She held him by the arm, but there was nothing she could do to help. He was crying and drooling. "Stop it!" she screamed at Lucifer.

Jaden abruptly relaxed, flopping onto his back and sobbing now. "Try again, Ms. Kwan."

Malia got to her feet and approached Ms. Knox. She had a feeling this *should* work—she'd been able to sense the Malor's thoughts, and Salvatore had heard hers. Melinda was half-human, and Malia had been able to penetrate her mind.

She considered each of those experiences and wondered if it was simply a matter of changing the frequency of her thoughts—almost like tuning a radio. Reaching out with her mind, she tried again to speak to Ms. Knox.

"It's me again—can you hear me?" Malia imagined pitching her telepathic voice higher. *"My name is Malia. Can you tell me your first name?"* Nothing. She tried a lower voice instead. *"How about now? Can you hear this?"*

Ms. Knox suddenly looked startled.

"I heard a voice—in my head! Was... was that you?"

"Yes! Now, answer in your head, not out loud."

"I can hear you! How are you doing this?"

"Well, you probably wouldn't believe me if I told you. What's your first name?"

"Bethany."

"It's nice to meet you, Bethany." Malia gave her a reassuring smile. Reaching out with her mind again, she tried to quell Bethany's fear.

"I can feel you in my head—what are you doing to me?"

"*Relax, I'm only trying to help you calm down,*" Malia told her. "*You have nothing to fear from Jaden or me.*"

"Well done, Ms. Kwan," Lucifer said. "Mr. Kwan, try again."

Jaden gave him a quick glance, then moved closer to Bethany.

"*Hey, it's me again,*" he said.

"*Imagine making your voice lower,*" Malia told him. "*That's what finally worked for me.*"

"*Okay, how's this?*" he asked.

Malia could sense something different but wasn't sure if he was doing the same thing she'd done.

"*Good, I think. Try talking to her. Her name is Bethany.*"

"*Bethany? It's me, Jaden. Can you hear me?*"

She gave no indication that she could hear Jaden.

"This is stupid, man," Jaden said out loud. "There's no—"

Jaden screamed, dropping to the floor again, his entire body convulsing.

"Leave him alone!" Malia screamed at Lucifer.

It ended as quickly as it had started. Jaden got to his knees, panting and sobbing.

"That will do for now," Lucifer told them.

Before Malia could do anything to stop it, the drugs hit her system, and she passed out.

Chapter Two: Venus

Venus stopped by the medical bay to check on Salvatore. A whole month had gone by already since she'd rescued him from the rubble of that building. She'd set his broken bones and performed surgery to repair the damage to his internal organs. His physical recovery had gone well, but he remained in a coma.

She was pretty sure the head trauma had brought on the coma. The accident had fractured his skull, and she worried there would be residual brain damage. There were ways to force him back to consciousness, but she had decided against trying this—yet. His brain needed to heal, and for now, the coma would give him the best chance of achieving a full recovery.

But damn, did she miss him.

They had been lovers and partners for centuries back on Mars before being selected for cryostasis. Being separated for so many years here on Earth had broken her heart. His sudden return to her life had shocked her to the core—she hadn't expected to see him again anytime soon. But of course, he was being noble, trying to protect those human teenagers and stop Lucifer from killing off humanity.

Venus sighed. She stroked Salvatore's face with the back of her hand and kissed him on the forehead.

"You'd better recover, you stubborn old codger."

A tear slipped down her cheek, and she left the medical bay. She went to the hangar to check on progress there. Her team had been making repairs to Salvatore's ship.

"We should be finished today," her chief mechanic told her.

Venus inspected the exterior of the craft; it looked as good as new.

"I've been thinking," she said. "Can we retrofit this antique with the weapon systems we have on my ship? The plasma cannons and fusion missiles?"

"I don't see why not," the mechanic told her. "We'll have to modify the control systems to accommodate them. But it should be doable."

"How long would that take?"

"A few weeks. Maybe a little longer."

Venus nodded. If Salvatore did recover, he'd want to go after Lucifer. Best to make sure he had the tools for the job.

"Do it."

Chapter Three: Malia

Malia woke with a start. She was back in the hangar bay again; Jaden was lying nearby. It was impossible to tell how long they'd been in the compound, now. Since she'd first acquired the ability to communicate telepathically with Bethany, Lucifer had matched her up with several other humans to repeat the skill. Jaden still hadn't been able to do this, although he had also managed to use basic telepathy with the hybrid, Melinda. Malia had allowed him to practice penetrating her mind, and while his facility with this had continued to improve, he'd not been able to do it with Melinda.

Lucifer had brought Malia here twice more with Wendy Bell, demanding that she try to stop Wendy's accelerated aging. The last time Malia had seen her, Wendy looked like a woman in her mid-sixties. Malia had been unable to help and learned from Melinda soon after that meeting that Wendy had died.

"Wake up, Mr. Kwan," Lucifer's voice said over the speakers. "I need a word with you."

Jaden stirred and groaned, finally sitting up.

"What the hell do you want now?" he demanded.

"I have a proposition for the two of you," Lucifer said with a smirk. "There are some things I need to do that I may not be able to accomplish on my own. To this aim, I have tried to give myself your powers, but as you know, other than self-healing, this effort has met only with failure. And considering the deleterious effects the effort had on Ms. Bell—"

"*Deleterious effects*?" Jaden shouted. "It killed her!"

"Yes, so you can understand why I'm reluctant to try the experiment with any of my hybrids," Lucifer drawled. "However, there is another way. If you were to join me, then with your help—"

"You think we'd help you kill all the humans?" Malia said with disgust.

"For the last time, we won't be killing *all* of them, only 99.9% of them—and at any rate, we don't need your help for *that*."

"What, then?" Jaden demanded.

"Let's just say it's a project that is much closer to my heart. Oh, and the body count will be lower by many orders of magnitude."

"Hah!" Malia blurted. "If you think we'd help you kill *anyone*—"

"You would be richly rewarded," Lucifer told them. "I would give you your freedom—well, the freedom to move around the compound, at least. You would live like a king and queen. No longer would you be kept sedated; instead, you could be my right-hand man—and woman."

"Forget it," said Jaden.

"Not a chance," Malia agreed without hesitation. "You're evil— we will never help you."

"Hmm. Well, I figured I'd give the carrot a try for a change. But I always have preferred the stick. Bring her in!"

A few moments later, Malia saw the door to the corridor open. Melinda walked in, forcing a woman into the outer chamber ahead of her. The woman was struggling mightily, her long blond hair flying all over the place. Melinda forced her into the hanger and threw her to the floor, quickly sealing the door again behind her.

"You bitch!" the woman screamed, regaining her feet. "I swear, if it's the last thing I do, you're going to pay for that!"

"Sydney?!" said Jaden.

As the woman pushed the hair out of her face, Malia realized he was right—this was their friend, Sydney Hastings. Or, more likely, one of Lucifer's hybrids using her emitter to create a flawless simulacrum of her.

"It's not her," Malia said to Jaden. "Don't forget about his holograms."

"Oh, right," he said with a scowl. "Yeah, we're not falling for *that* again."

"Malia, Jaden—it's me!" the woman said, approaching them.

But suddenly, she collapsed on the floor, screaming in agony.

"Mr. and Ms. Kwan, meet the stick," Lucifer drawled. "If you refuse to help me, I will torture Ms. Hastings within an inch of her life for as long as it takes for you to change your minds."

"Bullshit," said Jaden. "That's not Sydney!"

The woman's pain seemed to recede; she rose slowly to her feet, moving toward Lucifer.

"You son of a bitch," she screamed, pounding on the window directly in front of him.

"It's a convincing act you're giving," Malia told her, "but we're not falling for it. You must be one of Melinda's step-sisters."

"Malia, it's me," she said, turning to the twins again. "They abducted me—well, I let them this time. We've been trying to figure out who's behind all this. But how did you two get here? You should be in interstellar space by now..."

"I've had enough of this," Malia muttered.

"What are you gonna do?" Jaden whispered.

Malia reached out with her mind, trying to sense this woman's thoughts. She felt her anger more than anything else—she wanted to kill Lucifer and Melinda. Malia penetrated further into her mind. She found her memories of being abducted by Lucifer's flying saucer. And then she uncovered memories of her uncle, Brian Kwan—they were planning to send Sydney here with a tracking device. And there was another man present as well, but Malia didn't recognize him. Suddenly, a memory surfaced of Sydney making love to the man.

"Whoa, hey—what are you doing?" the woman said. "Can you see what I'm seeing? Because that's private!"

"Sydney!" said Malia, withdrawing from her mind. She ran to her and hugged her tight. "It's really you!"

"It is?" Jaden asked, approaching the two of them.

"Good," said Lucifer. "Now that we've established her identity..."

Sydney dropped to the floor again, shrieking in pain. Malia kneeled beside her, but it lasted only a moment.

"Now," said Lucifer. "You have two choices, Ms. and Mr. Kwan. Either you agree to help me, or you will watch as I inflict enough pain on our dear Ms. Hastings to reduce her to a quivering, drooling mass of flesh."

"You unimaginable bastard," said Malia, rising to her feet and moving toward Lucifer.

"We'll give you both some time to consider your options, shall we?" Lucifer asked with a smirk.

The sedative slammed into Malia's system, and she blacked out.

Chapter Four: Salvatore

Salvatore opened his eyes and gasped. Though he could see that he was lying flat on his back in a medical bay, he didn't recognize the place. He felt groggy; his vision was blurry.

"Where am I?" he said.

"In my compound, of course," a voice said.

Looking to his side, he saw Venus standing there, a tear streaming down her cheek. She reached out and stroked his head.

"What happened?" he asked. "We crashed... and the building collapsed on top of me. I don't remember anything after that."

"You were badly injured," Venus told him. "I was watching your progress with my oracle, but when you stopped moving for an entire day, I went to investigate. You were buried under the rubble. I rescued you and your ship and brought you back here. You've been in a coma..."

"How long?"

"Fifty-six days," she said, taking his hand in hers.

"Malia and Jaden—Lucifer must have captured them. We have to get them back."

Salvatore tried to sit up but found he was too weak.

"You need rest," Venus told him.

"I've rested long enough," he retorted. "It is time to take action."

"My dear, you had one foot in the grave when I found you. And for the first few weeks, I didn't think you'd pull through. It was only my care that saved you, and I'm telling you that you need more time to recover!"

Salvatore tried once more to sit up but couldn't manage it.

"Give me the elixir."

When they'd awakened from their cryostasis on Mars, the automated system had pumped a compound into their veins that assisted with their reanimation. It was a powerful stimulant, but the dosage had to be precise—too little would do nothing while too much would kill him.

"Salvatore, no!"

"You must."

"Lucifer will have taken whatever he needs from the twins by now. Whether we retrieve them now or a week from now will make no difference."

"No. It is my duty to rescue them. Give me the elixir."

Venus let out a long sigh.

"I would prefer to wait. I considered using it to bring you out of your coma, but the risk was too great."

"Only because my brain had not yet healed; what do the scans show now?"

"Well, there's no longer any sign of damage, but—"

"You are allowing your personal feelings for me to cloud your judgment. If I were anyone else, you would authorize the treatment."

"I could just knock you out again."

Salvatore fixed her with his steely gaze but said nothing more.

"Alright, fine," she said. "But this is damn irresponsible. Are you ready?"

Salvatore nodded. Moments later, he sensed the elixir hitting his system; it felt like his veins were on fire. He gritted his teeth, but the pain overwhelmed him. His entire body convulsed, and he screamed.

"Salvatore!"

Venus caressed his face; he barely noticed through the agony. But after a few minutes, the pain subsided. He could feel his heart racing, and his vision cleared. Sitting up, he took Venus's hand and squeezed it.

"Thank you."

"You're a fool," she told him. "But it's good to have you back."

"How soon can we leave for Lucifer's compound?"

"Right now, if you want," she replied. "But what is our objective? Rescue the twins and leave?"

"And destroy Lucifer and his compound."

Venus regarded him in silence for a moment, then nodded.

"I'm agreeing to this only because I know that if we don't eliminate him, he will never stop pursuing you. But there's one condition."

"Yes?"

"I'm in charge. We'll take my ship and my militia. And I call the shots."

"Very well," he agreed. "You'll need to download the data about Lucifer's compound from my ship."

"I already have."

"You were able to access the control systems?"

"Only because you designated me as the emergency operator. I initiated the override once I'd brought you here," she explained. "The system recognized your condition and allowed me to take control."

Salvatore followed her out of the medical bay and through the tunnel to the hangar.

"I'll have Captain Flint assemble a strike team," she told him. "He's recovered from his encounter with that girl; Perry will remain here with a small detachment."

Venus conferred with Flint. Salvatore noted his saucer docked next to Venus's—it looked like she'd saved the ship, too. Ten minutes later, Salvatore and Venus boarded her saucer with Flint and a dozen soldiers. Salvatore joined her in the cockpit; he noted her oracle sitting on the floor by her seat. She guided the ship out of the hangar bay, and they shot into the sky.

As they approached the Arizona desert, Venus took them in low. It was almost sunset, and the nearby buttes cast long shadows on the ground.

"The hangar bay is in the cliff face right over there," Salvatore said, pointing out the area. "You can blast through the doors with your plasma cannons?"

"Patience, darling," she replied. "First, we do some reconnaissance."

"For what purpose?"

"To help reduce our casualties, of course. If we're going to put my men in harm's way, we'll do everything we can to ensure their survival. Now. You say Lucifer is down to one saucer?"

"Yes. He used to use one to abduct the humans and the other for his own personal transport. My guess is that he must use the remaining ship for his own activities during the day, and for the abductions at night."

"Very well. We will monitor his activities for a few days and establish any pattern to his movements. It would be best to mount the rescue mission while Lucifer is away."

"But we must destroy him."

"Of course, darling. His minions will alert him when we infiltrate the compound. Once he returns, we will eliminate him and obliterate the complex."

Salvatore let out a long sigh.

"Your logic is unassailable as always."

They sat for a few moments in silence.

"Well, this is interesting," said Venus.

"What is?"

"There are two humans nearby. One due south of here, the other due north."

"What are they doing?"

"Nothing. Sitting around."

"That is strange," Salvatore observed. "They will be in grave danger should Lucifer take notice."

Soon after darkness fell, they saw Lucifer's saucer leave the hangar bay and launch into the sky.

"It must be going out to conduct the abductions," said Salvatore.

About an hour later, they saw a saucer appear out of nowhere in the canyon and move inside the hangar.

"That's odd," said Salvatore. "I've never seen him take the abductees in through the hangar before."

Only minutes later, another saucer appeared over the desert, only about a hundred yards from Venus's ship.

"Two ships," said Venus. "It appears you were mistaken."

"No," Salvatore replied. "We vaporized his second ship with a fusion grenade. He must have built a new one since then."

"So, Lucifer must have returned on the one that docked in the hangar bay," Venus observed.

As they watched, a man descended from the hatch in the bottom of the vessel. He floated toward a butte. As he approached, an opening appeared in the rock, and the man moved inside. Minutes later, a man and a woman emerged from the butte and floated over to the saucer. They disappeared inside, and the aperture in the butte closed again. Seconds later, the ship rose into the sky and streaked away.

Over the next several hours, the ship reappeared many more times, depositing one or two more victims per trip and flying away with one or two others. Finally, returning from one last voyage near dawn, it moved into the hangar after dropping off its passenger near the butte.

"Done for the night," Venus observed.

Just after sunrise, she reported that the two humans on the ground were moving away.

"Why don't you get some sleep," Salvatore suggested. "I will keep watch."

"Nonsense. You're the one who needs the rest."

"I slept for almost two months."

"Obstinate old man," she muttered.

Venus slept for a few hours. A little after noon, one of Lucifer's saucers shot out of the hangar.

"That should be Lucifer," said Salvatore.

Not long before sunset, the two humans returned to the area. And once darkness had fallen, the second spacecraft took off into the night. An hour later, the first saucer returned, moving directly into the hangar. And throughout the night, the abduction ship transported humans to and from Lucifer's compound. It docked in the hangar bay before dawn, and then the people on the ground departed soon after.

The process was repeated on the third day. But that night, when the abduction ship dropped off a blond woman, Salvatore started in surprise.

"What is it?" asked Venus.

"Bring up an image of that woman, please."

A hologram of the human appeared in the center of the cockpit.

"That's her," Salvatore said.

"Who?"

"Her name is Sydney—the twins' friend. When we infiltrated the compound, one of the hybrids disguised herself as this woman to deceive us."

After the saucer took off again, they noticed the humans on the ground moving toward the butte with the hidden entrance.

"And now I believe I know who one of those men might be," Salvatore said. "I need to go down there."

Salvatore hurried down to the bottom level. Venus had opened the hatch; he dropped down to the desert floor, moving toward the humans, pulling the hood of his sweatshirt over his head. As he drew closer, he recognized Brian Kwan from Lucifer's simulacrum; the second man was not familiar. They were examining the surface of the butte where Sydney had gone inside.

"This doesn't look naturally occurring," said Brian.

"The tunnel to the elevator is inside here," the other man said. "I'm certain of it. This is where they took me."

"Sydney must be in there," said Brian.

"Yes, she is," Salvatore told them.

They turned to face him, the unknown man pointing a light toward him.

"Who the hell are you?" he demanded.

"You may call me Salvatore," he said. "Your friend is in grave danger, and it is up to us to save her."

"You're not human," Brian Kwan said; it was not a question.

"Correct," Salvatore replied. "Please, come with me—we must hurry."

"Do you have something to do with the abductions?" Brian demanded.

"No—but one of my kind does."

"The man in black?" the other human asked.

"Yes. He is dangerous, and he is here—we need to move before he notices our presence."

"How do we know we can trust you?" the man asked.

"You don't yet. If you come with me now, I will explain everything, and you can decide for yourself. But I believe we share some common objectives."

Brian looked at his partner; he nodded.

"Lead the way," he said.

Chapter Five: Brian

Salvatore led them across the desert. After a few minutes, he stopped and said, "We're here."

"Where, exactly?" asked Brian, scanning the area. He could see nothing but desert.

In the next moment, a bright light shone down on them, and Brian found himself floating up into the air with Miguel and Salvatore. They moved inside a chamber with metallic walls but continued upward through a large, circular area with pods lining the walls; Brian noted about a dozen soldiers wearing camouflage uniforms on this level. Finally, they rose into a smaller circular chamber with transparent walls and plush seats. Sitting in one of the chairs was a woman with scaly skin like Salvatore's and long, dark hair.

"This is Venus," said Salvatore. "Venus, this is Brian Kwan—the twins' uncle, and, I'm sorry, I didn't get your name?"

"Miguel. Miguel San Juan," he said, nodding to Venus.

"A pleasure, I'm sure," Venus drawled.

"Please, have a seat," said Salvatore, sitting down next to Venus. Brian and Miguel took two seats across from them.

"This ship matches the description the abduction victims

have given," Brian observed. "Are the two of you involved with that somehow?"

"We are not," said Salvatore. "One of our brethren runs that operation. We call him Lucifer; you know him as 'the man in black'."

"His eyes—they're like yours," said Miguel. "Like a cat's. But his skin ain't scaly."

"Lucifer utilizes a holographic emitter to make himself look more human," Salvatore told them. "He keeps his eyes that way as a means of intimidation. Without the emitter, he looks like us."

"Where are you from?" asked Brian.

"This is a long story," said Salvatore. "My people come from Mars. The ecosystem there had been dwindling for millennia but collapsed completely tens of millions of years ago. Our civilization fell. The dinosaurs still ruled the Earth, so coming here would have been far too dangerous. Forty-five of us entered cryostasis. In 1938, television broadcasts from your planet triggered the reanimation sequence for our hibernation system. Only twelve of us survived; we came to Earth."

"I'm sorry, now, hold on," said Miguel, shaking his head. "You mean to tell me you folks are *tens of millions* of years old? How in the hell could you have lived this long?"

"We designed and built our technology to survive the ravages of time," Salvatore replied. "Every system had multiply redundant backup mechanisms. Still, only twelve of forty-five managed to last long enough to journey here.

"Originally, we had hoped to reveal ourselves to your people and peacefully co-exist. But it became immediately apparent that this would not be possible. Humans are violent and fearful of those who are different. Most of us decided it would be best to live in isolation. However, one of our number, Isis, felt differently. She believed we should conquer your planet and subjugate its people. Only Lucifer supported her."

"Isis was what you humans would call a 'psychopath,'" Venus told them. "And Lucifer with her."

"In the end, the only way we could stop Isis was to kill her," Salvatore continued. "Lucifer went on a murderous rampage to avenge her—he was her partner. He killed three of our people before the rest of us finally fled, scattering around the world. Since then, we have lived in hiding."

Brian was having trouble processing this information. Before the Malor invasion, he would have denied that there was any possibility this story could be true. He knew about the Drake equation and understood the incredibly long odds of technologically intelligent life springing up anywhere in the universe. But for it to do so on two separate planets in the same solar system... well, that seemed profoundly unlikely. And yet, here they were.

"And why is Lucifer abducting humans?" he asked.

"He is harvesting human sex cells," Salvatore replied. "Using those, he is breeding half-human, half-Martian hybrids. Only a tiny percentage of humans have compatible DNA. And even then, he must edit the genes before combining them with Martian sex cells. He uses his own cells along with the ones he took from Isis before her death to provide the Martian DNA. Hybrid women carry the fertilized eggs to term. Eventually, he plans to kill off the human population on Earth and install the hybrids as the dominant species."

"Well, this is all fascinating," said Miguel, "and I'm sure we'll want to find a way to stop him from doing that, but right now, we need to rescue Sydney!"

"Yes, we agree," Salvatore replied. "Along with the twins."

"*What?*" asked Brian. "What twins?"

"Your niece and nephew, Malia and Jaden."

This was too much for Brian to take in; they should have been well beyond the bounds of their solar system by now.

"What are you talking about? Lucifer has the twins in his compound?"

"There was a traitor among the Othali," Salvatore explained. "Bomani. Lucifer compromised him during the Malor invasion. He sabotaged the Othali engines, causing them to enter emergency orbit around Mars. When the Othali sent a team down to the surface to explore our abandoned underground city, Bomani accompanied the team—along with Malia and Jaden. He then commandeered one of their shuttles and took the twins back to Earth. I intercepted them and was able to keep them from Lucifer for a time, but in the end, he defeated me and captured the twins."

"When did this happen?"

"The day after the Malor invasion. I was injured in the battle with Lucifer. Venus rescued me and nursed me back to health; I only awoke from the coma a few days ago."

"What does Lucifer want with Malia and Jaden?" asked Brian.

"Can you not guess?"

"Their powers?"

"Yes. He hoped to fuse their DNA with his own and that of the hybrids to give them telekinesis and telepathy. Like us, the hybrids can already defy gravity; adding the twins' powers to their own would make them virtually invincible in battle."

"We need to get them out of there!" said Brian.

"Indeed," Salvatore agreed.

"You folks got a plan?" asked Miguel.

"Yes," said Venus. "We have established a pattern to Lucifer's movements. He departs each day during daylight and returns after nightfall. We will wait until he leaves and then blast our way into his hangar bay. Once inside, we will rescue the twins and your friend, plant explosives inside the compound, and then await Lucifer's return. Once he is inside, we will blow the entire complex to kingdom-come—Lucifer and his hybrids along with it."

"Do you know exactly where in the compound they're keeping them?" Brian asked.

"Yes," said Salvatore. "Venus?"

Suddenly, a holographic image appeared in the center of the cockpit.

"How did you do that?" asked Brian. "I didn't see you touch any controls."

"Neural implants," Salvatore told him. "We have direct mental access to our ships' control systems."

"Fascinating," Brian said with a nod.

"This is the entry where Salvatore found you," Venus told them, pointing to a butte at the top of the image. "There is an elevator inside of that formation that leads to the lower levels. This is the hangar level. They're keeping the abductees here, on the third level from the bottom. We'll use this access tunnel to move down from the hangar level."

"Lucifer keeps the abductees unconscious much of the time," Salvatore told them. "We have injections we will use to revive them."

"You two should get some sleep," Venus said to Brian and Miguel. "We'll wake you once Lucifer has departed."

"I ain't gonna be able to sleep now," Miguel replied. "I'm wired!"

"We can give you a sedative in the medical pod," Venus told him. "Come with me."

"I think we'd prefer to remain awake," said Brian. He was still having trouble believing all of this. Neither Venus nor Salvatore had given him any reason to doubt them, but he wasn't comfortable enough with the situation to surrender consciousness.

"Suit yourself," Venus said with a shrug.

"Hey, do y'all think Brian and I could have a few minutes alone?" asked Miguel. "Maybe we can go down to the surface?"

"As you wish," said Salvatore. "Follow me."

He moved to the chamber's center and disappeared through the floor; Brian and Miguel dropped down behind him. They gathered in the metal room on the bottom level.

"The gravity beam will lower you to the ground," Salvatore told them. "Wave at us when you're ready to return, and we'll bring you back up."

Brian suddenly found himself moving through the bottom of the ship and descending to the desert floor below, Miguel right behind him.

"What's up?" Brian asked.

"Not here," said Miguel. "Let's put some distance between them and us."

Brian followed him about a hundred yards away from the ship.

"You realize they can probably still listen to us if they want?" Brian asked. "Even humans have long-range microphones that would work at this distance."

"Guess you're right, but I had to get outta there anyway," Miguel replied. "Whole thing's kinda freaking me out. What do you think—do you trust them?"

"I think so," Brian said with a sigh. "They let us go just now, didn't they?"

"Yeah, I reckon that's a good point."

"You've got some doubts?"

"You'd better believe I do! Million-year-old Martians? I mean, we kinda had a feeling that man in black wasn't exactly human, but I dunno. This is a lot to take in. How the hell could they have survived that long?"

"Well, it's clear their technology is far more advanced than ours," Brian replied. "I'd like to know more about that, too, but for now,

Sydney and the twins must be the priority. They have a plan; I don't know how we'd get in there without them."

"So, you want to go along with this?"

"I don't see what choice we have at this point. If we leave, they're going to rescue them without us."

Miguel considered this for a moment.

"Alright. Yeah. Let's do it."

Brian and Miguel headed back to Venus's ship.

Chapter Six: Brian

Brian and Miguel spent the next few hours in Venus's cockpit, passing the time. Venus and Salvatore had moved to the main level to make preparations for their operation. Brian dozed off eventually but woke with a start to find Miguel shaking him by one arm.

"Hey, check it out," he said excitedly, pointing out toward the canyon.

Brian sat up, gazing out the window. He could see a flying saucer emerging from the hangar bay.

"Reckon that must be the man in black, right?" Miguel asked.

At that moment, the vessel streaked across the sky and disappeared.

"I think so," Brian agreed. "What time is it?"

"A little after three."

Just then, Salvatore and Venus rose through the floor.

"Hey, your buddy's ship just took off," Miguel told them.

"He's not our *buddy*," Venus told him with a frown. "But you're right, that was Lucifer."

"Where is he now?" asked Salvatore.

"Moving over Texas," said Venus. "Let's give it a few minutes and make sure he's not coming right back."

"I'm sorry, how can you tell where he is?" asked Brian.

"His emitter," said Salvatore. "It uses a frequency that is unique to this planet. He remains unaware that we can track him this way."

"He's moving over the Atlantic," Venus reported.

"How in the hell did he get there that fast?" Miguel asked.

"Gravitational propulsion," said Salvatore. "Our people have mastered the fundamental forces of nature."

"But he must be moving at about twenty times the speed of sound to have made it that far already," Brian observed.

"Mach 22, to be precise," Venus replied.

"Twenty-two times the speed of sound?" Miguel asked.

Venus nodded.

"That must produce extreme heat in the hull," said Brian.

"No," Salvatore replied. "A force field prevents the air from coming into contact with the exterior of the ship."

"But you must generate a significant sonic boom."

"No. Our ship diffuses the shock wave to eliminate that effect."

"I would love to pick your brain once we're done with all of this," Brian said with a grin.

"It's time," Venus announced twenty minutes later. "Lucifer has come to rest in Cape Town."

"South Africa?" asked Miguel.

"Yes," said Salvatore. "Let's go."

Brian and Miguel followed the two Martians down to the main level. The soldiers were waiting for them there, carrying what looked like bazookas strapped over their shoulders.

"You two will need to wait here," Venus said to Brian and Miguel.

"What?" said Miguel. "Not a chance!"

"This is going to be dangerous," Salvatore told them. "You will be safe here."

"That's our family in there," said Brian, noting the mutinous glint in Miguel's eye. "We want to go with you."

"You'll be a liability," said Venus. "Getting through the hybrids and rescuing the hostages will be tough enough as it is without my troops having to look out for you two."

"Give us weapons," Miguel suggested. "We can take care of ourselves."

Venus opened her mouth to retort, but Salvatore interrupted her.

"We can give them each a pistol," he said. "There are weapons to spare."

Venus glared at him for a moment but relented.

"Alright, but they fend for themselves. My men have enough to do without adding babysitting to their responsibilities. Flint—get a pistol for each of these men.

"And understand this," she added to Brian and Miguel. "I am in charge. You follow my orders without question, or I will have my soldiers put you down."

"Yes, ma'am," Miguel replied.

"Understood," said Brian.

Flint retrieved the weapons from a compartment in the floor. He handed one each to Brian and Miguel. The size and shape of the gun reminded Brian of a child's toy water pistol.

"You're kidding, right?" asked Miguel. "Why can't we get one of them bazookas your boys are toting?"

"Those are laser blasters," Venus told him. "One shot will be enough to knock out a hybrid. Point and shoot—just make sure the safety is disabled. I'm not giving you a plasma cannon—consider yourself lucky I'm allowing you to accompany us in the first place."

Venus moved off to join her men.

"I'd rather have a plasma cannon, too," Brian told Miguel. "But these will do."

Brian noted that neither Venus nor Salvatore was carrying a weapon, but Salvatore was holding a box.

"What's in there?" he asked.

"You'll see," Salvatore replied.

"Alright, men, be ready!" Venus called out to the group. "We're moving in now. I'll blast the hangar bay doors, and we'll continue inside. Alpha Team—you'll go with Salvatore and execute the rescue mission. I'll stay with Bravo Team and defend the hangar in preparation for Lucifer's return. Let's do it!"

Brian and Miguel followed Venus and Salvatore back up to the cockpit. Venus steered the ship out over the canyon's edge and hovered directly in front of the hangar. She fired a massive fireball that slammed into the bay doors, blowing them apart in one shot. The saucer moved into the hangar; Brian and Miguel followed the Martians down through the main level and out the ship's bottom.

"Brian, you're with me," said Salvatore. "Miguel, you'll stay with Venus's team."

"Now, hold on," Miguel protested. "I should come with you, too!"

"Flint, shoot him," said Venus.

Flint pointed his cannon at Miguel.

"Alright—forget it!" he shouted, putting his hands up in the air. "I'll stay here!"

"That's better," Venus said with a smirk. "Never mind, Flint."

"Try to behave," Brian said to Miguel.

He followed Salvatore and six of the soldiers across the bay. The area was empty except for Lucifer's abduction ship and the shattered remains of the doors strewn across the floor. There was an observation area at the front of the hangar, separated by enormous windows. As Brian approached the exit with the rest of the group, a dozen people burst into the area. They looked human, but as they drew closer, Brian realized their pupils were slitted like a cat's.

"Hybrids," he murmured.

A nearby soldier fired his plasma cannon at the closest hybrid; it ripped a hole through his chest, and he collapsed on the floor. Another ran straight for Brian; he pointed his weapon and fired. A laser blast hit the hybrid in the abdomen, launching her into the air; she hit the floor and didn't move.

By the time they'd reached the exit, they'd taken out all of the hybrids.

"Let's go!" said Salvatore.

Brian followed him and the soldiers out into a long corridor. The door they'd used was the only one in sight. Salvatore led them to the end of the hallway. To Brian's surprise, he poked his head right through the stone wall.

"It's clear," he reported to the soldiers.

One of them pulled a thick screw with a ring on its end out of his pocket. He held it by the ring, and it drilled itself into the floor. Each of the soldiers attached a metal hook to it; Brian noticed then that they were holding what appeared to be rappelling lines that they'd hooked onto their vests.

"What's happening, exactly?" he asked.

"The access tunnel to the lower levels is a sheer drop," Salvatore told him. "The Martians and hybrids have nanoparticles in their bloodstreams that allow them to manipulate gravity. But the soldiers will need to rappel down the tunnel wall."

"I've never rappelled before..." Brian told him.

"Don't worry," said Salvatore. "You're with me."

One by one, the soldiers disappeared through the wall. Salvatore instructed Brian to climb onto his back. He did so, and then Salvatore stepped through the wall.

Inside the tunnel, Brian could see the soldiers rappelling down the wall beneath them. Salvatore floated himself and Brian down the shaft, finally moving through the wall again and emerging inside another corridor. This one had metal doorways lining both walls along its entire length. Salvatore gathered the soldiers by the first door on the right.

"This is the command room," he told them. "There won't be

any abductees in here, but we should disable any hybrids that may be in here."

He led them into the room; Brian moved in last. There were only two people inside sitting at workstations on the far end of the area. They both turned to see who was there, jumping to their feet in surprise when they spotted the soldiers. The men hit them both with their plasma cannons.

They moved back into the corridor, and Salvatore led them through the door directly across from the command center. There, they found Sydney lying strapped to one exam table and a young woman Brian didn't recognize lying on another. Brian hurried over to Sydney.

"Brian!" she yelled when she saw him. "How did you get in here?"

"Long story—it'll have to wait," he said as he went to work on her straps.

"You've got to free Denise, too," Sydney said. "She's on that other table over there."

"We will," he assured her.

"You're not going to believe this, but Malia and Jaden are here, too!"

"Yes, I know. Do you know which room they're in?"

He released the final strap; Sydney sat up and swung her legs over the edge of the table. As she got to her feet, Brian held her by one arm to make sure she was steady, but she had no trouble walking.

"Sure do—follow me!"

Salvatore had freed Denise. They were about to move back into the corridor when several hybrids rushed inside.

Brian hit one of them with a laser blast; the soldiers quickly dispatched the others with their plasma cannons.

Sydney led the group to another room a little further along the hallway. They rushed inside and found Jaden and Malia lying unconscious on two of the exam tables.

"What are they wearing?" asked Brian. "Those look like wetsuits."

"Othali spacesuits," Salvatore told him.

Salvatore pulled a syringe from his pocket and hurried over to Malia. Pressing the needle to her neck, he gave her the injection and then moved to Jaden. A minute or two went by, but nothing happened.

"Lucifer must have increased the dosage of the sedatives," Salvatore suggested.

He gave them each a second injection.

Moments later, Malia's eyes fluttered open. She spotted Brian first, and then Sydney.

"Oh, my God!" she said, sitting up. "How did you find us?"

"We had a little help," Brian told her as Salvatore joined them.

"Salvatore!"

"We need to get back up to the hangar," he told them.

Brian helped Malia off the table, but she was able to stand on her own. He gave her a big hug. Jaden joined them a moment later, and he hugged him, too.

"You can get us out of here?" Sydney asked as they moved back into the corridor.

"Yes," said Brian. "We're going to wait for Lucifer to come back—that's the man in black—and then they're going to destroy the entire complex."

"What?" said Sydney. "But they've got other abductees in here! And there are *humans* working here! We have to get them out, too!"

"The workers are human-Martian hybrids," Brian told her. "And along with Lucifer, they're plotting to kill off most of humanity."

Salvatore had overheard Sydney.

"Do you know how many more abductees there are?" he asked.

"I'm not sure—maybe ten or twelve."

Salvatore sighed.

"This is going to be problematic," he told them. "I brought a couple of extra syringes, but I don't have enough to wake them all up. We'll have to hope we can do without."

"I can help," Malia told them. "My telepathy works on humans, now."

"Oh?" asked Salvatore.

"You remember when you were able to hear my thoughts?" Salvatore nodded. "Well, they gave us hormones to boost our abilities, and I was able to penetrate Melinda's mind. After that, Lucifer forced us to practice on some of the humans he captured. It worked."

"For you, anyway," said Jaden. "I haven't been able to do it yet."

"I'm confused," said Brian. "How is telepathy going to help if they're unconscious?"

"Have you ever seen any of the X-Men movies?" Jaden asked him.

"What? No—what does that have to do—"

"Forget it," said Jaden. "The point is, what Malia can do has gone way beyond just telepathy. She'll be able to wake those people up for sure."

Salvatore let the soldiers know they'd be rescuing the rest of the abductees and instructed them to guard the corridor.

Sydney led them into one of the rooms on the left side. There were two people here—a young white man and an older Black woman, both lying naked and unconscious on their exam tables. Salvatore hurried over to the woman first and gave her the injection. She woke up, saw Salvatore standing by her, and screamed.

Sydney hurried over and shushed her. The woman sat up, looked around the room, saw the other people, realized her nakedness, and screamed again, trying to cover herself. Sydney grabbed the woman's clothes from beneath the exam table and handed them to her.

Salvatore moved over to the young man and gave him the last injection. The man opened his eyes and recoiled at the sight of Salvatore, falling off his exam table.

"What the hell are you?!" he demanded, scrambling to his feet, realizing he wasn't wearing any clothes, and covering his groin with both hands.

"We'll explain later," Brian told him, handing him his clothes. "Get dressed—quickly!"

They moved to the next room. There was only one person here—a Chinese man who looked like he was in his fifties. Malia moved to his exam table, focusing intently on his face. After only a few moments, he opened his eyes and sat up. He spoke a few words in Chinese.

"Do you speak English?" Brian asked him, giving him his clothing. Unlike the others, he didn't seem troubled by his nakedness.

"No English," he replied, getting to his feet and putting on his clothes.

They continued down the corridor. Malia wakened everyone they found in the exam rooms. By the time they were done, they'd added fourteen abductees to their numbers.

"That's it—we must regroup in the hangar bay," Salvatore told them.

But as they made their way toward the end of the hallway, a child appeared through the wall. Brian guessed that he was only five or six years old. He looked human except for his cat-like eyes.

"Who are you?" the boy asked.

Before anyone could answer him, a woman emerged from the wall—a hybrid—and gathered the child to her.

"What are you people doing here?" she demanded.

"Leaving," Salvatore told her. "Get out of our way."

"You're going to destroy the compound, aren't you?" she asked. "That's what you tried to do last time you were here—I heard about the fusion grenades."

"*Fusion* grenades?" Brian whispered to Salvatore.

"Later," he replied, saying louder to the hybrid, "Step aside, or we will shoot you."

"No—take us with you! At least take my son!"

"There are children here?" asked Sydney. "Brian, we can't kill *kids*!"

"She's right," Brian told Salvatore. "We'll need to evacuate the children."

"And their parents!" added Sydney.

Salvatore looked from Sydney to Brian and let out a long sigh.

"Very well," he said. "What is your name?" he added to the hybrid.

"Vanessa."

"How many more children are here? And where are they?"

"Six in addition to my son. We live on the level below this."

Salvatore nodded.

"We will rescue the children and their mothers, but in exchange, you will help us."

"How?"

"We need to get these people up to the hangar level. You will give us access to the elevator."

Vanessa agreed. Salvatore directed the abductees to the opposite end of the hall. Vanessa and three of the soldiers accompanied them. The humans loaded onto the elevator, and Vanessa sent it up to the hangar level.

The rest of them moved into the access tunnel. Malia and Jaden took Brian and Sydney down to the next level; the remaining three soldiers rappelled down.

Arriving in the corridor, they found a group of hybrid women awaiting them with their children. Brian estimated that the youngest child was only two or three years old, and the oldest probably the same age as Malia and Jaden. Vanessa addressed the group and told them that they needed to leave the compound before Salvatore and Venus destroyed it.

"Traitor!" one of the women yelled at her. "Lucifer is on his way—we should fight these invaders until he gets here!"

"Fool!" Vanessa retorted. "They've breached the hangar bay—they're going to destroy the entire compound. This is the only way we can save the children!"

"No!" the woman yelled. She grabbed her daughter—one of the toddlers—and took off down the hall.

"Malia?" said Salvatore.

She nodded. A moment later, Brian saw the hybrid woman and her daughter rise a few feet off the floor and return to the group.

The woman screamed, struggling to escape Malia's control, but she couldn't do it.

"This is your final chance," Salvatore told her. "Come with us, and we will let you live."

"As your prisoner?!" she screamed.

"That is entirely up to you," he replied. "Your cooperation will determine your status. Decide now—we need to leave."

The woman stopped struggling and nodded. None of the others offered any resistance.

Salvatore directed the soldiers to take everyone to the elevator and up to the hangar bay.

"Malia, if you will come with me?" he added as the others moved away.

"Where are you taking her?" asked Brian.

"Bottom level to plant the explosives," he said.

"I'll go with you."

Brian ran down to the access tunnel with Salvatore and Malia. Malia used her telekinesis to transport him and herself down to the lowest level; Salvatore dropped on his own.

They moved into the corridor. Salvatore removed a small device that resembled a hockey puck from the box he'd been carrying. He affixed it to a nearby bulkhead; it appeared to attach magnetically.

"Fusion grenade, I presume?" said Brian.

"Yes."

"You're not setting the timer?" Malia asked as they hurried down the corridor.

"Venus will detonate them remotely," Salvatore replied. "And she has modified them—they cannot be removed from the bulkhead once they're attached."

"The fallout from these explosions is going to pose a risk to the surrounding population," Brian pointed out. "We should warn the government—they can evacuate the area."

"Not necessary," said Salvatore. "These are pure fusion weapons—there is no fallout."

"Incredible—what do they use as a triggering mechanism if there's no fission component?"

"High-powered lasers," said Salvatore.

They reached the opposite end of the corridor, and Salvatore planted a second device on the bulkhead there.

"That's it," he said. "Up to the hangar bay!"

Chapter Seven: Miguel

Miguel watched Brian hurry across the hangar with Salvatore and several soldiers. As they neared the exit, about a dozen people burst through the doors.

"Hybrids?" Miguel asked.

"Yes," Venus confirmed.

The soldiers made quick work of the hybrids using their plasma cannons; Brian even took out one with his toy-looking pistol. After that, they moved out of the hangar.

"Damn," Miguel muttered. "I guess these little things work after all. Hey, why don't them hybrids carry weapons?" he added more loudly to Venus.

"Lucifer believed his fortress to be impregnable," she told him. "And it was to anyone but me. He had no idea about the more advanced weapons I've been developing."

"So, if nobody could get inside, there was no need for them to be armed."

"Yes, precisely."

A few minutes later, more hybrids rushed into the hangar. Venus and her soldiers hurried over to engage them; Miguel hung back by the saucer. He thought this was hardly a fair fight—the soldiers picked off their unarmed opponents with ease. But suddenly, he noticed at least a dozen more hybrids emerging from openings in the wall and ceiling near the saucer—the other ones had only been a diversion.

"Hey!" he yelled. "We got more company over here!"

He watched the hybrids float down to the hangar floor from the wall and ceiling. The first few approached his position; he fired at them with his pistol, knocking them to the floor. Within moments, the soldiers returned, eliminating the rest with their plasma cannons.

"What did they hope to accomplish here?" Venus wondered out loud.

"Probably trying to commandeer your ship, I'd suspect," Miguel told her.

"Unlikely," she replied. "The security system won't grant entry to anyone but me or people I authorize."

"Good to know."

"Lucifer is on his way, as expected," Venus announced to her soldiers. "His minions here must have alerted him to our incursion. We've got about twenty minutes before he arrives. Be ready for more hybrids—they're sure to cause another diversion immediately before Lucifer's arrival."

Miguel felt his pulse quickening. He was no soldier; denied the opportunity to help rescue Sydney, he found himself wishing he hadn't come along. The minutes slipped by, and the tension in the group grew palpable.

"This is it," Venus announced. "He's here."

"I don't see him," Miguel said, frantically searching the hangar bay and pointing his pistol.

"At ease," said Flint, pushing his gun down. "You're going to hurt one of us if you're not careful."

"Sorry," Miguel replied. "But I don't understand—if he's here, where's his ship? Could it be invisible?"

"My ship's sensors would detect him at this close range even if he were," said Venus. "Tracking indicates that his coordinates match ours, but there's no sign of him."

"He could be holding position above the compound," Flint suggested. "There's no masking the missing bay doors—he must know we're in here. Probably avoiding an ambush."

"I'm sure you're right," Venus replied. "Stay here with the human; I'm going to take the others topside. We won't be able to use the elevator, but the men can use their ropes and ascenders in the access tunnel. I'm leaving the ship's plasma cannons set to fire automatically if another saucer enters the hangar."

Flint nodded; Venus led the rest of the group out of the hangar.

"This is more than my nerves can handle," Miguel said once they'd departed. He kept glancing back and forth between the hangar door and the observation room, expecting Lucifer to burst into the area at any moment.

"Stay calm," Flint told him. "Take slow, deep breaths."

Miguel tried to focus on his breathing but still felt like he was on the verge of a panic attack. Moments later, he spotted a dozen hybrids crawling into the hangar through the bay doors, approaching them along the walls and ceiling.

"Whoa, hey!" he shouted.

Flint had been focused on the opposite exit. Seeing the hybrids, he rushed toward them, firing his plasma cannon at the nearest ones. Miguel followed. He used his pistol to take out one of the hybrids. The rest dropped to the floor and surrounded them. Every time they eliminated one, another moved into the hangar. Miguel and Flint stood back-to-back, shooting anyone who moved toward them. For a few minutes, Miguel feared they'd be overwhelmed. But finally, new hybrids stopped entering the hangar. It took only moments to shoot the rest.

"What in the hell was the point of that?" Miguel asked. "Don't seem like they accomplished anything beyond adding to their body count."

"I'm not sure," said Flint, as they moved back toward Venus's ship. "This is puzzling."

Just then, Venus dropped out of the saucer, landing on the floor in front of them.

"Well, hey—when did you get here?" Miguel asked. "I didn't see you come in."

"Only a minute ago," she replied. "You had your hands full."

"Yeah, you can say that again..."

"I need the two of you to go up to the surface. The men need reinforcements."

"Did you find Lucifer?" asked Miguel.

"No, we haven't seen him. But he's brought in fifty more hybrids—heavily armed ones."

"From where?" Flint asked skeptically.

"I'm not sure, but we need to hurry—they're overwhelming us."

"Where is Lucifer now?" asked Miguel. "Are you still tracking his emitter thingy?"

Venus gazed at him for a moment.

"No. His signal disappeared. Let's go!"

Miguel followed Flint through the observation area and out into a corridor, Venus right behind them. Flint led him toward the far end. But suddenly, a group of people emerged through the stone wall at the end of the hall—Venus and her soldiers.

"What in the hell?" said Miguel, turning to look behind him—but the other Venus wasn't there anymore.

Flint pointed his plasma cannon at Venus.

"Who are you?" he demanded.

"What are you talking about? I'm your boss, you idiot—now drop your weapon!"

"I'm sorry, ma'am, but we just encountered you inside the hangar bay."

Venus looked puzzled for only a moment before saying, "Lucifer."

"What?" asked Miguel.

"You saw Lucifer, not me! I've been up on the surface with the men—there was nothing up there. No sign of Lucifer or his ship—he must have used his emitter to emulate *me*."

"Those hybrids were a diversion," said Miguel.

"The person we encountered gained entry to your ship," Flint told her, still pointing his cannon at her. "How can I know which of you is real?"

"*What*? That's impossible... Come with me. I'll take us all inside my ship and prove to you that *I'm* Venus!"

They followed her back to the hangar bay, Flint keeping his weapon on her the whole way. Once inside, they assembled beneath the saucer and moved up into the ship one at a time.

Venus waited till they'd all gathered on the main level, then activated a holographic display in the center of the chamber showing various graphs and gauges. Suddenly, one of the symbols began flashing in red. "Satisfied?" Venus asked, locking eyes with Flint.

"Yes, ma'am," the soldier replied.

"I don't get it," said Miguel. "How does that flashing light prove anything?"

"She armed the nukes," Flint told him. "Nobody can do that without her command codes."

"Command codes that are stored in my implants with gigabit encryption," Venus added.

"I'm sorry, ma'am," said Flint, finally lowering his weapon. "But we did see the imposter leave the ship—how did he get inside?"

Venus considered it for a moment.

"He must have scanned my body when we arrived. His emitter is good enough to fool the security system—this is not a good development."

"Well, you folks invented that tech. Don't you have a way to detect it?" asked Miguel.

"No—*Lucifer* and his people developed it. The rest of us don't have emitters, but you're right—we need to find a way to combat this."

"Lucifer must be inside the compound somewhere," Flint observed.

"Yes," Venus agreed. "Let's go find him."

They moved back down to the hangar. There was a third saucer here, now.

"Lucifer's ship," Venus observed. "Come on."

They followed her back out to the corridor. But at that moment, the elevator at the far end of the hallway opened, and three of Venus's soldiers escorted a group of humans toward them.

"Who the hell are these people?" Venus demanded.

"Abductees," one of the soldiers told her. "Salvatore ordered us to bring them up here for evacuation."

"Sentimental fool," Venus muttered. "Very well—let's get them on board the ship."

She led the whole group back to her saucer. One of the soldiers boarded with the humans.

"The rest of you with me," said Venus. "Let's find Lucifer."

She led them back out to the corridor.

"He's here in the compound somewhere, but I can't track him any more precisely than that. Let's move down—we'll clear the place one level at a time."

Flint kneeled and took something out of his vest. Miguel looked closer—it was a metal ring with a screw. He held it against the floor, and the device drilled itself into the ground. Next, the soldiers each attached a rope to the ring.

"Uh... what are we doing?"

"They're rappelling, dear," Venus told him. "But you're with me—climb onto my back."

"I'm sorry, what?"

"Stick your head through this wall and look down."

"Huh?"

Venus looked from him to the wall, saying nothing more; Miguel poked his head through. Below was a sheer drop of several stories with no ladder. He pulled his head out of the wall.

"On my back," Venus repeated.

"Yeah, okay—good idea."

Miguel climbed onto Venus's back. She moved them through the wall and down to the next level, the soldiers rappelling down around them. They emerged into another corridor—there were many more doors here.

Venus led them down the hall, Flint and the other soldiers right behind her. They had their cannons hoisted on their shoulders, ready to fire; Miguel kept his pistol drawn. One soldier checked each room as they moved. When they were roughly halfway down the corridor, the elevator doors opened. Miguel froze. Lucifer stepped into the hall, grinning at them.

"Welcome to my humble abode," he said.

"Shoot him!" Venus yelled.

Half a dozen fireballs answered her call, but Lucifer vanished before they'd reached him. A moment later, twenty hybrids appeared out of nowhere—they had the soldiers surrounded.

"Shit!" Miguel shouted.

He pointed his pistol at the nearest hybrid and fired, knocking him to the ground. All hell broke loose. The hybrids still bore no weapons; instead, they tried wresting the plasma cannons from the soldiers. A few of them succeeded, shooting the men at point-blank range.

"No!" Venus shrieked, firing her own weapon at each of the now-armed hybrids.

It took a few minutes, but they managed to take out the remaining attackers. Venus had lost three soldiers in the melee.

"Dammit," she muttered, taking in the carnage.

They cleared the rest of the rooms on this level and then moved back to the access tunnel to drop to the floor below.

Chapter Eight: Malia

Malia returned to the hangar bay with Salvatore and Brian.

"There's a third vessel here, now," Brian noted.

"Lucifer," said Salvatore. "He must be here in the compound somewhere."

They boarded Venus's ship and moved up to the main level. The area was a little crowded now—the human abductees were here, as well as the hybrid children and their mothers, Sydney, Jaden, and several of Venus's soldiers. Sydney joined Brian and Malia when she saw them.

"Where is Venus?" Salvatore asked one of the soldiers.

"She went to find Lucifer," the man reported. "Flint and most of the other men went with her. Oh, and your friend, too."

"Miguel?" asked Brian.

"I guess... I didn't get his name."

"Miguel's here, too?" asked Sydney.

"Yes—he and I found where they took you inside the butte, but we couldn't get in," Brian told her. "Salvatore here showed up, and we, ah... joined his team!"

"It's nice to meet you," Sydney said to Salvatore. Malia noted that if his scaly skin and cat-like eyes had alarmed her in any way, she didn't let it show. "So... I'm sorry, but who are you, exactly?"

"Salvatore and his colleague, Venus, are from Mars," Brian told her. "Just like the man in black, whose name is Lucifer, as it turns out."

Brian filled her in more about their background.

"Ah," said Sydney once he'd finished. "So, we were right—the man in black *isn't* human!"

Just then, Venus rose through the floor.

"It's time to leave," she announced.

"Where are the rest of your men?" asked Salvatore.

"Lucifer and his hybrids ambushed us—their numbers were too great, and they overwhelmed us. They took our weapons and killed my men—I barely escaped."

"What... what about Miguel?" Sydney asked fearfully.

"I'm sorry," said Venus. "They killed him, too."

"No..."

Sydney sobbed, tears rolling down her cheeks.

"We should leave and destroy the compound before Lucifer can escape," said Salvatore.

"What—no!" said Sydney. "What about Miguel and the soldiers?"

"What about them?" asked Salvatore. "They're dead..."

Malia could hardly believe his lack of tact until she reminded herself that he wasn't human.

"I know that—but we should recover their bodies!" Sydney said.

"There's no time," Brian told her. "I'm sorry. But we need to move quickly."

Sydney broke down sobbing; Brian gathered her in a hug. Salvatore moved up to the cockpit with Venus. Malia was torn. She wanted to console Sydney but had never met Miguel or been romantically involved with anyone—it felt like she was too young to be much help. Suddenly uncomfortable, she moved up to the cockpit.

"Where are you taking us?" Salvatore said to Venus when Malia arrived.

"Away."

"But we haven't completed the mission—why didn't you detonate the grenades?"

"What's going on?" Malia asked. Looking out the windows, she could see they were far above the clouds now, moving fast. "We didn't destroy the compound?"

"It's wrong," said Venus. "Killing all those people—I couldn't do it."

"You mean killing the hybrids?" asked Malia. "The ones who are planning on destroying humanity?"

"My decision is final."

Malia recalled Lucifer using his emitter to emulate Brian and suddenly felt highly suspicious. Reaching out with her mind, she tried to sense Venus's thoughts; it worked. She could feel only cold, menacing calculation. Malia was surprised that she could sense *anything* through the emitter.

"*You're not Venus,*" she said telepathically.

"Who else would I be?"

"*I'd like to wipe that smirk off your face permanently,*" Malia said, confident now that this was Lucifer.

"What's going on?" asked Salvatore, looking back and forth between them.

Malia penetrated Lucifer's mind—this worked despite his emitter. She saw a vision of another underground compound but couldn't identify its location.

"*Where are you taking us?*"

Suddenly, Lucifer forcefully expelled her from his mind.

"How did you do that?" Malia asked out loud. Only Jaden had ever been able to kick her out of their thoughts like this.

"Malia?" said Salvatore.

"This isn't Venus—it's Lucifer!"

At that moment, dagger-like claws extended from Lucifer's fingers, and he dove across the cockpit at Salvatore. Malia tried to use her powers to tear Lucifer away from Salvatore, but nothing happened—his emitter was still blocking her telekinesis; she dropped through the floor.

"Help!" she yelled. "It's Lucifer, not Venus—and he's trying to kill Salvatore!"

Before anyone could move, Salvatore dropped to the main level, blood dripping from multiple wounds.

"Where is Lucifer?" he demanded.

"He was with you in the cockpit!" Malia replied.

"He left—you didn't see him?"

"No!"

"I'm sorry—what's going on?" asked Brian.

"Lucifer used his emitter to disguise himself as Venus," Salvatore told him. "He moved us out of the compound—Venus must still be there."

"How did Lucifer get control of the ship?" asked Malia. "It belongs to Venus—nobody else should be able to do that, right?"

"Lucifer's systems must have scanned her when she entered his compound," said Salvatore. "His emitter must be able to trick the security system."

"We need to get back to the compound," said Brian.

"Yes," Salvatore agreed. "I cannot access the control systems—in Venus's absence, I should be able to do so. The ship should be able to detect that she's not aboard, and she designated me as the backup commander."

"Lucifer must still be on the ship," said Brian.

Salvatore considered this for a moment.

"Yes, that must be the case. But I'm not able to track him—I should be able to when he's using the emitter."

"Where are we?" asked Brian.

"Moving east over the Atlantic. He entered a heading only, not a destination, so I cannot determine where we're going. But we must regain control of the ship. Malia, Jaden—with me, please."

Malia and her brother followed Salvatore back up to the cockpit, Brian close behind.

"Can the two of you use your powers to stop our forward motion?" asked Salvatore.

"We can try," said Jaden, looking at Malia.

Malia nodded. The two of them stared out the windows. Malia tried to imagine she was out there among the clouds looking back at the ship. She reached out with her mind, trying to stop them; she felt Jaden's power joining her own. It felt like it should be working, but the ship's engines were fighting back.

"We're slowing," Salvatore told them.

Malia focused ever harder, trying to bring them to a complete stop. She felt herself starting to sweat with the effort, but it was too much. The engines were too powerful.

"We can't," she said finally, abandoning the effort. "It's too much."

"If we can find Lucifer and eject him from the ship, would you be able to take control?" asked Brian.

"Yes," said Salvatore. "But with his emitter making him invisible, I'm not sure the sensors will be able to detect him."

"But he's controlling the ship—the internal systems must be aware of his location, no?"

"Perhaps, but I cannot override his commands as long as the system recognizes him as Venus," said Salvatore.

"I think I can find him," said Malia. "I was able to penetrate his mind before—he kicked me out somehow, but I should still be able to sense him."

"We need to have a long discussion about your abilities once we get through this," Brian said.

Malia focused, reaching out with her thoughts to sense any other minds inside the cockpit.

"He's not up here," she said. "Must be down on the main level."

They dropped to the central chamber. Malia extended her thoughts, focusing methodically from one end of the area to the other.

"I don't get it," she said finally. "He's not here."

Salvatore eyed her for a moment.

"He must be in the airlock."

"The bottom level?" she asked. "In the metal chamber?"

Salvatore nodded.

"I'll go down with you."

"No—he wants to kill you. And you're the only one who can control the ship."

"I'll go," said one of the soldiers. "You let me know where he is, and I'll shoot the bastard."

"If you miss, you'll blow a hole through the hull," said Salvatore. "You'll be sucked out to the atmosphere."

"Don't worry—I'll save him if that happens," said Malia.

Malia dropped to the bottom level, the soldier right behind her with his plasma cannon at the ready. She searched the area with her mind and found Lucifer by the opposite wall. His thoughts were quiet but focused on getting them to that other compound.

Ready for his resistance, Malia penetrated his mind, bringing her full power to bear. She focused on making him visible—it worked. He appeared before them but still looked like Venus. The soldier aimed his cannon, but Lucifer dropped through the floor and out of the vessel.

"Damn!" yelled the soldier.

They moved back up the main level.

"We found him," Malia told the others. "I was able to force him to be visible, but he left the ship before we could do anything."

"He's gone?" asked Salvatore; Malia nodded. He focused for a moment, then said, "I've taken control. I'm taking us back to Lucifer's compound. Good work down there," he added to Malia; she beamed at him.

"You made him visible?" Jaden asked as Salvatore moved up to the cockpit.

"Yeah, but I think I caught him by surprise," said Malia. "He kicked me out of his mind before, so I knew I had to be fast."

"Damn," he replied, smiling appreciatively. "You've gotta help me learn to do all the crap you can do now. But I thought he made it so his emitter could block our powers?"

"I would have thought so, too—it did stop me from using telekinesis against him. But I dunno—telepathy worked."

Minutes later, Salvatore returned from the cockpit.

"We're back in Lucifer's hangar bay," he announced to the group. "Now, we need to find Venus and her team. I'll take one of you men," he said to the soldiers. "The rest of you stay here and guard these people. Malia, I'd like you to join me as well."

"I know she's powerful, but she's still a minor," Brian reminded him. "Please, look out for her."

"Of course," said Salvatore.

Malia followed him and the soldier down to the floor of the hangar bay. But before they'd made it to the exit, Venus charged into the area with Miguel and her remaining soldiers close behind.

"Where the hell did you go?" she demanded.

Salvatore explained what had happened with Lucifer.

"Damn him," she said, gazing across the hangar. "We got here to find both my ship and his missing. His ship's back now, too, but the tracking signal's gone dead."

"Yes," Salvatore agreed. "He must have remotely controlled his ship to follow us. But it would seem we no longer have any way to locate him."

"So, if we destroy this place now, we'll have no idea if we've taken him out with it," she observed.

"I believe we should proceed with our plan," said Salvatore. "We can still eliminate his compound and the hybrids. This will slow him down, at least."

Venus considered this for a moment, then nodded.

"Everyone on the ship!"

Malia followed her and Salvatore back inside the vessel. The soldiers regrouped with their comrades, and Miguel headed directly to Sydney. She held him tight for a moment before kissing him passionately.

"Aren't you going to introduce us?" Malia asked.

"Oh, sorry—Miguel, this is Malia Kwan and her twin brother, Jaden."

"It's a pleasure to meet you," Malia said with a smile.

"Hey," said Jaden.

"I've heard a lot about the two of you," said Miguel, shaking their hands. "Nice to finally meet you."

"We're out of the compound," Venus told them. "The fireworks show is about to begin if you'd like to join us in the cockpit."

Malia, Jaden, Sydney, Brian, and Miguel followed Venus and Salvatore up to the cockpit. They were hovering over the desert, a couple of miles from Lucifer's compound—Malia could see the hangar bay in the cliff face.

"Here we go," said Venus. "Fusion detonations in three... two... one..."

At that moment, Malia noticed something sliver streak out of the hangar bay and disappear into the sky. An instant later, the cliff face disappeared in a giant flash of light. When she could see again, an enormous mushroom cloud filled the sky. Only a gigantic crater remained where Lucifer's compound had been.

"And that's that," said Miguel.

"Something flew out of the hangar right before the explosion," Malia said to Salvatore. "Did you see it?"

"Yes," he replied. "Lucifer's ship. He must not have had time to get the second one out."

"I'm still not getting any tracking data," said Venus. "The signal went dead sometime before you left with my ship before."

"I don't understand it," Salvatore said with a frown. "We should be able to track him when he's using the emitter."

"Hey, uh... I just realized it," said Miguel, "but that might be my fault..."

"What? How?" asked Venus.

"Well, when I was with the soldiers, and he showed up as you... I asked him if you—that is to say if *he* was still tracking Lucifer's emitter..."

Venus stared at him for a moment in silence.

"That's lovely," she muttered finally, dropping into one of the chairs. "He must have altered the emitter to block the signal."

"I'm really sorry—we thought it was you!" said Miguel. "I feel terrible..."

"It's not your fault," Salvatore told him. "That was a useful tool while it lasted, but we'll have to do without."

Chapter Nine: Brian

"What do we do now?" asked Brian. "Lucifer got away—will he set up shop somewhere else?"

"I think he already has another compound," Malia told them.

"What makes you say that?" asked Salvatore.

"I penetrated his mind when he hijacked the ship. He was thinking about some other place that looked a lot like his compound—I think that's where he was taking us."

"Could you tell where it was?" asked Salvatore.

"No, he kicked me out of his head before I could get that far."

Salvatore considered this for a moment.

"This could explain where the replacement saucer came from."

"Yeah—I was wondering about that, too," said Malia. "We blew up one of his saucers before he captured us, but then he had two again. There were also way more hybrids in Chernobyl than there should have been."

"Perhaps they came from this other compound as well," Salvatore suggested.

"Well, I don't know about the rest of you," said Miguel, "but I've had about enough of this shit. Y'all think you could drop us off at Brian's ranch?"

"That would not be wise," Salvatore replied. "You will be unable to protect Malia and Jaden there—Lucifer *will* come for them again."

"Do we know that for sure?" asked Miguel. "He had them for almost two months—that must've been enough time for him to get whatever he wanted, right?"

"We just destroyed his work," said Brian. "He's going to have to start over from scratch. Unless he was carrying samples of their DNA on his ship, he's going to need them back."

"Not only that," said Malia, "but he told us he needed us to work for him. He gave himself our DNA, but it only gave him our healing powers—nothing else. And the human he tried it on aged very quickly and died, so he was reluctant to try it on his hybrids. He said that with our powers, we could help him with some sort of project, but he wouldn't tell us what it was."

"Before we do anything else," said Salvatore, "we need to remove everyone's tracking devices."

"They didn't abduct Brian or me this time, so we don't have them," said Miguel, feeling the back of his neck as if to be sure there wasn't a new scar.

"No, but anyone who spent time in his compound will," Salvatore replied.

They moved down to the main level. Salvatore told the group what they needed to do.

"I'm sure *we* don't have any tracking devices," Vanessa told him. "We've always been loyal to Lucifer—he wouldn't do that to us."

"We will see," said Salvatore.

Malia, Jaden, Sydney, and all of the hybrids took turns in the pods lining the walls. Sure enough, the hybrids had the devices, too. It took a few minutes, but Salvatore removed the chips from everyone's necks and deposited them in the center of the chamber. An energy beam fired from the ceiling, vaporizing them.

"Now, we can decide our next moves," said Salvatore.

"No, no, no," said Venus. "I agree with the human—I'm tired of this shit, too. I want to go home. After a meal and some sleep, then we can figure out this mess."

"Fair enough," said Brian. "Where's home?"

"Down south," she said, waving her hand dismissively and moving back up to the cockpit.

Malia giggled.

"You know where her home is?" Brian asked her.

"Oh, we do—we've been there," she replied; Jaden was grinning now, too.

"Are you going to fill us in?" asked Brian.

"You'll see," Jaden told him as he moved up to the cockpit with Malia.

Brian turned to Miguel and Sydney.

"Don't look at us, chief," Miguel told him. "But a meal and some sleep do sound good right now."

Brian moved up to the cockpit. They were far above the clouds, which were racing by unimaginably fast. Soon, the weather cleared, and he could see the ocean extending beneath them. Minutes later, they passed over a frozen landscape and slowed to a crawl.

"Are we in the arctic?" he asked.

"The *Antarctic*," Malia replied.

Venus moved the ship into a hangar bay in the side of a rocky hill.

"Perry, we've got incoming," she said out loud. "Seven hybrid children and their mothers. I want them contained to level five with force fields. Make sure they're fed and comfortable, and they can move about freely, but only on that level."

"Yes, ma'am," a voice said through a speaker somewhere.

"We also have a bunch of humans to house until we can decide what to do with them," she added. "Put them on level four. Same restrictions."

Brian followed Venus, Malia, and Jaden down to the main level. Salvatore directed Brian, Miguel, Sydney, and the twins out of the ship. Down on the hangar floor, he led them away from the saucer. Brian noted a second flying saucer hovering nearby.

"We'll stay out of the way," Salvatore told them. "Some of these people may offer some resistance."

The hybrids emerged from the ship next. A few of Venus's soldiers herded them out of the hangar through a tunnel. The human abductees came next, and another group of men led them away.

Venus left her ship alone and said, "Let's eat."

"Hey, do you still have our clothes on your ship?" Malia asked Salvatore. "I'd really like to get out of this spacesuit!"

"Yeah, me too," Jaden added.

"I do," said Salvatore. "Come with me."

The twins followed him over to the other spacecraft. Venus

"But Lucifer is the head of the serpent, so to speak," Venus added.

"I don't know," Sydney replied. "We've had some run-ins with a CIA officer named Babcock. He told me that he's been compromised—and that he works for the same people that Lucifer does. The way he said it—he didn't make it sound like Lucifer was the leader."

"I believe he must be mistaken," said Salvatore. "We have no evidence of anyone but Lucifer being in charge. I cannot imagine him bending the knee to anyone else."

"We have no idea where this other compound might be—the one that Malia saw?" asked Brian.

"No," Salvatore confirmed. "This is the first we've heard of it."

"Some of the hybrids have emitters like Lucifer's," said Malia. "Can you track them? You might be able to find the compound that way."

"It should be possible," Salvatore replied. "I believe each emitter has a slightly different frequency. When I first discovered the signal coming from Lucifer's device, I did try scanning his compound but couldn't detect any of the other emitters that way."

"So, you'd have to know a specific device's frequency first before you could scan for it?" said Brian.

"Yes. And now that Lucifer knows about that exploit, I suspect he'll modify the rest of the emitters to correct for it."

"Hey, speaking of Bomani, do you think we can contact the Othali now?" asked Jaden.

"Perhaps," said Salvatore. "We face the same risk now that we did before—if we use enough power to achieve escape velocity and leave the planet, Lucifer will be able to detect us. He could follow us to Mars."

"Where is Bomani?" asked Brian.

"He's here," Venus told him. "Having a long sleep in my medical bay."

"He could use one of the power stations to contact the Othali," Sydney suggested.

"That's not a bad idea," said Brian. "We could use their help at this point. And it would be best to reunite Malia and Jaden with their mother."

"We also have to get the human abductees to their homes," said Sydney.

"We will have to find out where they're all from," Salvatore replied.

"Probably spread out all over the world," said Venus. "Let's drop them off to the U.S. government and let them sort it out."

"Speaking of the government, we should consider alerting them to Lucifer's plan," Brian suggested.

"They'll think we're crazy," said Miguel. "A million-year-old Martian building an army to kill off all of us?"

"After the Malor invasion, I think they'll be receptive," Brian countered. "And if they see Salvatore... well, the evidence is hard to refute."

They sat in silence for a few moments. Brian yawned—it had been a long time since he'd slept.

"Me, too," said Miguel through a yawn of his own. "Listen,

why don't we sleep on it and reconvene tomorrow to make some decisions?"

"Good thinking," said Sydney, getting up and stretching.

"Very well," Salvatore agreed.

Venus had one of her men lead the humans down to one of the lower levels where she had sleeping accommodations. Malia and Jaden each had a room of their own, Miguel and Sydney shared a room, and Brian ended up in a room across the corridor. He went to bed and fell asleep almost immediately.

Chapter Ten: Malia

Malia went to bed but couldn't fall asleep; she had too much on her mind. Her entire world had been turned upside down these last two months. She'd spent the majority of that time as a prisoner in a Martian's underground bunker. More than anything, she wanted life to go back to normal. She wanted to go home and go back to school and reunite with her friends...

If only they'd detonated the grenades a little sooner, they would have eliminated Lucifer. But Malia knew that even with him out of the picture, it would never be possible to go back to how things were before the invasion. With the powers she now possessed, someone would always be hunting her. If not Lucifer, then Babcock—there would always be someone.

"Hey, Malia—are you awake?" Jaden's voice said in her mind.

"Yeah, I can't sleep."

"Me neither."

Moments later, there was a knock on her door; it was Jaden. He came inside and sat on the floor across from her bed.

"So, why can't *you* sleep?" Malia asked.

"I dunno... shit's just weird."

"Yeah."

Jaden let out a long sigh.

"Have you been able to communicate with Mom?"

Malia shook her head.

"I've tried, but it's no use."

"You could probably do it if you use the magnetic field."

"Yeah, but I don't know how to do that. Well, not consciously, at least."

"Hmm."

They sat in silence for a moment.

"We should practice while we're here. You gotta help me with all that telepathy shit you can do now, and you should work on using the magnetic field."

"That's not a bad idea. We can do it tomorrow."

Jaden nodded.

"I was thinking... Once we do find Mom—if Bomani can use the power stations or whatever... I'm not so sure I want to go off with the Othali to some other planet. I mean, these Martians found a way to live here without any humans finding them. Why can't we?"

"That's a good question. Even Lucifer hasn't been able to find them—and he's got better tech than Babcock."

"Yeah, exactly!" said Jaden. "I bet if we team up on Mom, we can convince her that we should stay here."

"It'd have to be somewhere remote and hidden like this place or Lucifer's compound."

"That's fine. Better than being a hundred years away or whatever."

"Well, we still have to find Mom first."

"Right."

Jaden left to go back to his room a few minutes later. Malia drifted off to sleep soon after.

The following day after breakfast, Malia and Jaden went to the hangar bay to practice. Brian and Salvatore accompanied them.

"So, if you don't mind, I'd like to take stock of everything the two of you can do, now," said Brian.

Malia nodded; Jaden said "Sure."

"You both started with telekinesis and simple telepathy—meaning you could speak to others with your mind—but only each other and the Othali, right?"

"Yes," Malia confirmed. "But now we can both talk to the hybrids that way, I can talk to the Martians and humans, and I'm able to penetrate people's minds."

"But Jaden can't do that yet?"

"Nah, man," Jaden replied, rolling his eyes. "I want to, though."

"You were able to penetrate *my* mind," Malia reminded him. "So it should work on other people, too."

"Malia, are you able to *control* people that way, or is it more just a matter of reading people's minds?" asked Brian.

"Well, I was able to force Lucifer to make himself visible, but that's the first time I've tried something like that. But he kicked me out of his mind—other than Jaden, nobody else had done that before."

"Also, we can fly like Superman, and we have healing powers like Wolverine," Jaden told him.

"You can *fly*?" asked Brian, his eyebrows raised.

"Using telekinesis on ourselves," said Malia. "And I can heal other people once I'm inside their heads—that's how I was able to wake those people up in Lucifer's bunker. I made their systems remove the sedatives from their bloodstream."

"That's incredible," Brian muttered. "When we first met the Othali, we found out that the planet's magnetic field was amplifying your thoughts. Is that something you're able to do at will?"

"No, I wish," said Malia with a sigh. "It makes our telekinesis way stronger too, but so far, it's happened on its own when we're under a lot of stress. It's not something we can control."

"I believe you should be able to control it," said Salvatore. "It will take practice."

"I agree," said Brian. "Now, I understand that Lucifer has found a way to shield himself from your powers?"

"Well, the shielding in his hangar bay blocked *everything*," said Malia.

"Just like Babcock's testing room in Area 51," Jaden added. "Or at least, that's what they told us—I don't think we ever tried our telepathy in there, did we?"

"No, we didn't," Malia confirmed. "He also modified his emitter to block our telekinesis, but I was still able to penetrate his mind when he was using it."

"Oh, and our telekinesis doesn't work against his flying saucers anymore, either," said Jaden.

Brian nodded.

"Alright. So, Jaden, the main thing for you to work on will be using your telepathy on humans and Martians and penetrating people's minds. I believe that ability will provide you both with a powerful weapon to use against Lucifer."

"Agreed," said Salvatore.

"And Malia—"

"Using the magnetic field at will," she said.

"Yes, exactly," Brian replied. "That seems to amplify your powers exponentially, and I suspect it may be enough to overpower Lucifer's shielding—if you can tap into it consciously."

"Right, but how do I do that? Every time it's happened so far, we've been under extreme stress."

"Yes, and you have the ability to control your body's internal workings to simulate those conditions."

"How?"

"Adrenaline," Brian said. "If you can consciously stimulate your adrenal glands, it should recreate your body's typical stress response."

"That's right—adrenaline increases heart rate and muscle strength! We learned about this in school!"

"I'm willing to bet that's what's giving you access to the magnetic field," Brian told her.

"Remind me where the adrenal glands are again?" said Malia.

"Right on top of your kidneys," Brian told her.

"Hey, I got a question," Jaden said to Malia. "I know you can wake people up when they're unconscious, but can you knock them out? You know, using your powers?"

"I don't know," she said with a shrug. "I've never tried."

"We'll add that to the list," said Brian.

"How about this," said Salvatore. "I'll go outside with Malia, and we'll use my ship for her to practice on. You two stay here and see if you can help Jaden communicate with you telepathically."

"Sounds like a plan," said Brian.

"Remember, imagine modulating the pitch of your voice," Malia said to Jaden. "Try a lower pitch—that's how I got it to work."

"Got it," Jaden replied.

Malia went with Salvatore to his flying saucer. They moved up to the cockpit, and Salvatore guided the ship out of the hangar bay and over the frozen landscape.

"I propose a simple exercise," he told her. "You will change into your spacesuit and go down to the ground. Using your powers, you will move my vessel. I will then use the engines to counteract you. As you push harder, so will I. You will reach your maximum output, and at that point will need to tap into the magnetic field to continue."

"You make it sound so simple," Malia replied with a sigh. "Okay."

Malia grabbed the spacesuit and moved down to the main level. Once she'd changed into the suit, she dropped down to the ground.

"Can you hear me?" she asked Salvatore in her mind once she'd moved about fifty feet away from the vessel.

"Yes. Are you ready?"

"Give me a minute."

Malia focused inside herself, imagining her adrenal glands sitting on top of her kidneys. She tried to visualize them pumping their hormone into her bloodstream. It didn't feel like anything was happening.

"Alright," she said to Salvatore, letting out a long sigh. *"Let's try it."*

"Go ahead."

Malia concentrated on the flying saucer, pushing it away from her with her mind. This felt relatively easy. She could sense it when Salvatore engaged his engines—she had to try harder to keep the ship moving away. Over the next minute or so, Salvatore continued increasing his engine output; Malia was able to match the escalation, keeping the vessel moving away from her. But finally, his engines surpassed her power; the ship came to a standstill.

Malia focused again on pumping adrenaline into her system, but nothing happened. Salvatore's ship slowly accelerated toward her, and no matter how hard she pushed back, she couldn't stop it.

In the end, the vessel overran her position and streaked off into the sky. Malia collapsed in exhaustion.

"Are you alright?" Salvatore asked in her head.

"Yeah, I'm fine. Just tired."

"Rest for a few minutes, and we'll try again."

"Ugh," she said out loud.

Malia could feel her heart hammering in her chest and knew for sure there was adrenaline flowing through her veins right now. But it wasn't enough—she needed a massive amount. She had to create a fight-or-flight response within herself artificially.

Getting to her feet, Malia focused again inside her body and tried to sense the adrenaline already moving through her system.

She thought she could identify the hormone—it was making her feel strong.

"*Ready for round two?*" Salvatore asked in her head. His ship was right in front of her again.

"*Yes.*"

Malia took a deep breath and focused. Reaching out with her mind, she pushed his vessel away from her again. As before, Salvatore increased power to his engines. Malia continued pushing harder and harder but eventually could not keep up. The flying saucer came to rest and then slowly started creeping back toward her position.

Malia concentrated as hard as she could on pumping more adrenaline into her bloodstream. She screamed on the top of her lungs, and suddenly it happened—she could feel the hormone flooding her system. And a moment later, she sensed immense power flowing through her—it was indeed as if she'd tapped into the energy of the planet itself.

Shifting her focus to Salvatore's ship, she directed the fullness of her power at moving it away from her. She could feel Salvatore kicking his engines to maximum output, but she overwhelmed them. With another scream, she hurled the vessel far across the desolation and out of view. Collapsing on the ground again, she basked in the moment: she'd done it. Finally, she knew how to tap into the magnetic field at will.

Salvatore returned a minute later.

"*That was quite impressive,*" he told her. "*You threw the ship several miles away. Ready to try again?*"

"*Not a chance,*" she replied, grinning from ear to ear. "*I'm spent! I don't think I can lift myself off the snow at this point, much less move your spaceship again.*"

"*Very well. Come aboard, and we'll go check on your brother's progress.*"

He moved the ship directly over her, and Malia floated up through the entry. Once inside, she made her way up to the cockpit.

"I'd like to try one more thing before we go back," she said, plopping down in one of the chairs.

"Yes?"

"I want to see if you can kick me out of your head... and if I can stop you from doing it."

"Understood. You may proceed."

Though wiped out from her effort with the spacecraft, Malia found it didn't take much energy to penetrate Salvatore's mind. His thinking was sharply organized—there were no stray thoughts as she'd sensed in others.

Malia focused on Salvatore's memory of her recent accomplishment. She saw the events from his perspective and felt his surprise when she managed to hurl his vessel so far away.

"*Can you sense my presence in your mind?*" she asked.

"*Yes. This is disconcerting. I feel... violated.*"

"*I'm sorry—see if you can push me out.*"

And just like that, he ejected her from his mind.

"Wow—that seemed like it was easy for you," she observed.

"It was."

"Can we try again? This time I want to see if I can stop you from doing it."

"Go ahead."

Malia reached out once more with her thoughts, penetrating Salvatore's mind with ease. Focusing on his body this time, she sensed the blood pumping through his veins. She tried to imagine anchoring herself here as if she were physically holding onto something.

"Okay, see if you can kick me out again."

She felt Salvatore pushing against her consciousness, trying to eject her from inside of him. Malia fought back, trying to hold her ground. It took longer this time, but in the end, it was impossible to resist; he kicked her out of his mind again.

"It was more difficult this time," Salvatore observed. "I wonder if tapping into the magnetic field would enable you to overwhelm me."

"It might, but I don't have the energy for that right now," she said with a sigh. "Let's save that for next time."

Salvatore nodded.

"See if you can render me unconscious."

"Oh, right."

Malia penetrated his mind again. When she woke people up, it felt like turning on the lights. So, instead, she focused on dimming the light of his consciousness. This took a little time, but it worked—Salvatore was out. Malia woke him up again.

"Well done," he said.

"I'd like to try again—that took too long."

"You may proceed."

This time, Malia tried to imagine putting out a fire with a strong wind. Thinking of it this way, she was able to put him under in only a couple of seconds.

"That's better," she said once she'd awakened him again.

"Yes. This could prove useful against Lucifer when he's wearing his emitter."

"My thought exactly."

Chapter Eleven: Jaden

"Are you ready?" Brian asked once Salvatore and Malia had left.

"Yeah, I guess," said Jaden.

He focused on his uncle, reaching out with his mind.

"*Can you hear me?*" he asked.

No response.

Jaden imagined lowering the pitch of his mental voice and tried again.

"*Uncle Brian?*"

Nothing.

"I'm ready whenever you are," Brian said out loud.

"I've already been trying," Jaden told him.

"Oh, I'm sorry. Please, continue."

Jaden imagined pitching his voice *higher* instead.

"*Can you hear me, now?*"

Brian showed no reaction.

"This is useless," Jaden said with a sigh. "I'm never gonna get it."

"Nonsense," said Brian. "You know it's possible because your sister can do it."

"Yeah, that's just it—she can do loads of stuff I can't."

Brian regarded him in silence for a moment.

"Let me ask you something," he said finally. "If you were teaching a young child to walk, how long would you work with him before giving up?"

"What?" Jaden replied with a chuckle. "I *wouldn't* give up—he's obviously going to walk eventually."

"Precisely," Brian said. "I'm not sure exactly why Malia seems to come into each of these powers before you, but the fact that she can do this *proves* that you can, too—in time."

"I'm pretty sure it's hormones," Jaden told him. "Lucifer gave us some sort of hormone treatment to increase our powers."

"That makes sense," Brian said with a nod. "Girls do tend to mature a bit faster than boys, so it may well be that Malia's hormones have developed more than yours."

"Yeah, yeah, I know. Alright, let me try this again."

This time, Jaden imagined pitching his voice extremely low.

"*Uncle Brian, can you hear me?*"

"Yes!" Brian looked startled. "That was it—I heard you!"

"*Say something back to me in your mind,*" said Jaden.

"*This is very odd. The only voice I've ever heard in my head before is* mine!"

"*Yeah, it is a little strange at first,*" Jaden replied.

"I'm not entirely comfortable with the idea," Brian said out loud, "but see if you can penetrate my mind the way Malia does."

Jaden nodded—he'd been hoping to work on this next. He focused on Brian, trying to hear his thoughts, but without Brian actively communicating with him, he couldn't sense anything.

"I've only done this a few times with Malia—talk to me in your mind again so I have something to focus on."

"Very well," Brian replied. *"I'm right here. Use my words and try to locate my mind."*

Brian kept talking, giving him a steady stream of observations about Venus's compound and their current situation. Jaden focused on his "voice," and within moments, was able to sense Brian's mind. He penetrated his thoughts with ease once he'd done that, now seeing the images that accompanied Brian's words.

"Oh!" Brian said out loud. "Is that you?"

"Sure is," Jaden told him.

"This is a profoundly disturbing sensation..."

Jaden focused on surfacing a memory... he wanted to see his dad. Suddenly an image formed of his parents standing in front of an altar, his mom wearing a flowing, white dress. His dad lifted her veil over her head and kissed her.

"Whoa—is that their wedding?"

"Yes—I'd been thinking about that day last night... Jaden, while I'm delighted that you're able to do this, it's making me deeply uncomfortable."

"I know what you mean—but let's try something. See if you can force me out of your head."

"Good idea."

Jaden could feel him trying to expel him from his mind, but he couldn't manage it.

"*I wonder if perhaps this ability is unique to the Martians,*" said Brian.

"*Malia was able to do it,*" Jaden pointed out.

"*Hmm. Yes, well, let's try one more thing. See if you can control my body this way. Make me stand on one leg.*"

Jaden had to focus—he could easily do this telekinetically. But he concentrated on staying inside Brian's mind and causing his leg to lift from there. It worked.

"*Try to fight it,*" Jaden suggested. "*Put your foot down.*"

Jaden could feel Brian trying to overpower him, but he wasn't able—Jaden had no trouble forcing him to keep one leg in the air. Brian had to hop around a bit to maintain his balance.

"*Okay, Jaden, I think that's enough.*"

Jaden removed himself from his uncle's mind.

"This is pretty cool," he said with a grin.

"Let's go find Sydney and Miguel," Brian suggested. "I'm curious to see if either of them can eject you from their mind."

They found the two of them in the dining room eating breakfast. Brian explained what he wanted to attempt.

"Yeah, I'm game," said Miguel.

"No digging around in my memories, though," Sydney told him. "I had Malia in my head before, and it was a little... embarrassing."

"No worries," Jaden replied. "I don't want to see any private stuff."

"Excellent," said Brian. "Miguel first?"

"Sure, why not. Hit me with your best shot, kid."

Jaden reached out to him with his mind. This time, he didn't need Miguel to communicate with him to find his mind. He sensed his thoughts and a deep apprehension when Miguel realized that Jaden was inside his head.

"I'll be damned," Miguel muttered, his eyes wide.

"See if you can force me out," Jaden told him.

Like with Brian, Jaden could feel Miguel trying to push him out of his mind, but his effort was fruitless.

"No can do," Miguel said out loud. "So... is my brain like an open book to you now, or what?"

Jaden tried to surface Miguel's first memories of Sydney. Suddenly he was looking out the window of what he knew to be Miguel's mobile home. He saw Sydney approaching his front door. Next, he was in Miguel's pickup truck, speeding down the road, trying to get away.

"Yep, open book," Jaden told him.

"Alright, this sure is impressive, but I'm ready for you to stop now."

Jaden exited his mind.

"Sydney?" said Brian.

"Yeah, go ahead," she said with a sigh.

Jaden reached out and penetrated her mind.

"Hey, Sydney," he said.

"I'll never get used to this. Let me see if I can push you out..."

Again, Jaden could feel her trying to eject him, but it had no effect.

"No good," she said out loud. *"Now get out—please."*

Jaden chuckled, removing himself from her thoughts.

"Fascinating," Brian said with a frown. "Well, let's go see how Malia's doing. Thank you, both."

By the time Jaden and Brian had reached the hangar bay again, Salvatore's ship was just returning. They waited a few moments until Malia and Salvatore emerged from the portal.

"Hey, how'd it go?" Malia asked as they approached.

"I did it!" Jaden told her, swelling with pride. "Got into Brian's mind, and Sydney's and Miguel's, too."

"Awesome, I knew you could do it!"

"None of them could kick me out, either," added Jaden.

"I'm wondering if there is something about the Martian mind that makes that possible," said Salvatore. "Lucifer and I have both been able to eject Malia."

"Precisely what I was thinking," said Brian. "Jaden was also able to control my body telepathically. I couldn't stop him."

"That's probably not too useful, though," said Jaden. "I mean, we can do that way easier with telekinesis."

"Not with Lucifer," Malia pointed out. "As long as he's got his emitter, telepathy is the only way we could control him that way."

"Okay, good point," Jaden replied.

"How about you, Malia? Any progress?" Brian asked.

"She can now tap into the magnetic field at will," Salvatore reported.

"Yeah, but it's super draining," Malia added. "I wouldn't be able to do it more than once without some rest in between."

"We'll have to hold some regular training sessions for the two of you," Brian suggested. "I'm sure with time and practice, you'll both continue getting stronger."

Chapter Twelve: Brian

Brian felt a deep sense of foreboding after helping Jaden practice. He wanted to see his niece and nephew develop their powers to the fullest extent possible. Exploring one's potential was a worthy goal for anyone, and for the twins, these powers were a part of who they were. Yet, there were implications that troubled him deeply.

Babcock and the CIA had been right: they were weapons. Or could be, at least, if used by the government to combat its adversaries. But more importantly, they were sentient beings. They were only teenagers, not yet fully developed adults, and still had much to learn about life. It would be imperative to guide them concerning the responsible use of their powers. They were good people. As long as the adults in their life could nurture that goodness as they continued to mature, Brian felt confident they would make good decisions.

Yet as long as they remained on Earth, there would always be people trying to gain control of them and their powers. Right now, Lucifer was that person. If they managed to eliminate him, there was still the CIA. And even if they could somehow remove that threat, others were sure to arise.

Brian couldn't help but feel that it might be best to reunite Malia and Jaden with the Othali and carry through with their original plan to move the twins off-planet. Humanity wasn't ready to integrate alien life into its societies, and it probably wasn't prepared to do so with beings like the twins, either.

By the time Brian gathered with the others in Venus's dining room that afternoon, he still hadn't managed to shake his sense of foreboding. The twins' fate was something they would need to address.

Venus provided them with a great feast. Once they'd finished eating, she sat back in her chair, gazing around the table at them. Sydney and Miguel were here, as well as Salvatore, Malia, and Jaden.

"Well, it's time to make some decisions. Salvatore?"

"Our top priority must be finding and eliminating Lucifer. This has not changed."

"How do we find him now that we've lost our ability to track him?" asked Brian.

"Data," said Salvatore. "Our ships travel faster than anything humankind has built. And they do show up on radar."

"Yeah, why is that, exactly?" asked Miguel. "I mean, you've got shields that can make them invisible—why don't they block radar signals?"

"They do when they're engaged," Salvatore replied. "But Lucifer doesn't bother using his shields as his ship travels to and from the abduction sites."

"I wonder why that is," said Miguel.

"He doesn't need to," Brian suggested. "Nothing on this planet could possibly catch him."

"Well, Brian tried using radar to track that abduction ship, and it was no good," said Miguel. "Thing was too quick."

"Yes, but the signature *was* there," said Brian. "It just moved too fast to track its trajectory in real-time."

"Precisely," said Salvatore. "We have accessed the data banks for the entire North American radar grid. Right now, we are compiling the data to search for any radar signatures traveling above the speed of sound since the destruction of Lucifer's compound. This data will include supersonic military aircraft and meteors, but we will be analyzing patterns. Meteors are distributed randomly. Military activity centers around known installations and training areas."

"And so once you filter those out, what remains should be Lucifer," Brian observed.

"And that will tell us where he's been," said Sydney. "But how do we use that to figure out where he is *now*?"

"Malia reports that there is another compound somewhere," said Salvatore. "There is a good chance Lucifer will have moved his base of operations there. One would then expect to see a nexus of activity around that location."

"Ah... do we know for sure that that's in North America?" asked Sydney.

"We do not," Salvatore replied. "When Lucifer hijacked Venus's ship, he was taking us across the Atlantic. So the new compound may be overseas somewhere, but we'd like to be thorough. If we fail to find a nexus in North America, our next step will be to access radar data for other continents."

"I believe we should notify the U.S. government and get them involved as well," said Brian. "They've been very successful rounding up the rogue Malor since the invasion. I'm sure they'll want to eliminate Lucifer, too."

"But who would you contact?" asked Sydney. "We know Babcock's been compromised—there could be lots of other people in the government covertly working for Lucifer's organization."

"This is bigger than Babcock," Brian replied. "And you're right; they could have infiltrated other agencies, too. We should get in touch with the White House. I've got a contact in the Defense Department who may be able to arrange it. We can let them know about Lucifer and his organization's spies inside the government."

"Don't mention Babcock specifically, though," said Sydney. "Lucifer threatened to kill his family if he didn't cooperate."

"Fair enough," Brian agreed.

"Wait—the Malor destroyed Washington in the attack," said Malia. "The White House is gone..."

"They've moved the seat of government to New York City," Brian told her. "They're still calling it the 'White House,' but the president's offices are now located in the Empire State Building."

"Good, we can drop off the abductees while we're there," noted Venus.

"We should contact the Othali, too," Sydney suggested.

"Yes," Salvatore agreed. "Due to their experience with the Malor, there is a good chance that their weapons are stronger than ours. They could prove quite helpful in eliminating Lucifer."

"And we also need to reunite Malia and Jaden with Melissa," Brian pointed out.

"Malia and I were talking," said Jaden, sounding uncomfortable addressing the whole group, "and we thought that maybe we could convince our mom that we should stay here... you know, on Earth, instead of going out into space with the Othali. Do you think you guys could help us out with that? Mom seemed pretty set on finding that new planet."

"Aw, of course, we can," said Sydney with a smile. "We'd love to see you stay here with us."

"I'm not so sure that's the best idea," Brian told them. The room went quiet; all eyes turned to him. The stricken look on Malia's face drove a dagger into Brian's heart. "Don't misunderstand me—I'd love nothing more than to keep the two of you here. But you must recognize that with the powers you possess, there will *always* be someone trying to control you for their own aims. Whether it's Lucifer or the CIA or whoever comes next—you would forever be on the run."

"Now, hold on," said Venus. "There are ways around that. We're living proof—Salvatore and I, as well as our brethren, that certain measures can be taken to avoid that."

"Yeah, exactly!" said Jaden. "I get that we can't go back to a normal life—but living underground in Antarctica would be better than going somewhere it takes hundreds of years to get to, ya know?"

"I agree," Malia added.

Brian still harbored doubts but decided to keep them to himself.

"That's a fair point. But Melissa will be the one to make this decision."

"What will you do with the hybrids we brought here?" asked Sydney.

"They'll have to remain here until we get rid of Lucifer," said Venus. "If we let them go now, they'd find their way back to him, I'm sure. But once he's gone..." She shrugged.

"How long will it take to locate Lucifer with the radar data?" asked Sydney.

"That remains to be seen," said Salvatore. "Hours. Days, perhaps, if we need to move beyond North America."

"In the meantime, we can contact the Othali and visit New York," Venus told them.

"I'll try to arrange a meeting with the White House," said Brian. "But my phone doesn't work here—I can see that you have a wireless network, but I'll need access."

"Not a problem, dear—I'll help you with that when we're done here," Venus replied. "But honestly, *arrangements* won't be necessary. When our ship shows up hovering over Thirty-fourth Street, they'll be more than happy to accommodate us."

Miguel chuckled.

"Yeah, I don't reckon we'll have any trouble getting a meeting."

"Fair enough," Brian said. "But let me notify them, at least, to make it clear there's no hostile intent."

"Very well," Venus replied with a sigh. "Do as you will. We will depart in the next day or two—I'll keep you all posted. I believe that should conclude our business?"

Salvatore nodded.

"Have you had a chance to, ah, consider my request?" Miguel asked as everyone got up from their seats.

"Ah, yes," Venus replied, rolling her eyes. "Approved. Flint will be waiting for you in the hangar bay."

"Excellent—thank you much!"

Brian moved next to Venus as the others left the room. He opened his phone and handed it to her. Venus entered the network password and returned it to him. Before he could open his contacts, a notification popped up.

"Well, this is strange," he muttered.

"What is it?" asked Venus.

"The alarm system at my ranch went offline last night. I can't bring up the cameras, either."

"Probably a power outage, dear."

"I have backup generators. Something's wrong."

He logged into the live satellite network and entered the coordinates for his property. It took a few seconds to load, but once the image resolved, he gasped. A plume of black smoke was rising from the building. He showed Venus.

"Lucifer could have done this," he said.

"Why would he bother?"

"He might have gone there looking for the twins—he knows that's where I live."

Venus considered this for a moment.

"Let's go see how soon Flint can be ready to move out."

Chapter Thirteen: Sydney

"Where's Miguel going?" Malia asked as she and Jaden followed Sydney down the tunnel.

"He's getting a plasma cannon," Sydney replied, rolling her eyes. "They're going to teach him how to use it."

"It's easy," Jaden told her. "Me and Malia used them before."

"Well, let's hope he doesn't incinerate his foot or anything," said Sydney. "Hey, you guys wanna hang out? We have a lot of catching up to do!"

"Yeah, we do," Malia agreed.

When they got to Sydney's room, Malia and Jaden plopped down in her bed. Sydney sat on the floor across from them.

"So, where did you meet *Miguel*?" asked Malia.

"It's a bit of a long story," Sydney told her, smiling ear to ear. "A woman named Martha came to see me—she was investigating these alien abductions, and Lucifer was harassing her. He killed her in the end, but she told me to find Miguel right before she died. Your uncle and I picked up her investigation, and it took a while, but we finally found him."

"Why did she want you to find him?" asked Jaden.

"He'd been abducted. But unlike most of the victims, he

remembered most of the experience. He thought it was the Malor doing it, and he found a camp they'd established out in the desert near Monument Valley."

"We found that place, too!" Malia told her. "They captured us, but we escaped."

"Well, they grabbed Miguel and me, too, but Brian called in the military. They rounded them up—the camp's not there anymore."

"So, are you and Miguel *in love?*" Malia asked with a knowing smile.

"That's none of your business," Sydney said, feigning a shocked expression. "But it so happens that we are very much in love."

"Aw, I'm so happy for you," Malia replied.

"When are you gonna get married?" asked Jaden.

"Oh, I don't know," said Sydney, feeling herself blush now. "I'm not sure if we will, but if we do, it'd have to wait till after this craziness settles down."

"Yeah, if it ever does," said Malia.

"What was up with Uncle Brian before?" asked Jaden. "I can't believe he wouldn't want us to stay on Earth. I mean, he's the one with all the crazy security systems and stuff. I figured he'd think of some way to hide us here."

"I'm sure it's not that he doesn't *want* you to stay here—he's only concerned for your well-being," said Sydney.

"He does have a good point," said Malia. "People *will* keep trying to take us because of our powers. Babcock and Lucifer won't be the only ones."

"Yeah, I guess," Jaden replied. "But Venus is right—we could live somewhere like this, and nobody could ever get to us."

"And Brian did seem agreeable to that idea," Sydney pointed out.

"I don't know, though," said Jaden. "When I was practicing with him earlier—I was inside his mind. And it almost felt like he was *afraid* of us... or something."

"Afraid of you and me?" asked Malia, looking confused.

"Yeah! Like he's worried about what *we* might do with our power—not just what other people might try to make us do."

They sat in silence for a moment.

"That's a reasonable fear," Malia said finally. "I mean, think about it. We can do some pretty crazy things, now."

"That is true," Sydney agreed. "It was disconcerting when you were inside my head. You two could uncover any secret from someone's mind or make them act against their will. If you were inclined to take over the world, you probably could..."

"I would never do that," said Malia. "I don't know about Jaden, though..."

"Oh, come on," he said. "We're not like Lucifer. Uncle Brian *knows* we're not like that. Right? Or do you think he wants us to leave Earth because he's worried we could be like him someday?"

Sydney opened her mouth to speak, but just then, there was a knock at the door. She got up to answer it and found Brian standing in the corridor.

"There's been a development," he told her. "We're leaving first thing in the morning."

"What happened?" asked Sydney as Malia and Jaden gathered behind her.

"Someone's attacked the ranch. We believe it might have been Lucifer."

"Charlie's still there!" Sydney felt tears welling up in her eyes.

"Uh... who's Charlie?" asked Jaden.

"My cat!"

"Oh, no!" said Malia.

Chapter Fourteen: Malia

Malia returned to her room and went straight to bed but had difficulty sleeping. She'd imagined having a longer break from Lucifer, but it seemed that was not to be. Dozing off eventually, she suffered nightmares of her time in his compound, reliving the pain and trauma she'd endured during his experiments in the hangar bay.

Waking with a start, she checked her watch—it was time to get up. She felt like she'd barely slept.

Minutes later, she met the others in the hangar bay—Jaden, Brian, Sydney, Miguel, and Salvatore were there; only Venus was missing. Captain Flint was in the process of loading the human abductees onto Venus's ship.

Venus joined them moments later.

"I'm leaving Perry here with a team to guard the hybrids," she told them. "Bomani is already on my ship, in one of the medical pods. We can wake him when we're ready for him."

Flint and several other soldiers boarded the vessel a few minutes later. Malia was about to follow them up when Salvatore grabbed her by the arm.

"We'll be going in my ship."

Malia followed him along with Jaden, Brian, Miguel, and Sydney.

They boarded his saucer and moved up to the cockpit. Moments later, the ship moved out of the hangar and streaked into the sky.

"Why are we taking two saucers?" asked Jaden.

"Lucifer may still be there," Salvatore replied. "If so, having two ships will give us the advantage."

"We'd like the two of you to accompany us on the ground when we get there," Brian told her and Jaden. "It may be dangerous—even if Lucifer is gone, his agents may still be there. You'll need to keep your guard up and be prepared for an ambush."

"We're ready," Jaden told him.

"Malia, if we do encounter anyone, we'd like you to see if you can access their memories. Try and locate their new compound."

"Got it."

The ship raced to its destination, nothing but clouds visible below. The sky cleared eventually, and Malia spotted a plume of black smoke as they arrived at Brian's ranch. Much of the roof had caved in.

"I'm not detecting any other ships in the area," Salvatore told them. "But Lucifer's shields would make him invisible."

Brian nodded, his expression grim.

"Let's go."

"Be careful down there," Sydney told Malia and Jaden.

They followed Salvatore and Brian down to the lower level and descended to the ground. Meeting up with Venus and her soldiers, they approached the building. Someone had blown a hole in the front wall by the door.

Venus and Flint led the way inside, the others following cautiously. Malia couldn't believe the damage—they'd destroyed the furniture, knocked down the interior walls, and blown holes in the floor. The sky was visible through the gaping hole in the roof.

"What were they looking for?" Brian asked out loud. "It must have been obvious that the twins weren't here."

"Information, probably," Salvatore told him. "Clues about where we might have taken them."

They moved room to room but found nobody. The entire house had been thoroughly ransacked. Suddenly, Malia heard a noise—everyone froze. Listening intently, she realized it sounded like a cat.

Brian pointed toward the attached garage. Moving quietly, he opened the door, the others following. Malia could see that the exterior doors had been blown into the backyard. She heard the cat again—it sounded like he was in the shadows in the far corner.

A man stepped out of the darkness, holding the animal. His pupils were slits.

"Lucifer was right," the man said with a smirk. "He figured you'd come calling."

"Where is he?" Salvatore demanded.

"On his way."

"Let the cat go," Brian told him.

"I don't think I will."

"Malia?" said Brian.

Malia reached out with her mind, penetrating the hybrid's thoughts. She tried to surface a memory of their new compound.

But she found only images of the man hurriedly boarding Lucifer's saucer right before they destroyed his old compound.

"*Where is the new bunker?*" she asked.

"*I don't know what you're talking about.*"

Malia focused more intently, summoning any strand of recollection about a second compound but found nothing. It didn't seem like this hybrid had ever left Lucifer's bunker before.

"Any luck?" Brian asked.

"No," she said out loud. "He doesn't know anything."

"That's not nice—I know plenty of things."

"Shut up and drop the cat," said Brian.

"Make me," the hybrid said with a smirk.

Malia pushed deeper into his mind. She could sense his arms holding Charlie. Focusing, she forced him to release his grip. The cat dropped to the floor and trotted over to Brian, rubbing his head against his leg. Brian squatted down and scooped him up.

"Your mama's going to be very happy to see you," he cooed.

Salvatore nodded to one of the soldiers; he fired his plasma cannon, blowing the hybrid's head into oblivion. The corpse collapsed on the floor.

"Let's get out of here," said Brian, leading the way back through the house. "If Lucifer is coming, we should get back to the ships."

"Agreed," said Salvatore.

They moved outside and boarded the flying saucers. Sydney was waiting for them on the main level—Brian handed Charlie to her. She hugged him close to her, tears streaming down her face.

"Oh, my good boy, I missed you so much! Thank you for saving him!"

"My pleasure," Brian replied.

Malia and Jaden followed Salvatore and Brian back up to the cockpit.

"We've still not had any sign of Lucifer's ship in the area," Salvatore reported.

"There's no guarantee he'll show up here," Brian observed. "The hybrid could have been lying."

"Yes," Salvatore agreed. "We'll give it a few minutes, but then we should move on."

Malia suspected that Lucifer had probably moved on to his next target, whatever that might be. He had to know that Salvatore and Venus would be keeping her and Jaden heavily guarded. Salvatore confirmed with Venus that she hadn't detected Lucifer, either, and then they headed to New York.

"Were you able to arrange a meeting with the White House?" asked Malia.

"No, my contact in the Defense Department hasn't returned my calls," said Brian.

"So, let me get this straight," said Jaden with a grin. "We're about to show up unannounced and just drop in and ask to meet with the president?"

"Yes, we are," Brian replied with a nod and a shrug.

Only minutes later, they slowed down, and the Manhattan skyline came into view. They passed over the city, coming to rest in front of the Empire State Building. Salvatore took them lower, finally hovering twenty floors over Thirty-third Street.

"I'm receiving a transmission from the United States military," Salvatore told them. "They are warning us that we have entered restricted airspace and that they will shoot us down if we don't depart immediately."

"Heh, I'd like to see them try it," Jaden muttered.

"Let's move down to the street—and take the abductees with us," Brian suggested. "No soldiers and no weapons. We want to make it clear we're not a threat. But Malia and Jaden, you'll come with us—and be ready to act. There's a good chance they'll try to apprehend us."

"I'm assuming we shouldn't let them?" asked Malia.

"Ah, no," Brian confirmed. "Try not to injure anyone, but if they won't listen to us, then we'll be leaving."

Once Salvatore had communicated their plans to Venus, they dropped down to the main level. They let Sydney and Miguel know their intentions, and then Malia and Jaden followed Salvatore and Brian down to the street. They found Venus there with the human abductees.

Malia took in their surroundings. They were standing in the middle of Thirty-third street, directly in front of the lobby entrance to the Empire State Building. There were barricades at both ends of the block, preventing motor vehicle access—Malia guessed that made sense, with the president working here, now. However, there was still foot traffic, and scores of people had gathered to get a look at them and take photos and video with their phones—although they were keeping their distance. Malia found it strangely quiet for such a large crowd.

But the next moment, a group of twenty men and women charged out of the building and surrounded them, guns drawn. Several wore dark suits, the rest, police uniforms.

"On your knees, hands on your heads—all of you!" their leader shouted. "NOW!" he added when nobody moved.

Malia dropped to her knees immediately, as did Jaden and the abductees. Salvatore, Venus, and Brian put their hands on their heads but remained standing.

"We mean you no harm," said Salvatore. "There is a dire threat to the people of your country, and we are here to warn your president."

The agent seemed to suddenly take in Salvatore's appearance—his scaly skin and catlike eyes—and froze in his tracks. But he recovered quickly.

"On your knees, or I will fire!"

"Sir, my name is Brian Kwan—the president knows of me. My niece and nephew helped defeat the Malor—"

"I know who you are, but this is your final warning—on your knees, now!"

"Malia, Jaden?" said Brian.

Salvatore caught Malia's eye.

"*What is it?*" she asked telepathically.

"*There are snipers on the rooftops across the street.*"

"Jaden—you get the snipers," Malia told her brother in her mind, *"I'll take care of the ones on the ground."*

"On it."

Malia focused on the agents surrounding them. Using her mind, she snatched the weapons out of their hands, collecting them in a pile on the ground, and lifted the people a few feet into the air. Moments later, several rifles landed on top of the handguns, and the snipers floated down toward the street.

"Now," said Brian. "Let's try this again. We are here to warn the president about a new alien threat that could prove vastly more devastating than the Malor attack. Can you arrange a meeting for us?"

"I... uh... put me down, and we can talk," the agent replied.

Brian nodded to Malia. She lowered the agent to the ground. Brian approached the man, his hand extended. The agent regarded him in silence for a moment, then shook his hand.

"Agent Crickson, Secret Service," he said. "Who are these people?" he added, nodding toward the abductees.

"Victims," Brian told him. "An alien invader abducted them; we rescued them."

"And what about those two?" he asked, indicating Salvatore and Venus.

"That will take some explaining... but they're on our side. They made the rescue mission possible."

Crickson considered the situation for a moment.

"Alright. Put my people down, and I'll have them take care of the victims. You and your, ah, friends will need to come inside with me."

"Fair enough," Brian said, nodding to Malia and Jaden.

Malia returned the rest of the agents and officers to the ground.

Crickson headed into the building, speaking into his wrist microphone. Salvatore and Venus followed him in, Malia, Jaden, and Brian close behind. Once inside, Crickson directed them down the main corridor and into a small office.

"Please, wait here, and someone will be with you shortly."

He left the room, closing the door behind him.

"So far, so good," Brian said with a nervous smile.

"Do you think they'll let us talk to the president?" asked Malia.

"Probably not," said Brian. "I'm guessing we'll speak to an aide, but that's fine. We'll deliver our warning, and they can do what they will with the information."

Only a few minutes later, the door opened, and a man in a suit walked in.

"Good morning. I'm Andrew Stetson, the White House chief of staff," he told them. "We were arranging for you to meet with representatives from the Pentagon and National Security Council, but President Ferris stepped in. She insists on seeing you herself."

"That's terrific," said Brian. "Surprising, though."

"To say the least, yes. You will be meeting the president and vice president and nobody else. Usually, there would be aides and advisers present—at the very least, someone to record the conversation. But she has decided to dispense with all of that.

"There are a couple of conditions, however. First, your ah... foreign friends will need to leave the building. We have vetted you thoroughly, Mr. Kwan, after the Malor incident, as well as your niece and nephew. However, we have no information on these two, and allowing them access to the president is simply out of the question."

"I can vouch for them," said Brian.

"Irrelevant. If they do not agree to leave the building immediately, it will force a confrontation that I don't think either of us wants."

Brian turned to Salvatore and Venus; Salvatore nodded.

"Very well," said Brian. "What's the other condition?"

"They need to move the alien spacecraft out of restricted airspace. No unauthorized aircraft are permitted within a thirty-mile radius of this building."

Salvatore nodded again.

"Alright," said Brian.

"Two Secret Service agents will escort them from the building, and you three can follow me," said Stetson, opening the door again.

Salvatore and Venus followed the agents back toward the entrance, while Brian and the twins went the other way with Stetson. At the end of the corridor, they boarded an elevator. They got off on the twentieth floor and walked halfway down the hallway. Stetson opened a door for them and stood aside to let them enter. He remained in the hallway, closing the door behind them.

Malia looked around in surprise; this room looked exactly like the Oval Office from the actual White House—at least, the way she'd seen it portrayed in movies. A door across the room opened, and President Ferris walked in, Vice President Roberts behind her.

"Good morning," said the president, shaking Brian's hand first and then Jaden's and Malia's. "I'm Valerie Ferris, and this is the vice president, Nick Roberts." They shook hands with Roberts, too. "I've always wished I could meet the three of you. Please, have a seat."

The president and vice president each sat in one of the chairs by the fireplace. Brian sat down on one of the small sofas adjacent to them, while Jaden and Malia sat across from him.

"Forgive me, but I thought you two were on your way to another star system?" said Ferris.

"We were," Malia replied. "But there was a traitor on the Othali ship. He sabotaged the engines and took us back to Earth."

Ferris nodded.

"My people briefed me about the two of you during the invasion. I was shocked to find out about the CIA project—the plan to turn you into weapons had been kept hidden from my predecessors as well. But it turns out that wasn't the only thing being kept secret from our elected officials. After the pardons for your uncle and Ms. Hastings, I also issued an executive order requiring our intelligence agencies to brief the president directly about any new projects involving aliens, alien technology, or enhanced human beings."

"Good thinking," said Jaden.

Malia smacked him on the leg.

"Thank you, Madam President."

"So, tell me—what the hell is going on here?"

Brian gave her a summary of the events involving the Martians, Lucifer, his compound, the hybrids, and the abductions. Ferris and Roberts heard him out, their expressions growing graver by the moment.

"And do we know *how* exactly this Martian plans on eradicating humanity?" Ferris asked once he'd finished.

"I'm sorry, Madam President—we don't. Based on the experiments he was conducting in his compound, we suspect he may have developed some sort of chemical or biological agent. But we honestly don't know."

"And you're sure these other Martians are not in league with him?" asked Ferris.

"No, as I said, they're the ones who destroyed his compound and tried to eliminate him as well," said Brian. "And we are planning to resume the hunt. But Lucifer has said some things that make us believe he has agents operating within the government. When the time comes, we would expect him to use these people to help facilitate his plans."

Malia thought the president's expression had become rather stone-faced in response to this.

"Forgive me," said Roberts, shaking his head, "but I find this entire story difficult to believe. Million-year-old Martians? Human-Martian hybrids infiltrating our government? This sounds more like a second-rate science fiction movie than reality."

"Surely you saw their flying saucers hovering over Thirty-third

Street?" asked Brian. "And I have no doubt your Secret Service agents will have reported the appearance of our friends—"

"Yes, yes—scaly skin and cat-like eyes," said Roberts, waving his hand dismissively. "All it would take is a little stage make-up and some contact lenses—"

"I would have been quite skeptical myself before the invasion," Ferris interjected. "We will launch an investigation into these matters—thank you for bringing them to our attention."

"Yes, ma'am," Brian replied.

"Now, do you think we could have a little demonstration of your abilities?" she asked Malia and Jaden. "I've been extremely curious about this since learning about the two of you."

"Sure," said Malia. Reaching out with her mind, she lifted the president's and vice president's chairs a few feet in the air.

"Oh!" said Ferris, startled, holding onto the arms of the chair. "Very impressive!"

"Please, put us down, now," said Roberts, looking stern.

Malia returned them to the floor.

"And how about telepathy?" Ferris asked.

"*Can you hear me, Madam President?*" Malia asked with her mind.

"*Yes—can you hear me, too?*"

"*Sure can!*"

"*Listen to me very carefully. Your uncle is right: there are spies embedded in my administration. I've had orders countermanded and initiatives undertaken without my authorization. I no longer know whom I can trust. Although I will order investigations into this Martian and his organization, it's unlikely those orders will be carried out. Will you let your uncle know?"*

"Yes, of course! But you should know—Lucifer and his hybrids have holographic emitters they can use to disguise their appearance. They can masquerade as anyone they want—and the devices are very advanced. They fooled the other Martians' biometric scanners!"

Ferris looked suddenly thoughtful.

"That could explain a lot... thank you."

Malia shifted her gaze to Roberts; he was staring at her with a shrewd expression. But suddenly, he grinned, shaking his head slightly.

"No telepathy for me, thanks."

"Well, thank you for that," Ferris said out loud. "Is there anything else we should know?"

"I think that covers it," said Brian.

"I would consider asking the three of you to work with our officials to decide how to combat this, but at this point, I think I'd be putting you in danger—more than you're already in."

"We'll continue working with our Martian friends," said Brian. "They have a vested interest—killing them, and the rest of their brethren is one of Lucifer's stated goals."

"I will instruct the Joint Chiefs to give you folks a wide berth," said Ferris, getting to her feet. The rest of them rose as well, but as they did so, Malia noticed the president catching her eye.

"Madam President?"

"*Warn your uncle,*" Ferris told her telepathically. "*If I'm right, the military will take steps to obstruct your efforts. And I don't think I'll be able to stop them.*"

"*I'll let him know,*" Malia assured her.

"Good luck, Madam President," said Brian, shaking her hand again.

Malia and Jaden followed Brian back into the hallway. They met Stetson, and he escorted them back to the elevator.

"*Uncle Brian—the president told me there are definitely spies in her administration!*" Malia told him with her mind as they rode down to the ground floor. "*She said that the military would probably disobey her orders and work against us!*"

Brian fixed her with a worried look.

"*That would explain why she wanted to see us privately. I wonder...*"

"*What?*"

"*The fact that she didn't give us this warning out loud makes me suspect that she doesn't trust the vice president, either.*"

Malia shared his concern.

Once they'd said farewell to Stetson, they went back outside.

"And now how are we supposed to find Salvatore and Venus?" asked Malia, scanning the sky for the flying saucers.

"We're right here, darling."

Malia turned to see Venus and Salvatore leaning up against the building.

"I thought they made you guys leave!" said Jaden.

"They only said we had to leave the building," Venus told

him. "We had to move our ships out of the no-fly zone, but not our persons."

"How did you move the ships if *you're* still here?" asked Jaden.

"Our neural interfaces work remotely, dear."

"Where'd all the people go?" asked Malia. The street was clear now. She could see crowds gathered at both intersections, but they'd barricaded the sidewalks.

"They announced that they were closing the street due to a security concern when we came outside," said Salvatore.

"Well, we've warned them, and the president herself has granted us free rein," said Brian. "Let's get out of here before someone countermands her decision. How do we get to the saucers?"

"We fly, of course," Venus told him.

"Fly? Oh—you mean like Superman?" Brian asked, his eyes wide. "I don't know if I'm ready for this..."

"Relax, Uncle Brian," said Jaden. "It's fun. We won't let you fall."

At that moment, there was a commotion at the far end of the block—someone was trying to get through the crowd. They made it to the barricade, but the police officers stopped them. Suddenly, a figure rose into the air, crossed the barrier, and landed on the sidewalk.

"Uh-oh," said Jaden.

A woman with long, blue hair ran toward them.

"Venus—Salvatore—is that you?!"

Chapter Fifteen: Jaden

"Vesta?" said Venus as the woman drew closer.

"Yes! Thank God I found you two!"

Venus drew the woman into a hug. Salvatore nodded to her, but Vesta hugged him, too.

"I don't understand—what are you doing here?" asked Venus.

"I need your help—Lucifer found me!"

"*What*?!" said Venus.

"How?" asked Salvatore.

"I have no idea—I was hoping one of you could tell me..."

"I'm sorry, who is this?" Brian asked.

"Brian Kwan, this is Vesta," said Venus. "One of our people."

"You're a Martian?!" Jaden blurted out. She looked human. Her pupils were round, and her skin had no scales. The only thing about her appearance that stood out in any way was her blue hair.

"Born and bred," she said.

"But you look human..." Malia observed.

"Contact lenses and make-up," Vesta told her.

"Just like Roberts said," Jaden muttered.

"What?" asked Vesta.

"Oh, nothing..."

"Where is Lucifer now?" asked Salvatore.

"He was at my place—I own an apartment building in Brooklyn."

"He didn't follow you here?" asked Brian.

"I don't think so. I live in the sub-basement. I had it built when I bought the building, and nobody ever goes down there. Anyway, I've got this insane security system, and he tripped the motion sensor. He didn't show up on the cameras, though. But I heard him—I'd recognize that voice anywhere. So, I left through the escape tunnel and flew here."

"How did you know where to find us?" asked Jaden.

"You're all over the web—if you show up over the Empire State Building with a couple of flying saucers, you're going to attract attention! Every news station in the city is covering it."

"How did your motion sensors detect Lucifer?" asked Brian. "Mine couldn't!"

"I use lasers instead of infrared—cloaked or not, you're gonna trip them if you disrupt the beam."

"Ah..."

"We should go to your building now," Salvatore suggested. "Together, we can take him out."

"What about the kids?" asked Vesta. "It won't be safe for them."

"This is Jaden Kwan and his sister, Malia," Salvatore told her. "They're not normal humans."

"Yeah, we've got special skills," Jaden added.

"Oh—you two were on the news!" said Vesta, suddenly

recognizing them. "You were the ones who helped defeat those aliens!"

"That's us!" Jaden confirmed.

"Great! Well, let's go—where are your ships?" asked Vesta.

"No time for that," said Venus. "We can move them to our position when we get there—we'll want my soldiers to join us."

"We'll have to fly," Salvatore added. "Lead the way!"

Vesta took to the air, and the others followed; Malia took Brian with her. They climbed high above the Empire State Building and headed south. Once across the East River, Vesta took them in lower. They passed above a neighborhood full of row buildings, finally landing in front of a four-story brownstone.

"This is it," Vesta told them.

"I don't see any signs of Lucifer," Brian observed.

"He could be inside, waiting for Vesta to return," Venus pointed out. "Our ships are here now; I'm sending the soldiers down."

"Could they bring me a weapon?" asked Brian.

Venus nodded. Moments later, six men floated down from the sky, led by Captain Flint. He handed Brian a pistol.

"Let's go in," said Venus.

The basement opened at grade; Vesta led them up the front steps to the first-floor entry. She produced a key and unlocked the door. They followed her inside. She led them to the rear stairway and down to the basement level. There was a trapdoor in the floor that led to her sub-basement—it blended into the tile perfectly, and Jaden didn't think he would have noticed it if Vesta hadn't pointed it out.

"Where does your escape tunnel come out?" asked Salvatore.

"Backyard," Vesta told him.

"Let's split up," said Venus. "If Lucifer's still down there, he'll be trapped."

Salvatore nodded.

"I'll enter from the backyard. Jaden, come with me, please?"

"Take three of the soldiers, too," said Venus.

Vesta opened the trapdoor. Jaden caught a glimpse of a spiral stone staircase before heading out the back door with Salvatore and three soldiers. Behind the building, Salvatore found a manhole in the rear corner of the lot. Moving the cover aside, he revealed a shaft delving straight into the ground. He climbed in and descended the metal ladder. Jaden followed, the three soldiers bringing up the rear.

At the bottom, they found a tunnel heading toward the building. Salvatore led the way, creeping along silently. Jaden did his best not to make any noise. They came to a dimly lit area that looked like a typical cellar with bare stone walls and a concrete floor. There was a door at the far end. Salvatore opened it slightly, peering beyond for a moment, before signaling the others to follow.

They moved into what must have been Vesta's kitchen. Salvatore led them through the apartment, and they found Venus and the others in the living room. There was a giant fireplace at one end. The door leading to the front steps was hanging from one hinge.

"There's nobody here," Venus told them.

"The place is exactly how I left it," Vesta added, "except for the front door."

Salvatore considered this for a moment.

"We need to get back to our ships—Vesta, you should come with us. I don't know how he found you, but the rest of our people are in danger. We need to find them and warn them."

At that moment, Lucifer appeared in the doorway leading back to the kitchen. Several hybrids became visible as well, surrounding them.

"You people are so predictable," Lucifer said with a smirk.

The hybrids charged them; Lucifer launched himself toward Vesta. Jaden tried using his powers to repel them, but it was no use—their emitters must have been blocking his telekinesis. Brian fired his pistol, dropping a hybrid, and one of the soldiers shot another with his plasma cannon, but the others managed to overwhelm the rest of the soldiers before they could use their weapons. Jaden scanned the room for something he could use as a weapon; he spotted the fireplace tools. Reaching out with his mind, he grabbed the poker and launched it at one of the hybrids like a spear. It impaled him through the back, the point sticking out of his chest. He looked down at it for a moment in surprise before collapsing on the floor.

Salvatore was fighting Lucifer now; they were swiping at each other, their claws extended. Vesta was battling two hybrids; a third had pinned Venus on the floor. Jaden used his powers to remove the fireplace poker from the dead hybrid and launched it at Venus's assailant. It ripped through his torso, landing on the floor beyond. Venus pushed the corpse off of her and regained her feet.

One of the soldiers had managed to overcome the hybrid

attacking him. He hoisted his plasma cannon onto his shoulder and began firing at the others. But once he'd taken out four of them, Lucifer sprang on him from behind, impaling him in the back with his claws. Salvatore pulled him off the soldier, but it was too late; the man fell to the ground and didn't move.

Jaden hurried over and grabbed his plasma cannon. Raising it onto his shoulder, he pointed it at Lucifer. But he didn't have a clear shot—Salvatore was grappling with him.

"Jaden! Look out!" someone screamed.

Turning, Jaden spotted the hybrid flying toward him in the nick of time. He bludgeoned her with the cannon, then shot her when she hit the floor.

Looking up, he realized it was Malia who'd warned him—she was wielding the fireplace poker, now.

"Thanks!"

At that moment, a hybrid rushed her; she stabbed him in the heart with the poker.

"No problem," she replied as the hybrid collapsed.

Jaden returned his focus to Salvatore, but Lucifer had disappeared. Looking around the room, he realized the remaining hybrids were gone, too.

"Where did they go?" Venus demanded. "Are they still here?"

Malia scanned the room slowly, and Jaden knew she was reaching out with her mind to find their opponents. Jaden took stock of their situation while she was doing that. They'd lost three soldiers, and

Vesta was bleeding from the forehead. But Salvatore, Venus, and Brian had escaped unscathed.

"We're missing two plasma cannons," Venus noted. Jaden noticed then that all three fallen soldiers were missing their weapons; he had one, but the other two were nowhere to be seen. "Lucifer must have taken them."

"I'm sure we'll be encountering those in battle," said Brian.

"Lucifer and his hybrids are gone," Malia reported when she was done.

"How the hell did he find me?" Vesta asked. "I've lived here undercover for decades, and I've been very careful to cover my tracks."

"I don't know," said Salvatore. "But we need to warn the others. This must be the secondary project he was planning when he tried to recruit the twins."

"We're only his *secondary* target, now?" asked Vesta. "What's his primary goal?"

"Destroying humanity," Salvatore told her.

"Oh, well, that's lovely," Vesta said sarcastically.

"Those hybrids were able to block my telekinesis with their emitters," Jaden told the others.

"Yeah, mine, too," Malia added.

"That's not entirely unexpected," said Salvatore. "Once he'd tested that with his own emitter, it was only a matter of time before he modified the others."

They headed out the front door and back up to the street. Venus engaged her ship's gravity beam, and they floated into the air. Once on board, Venus headed up to the cockpit. She returned to the main level moments later.

"My oracle is gone," she announced.

"Lucifer must have taken it when he boarded your ship back at his compound!" said Malia.

"How would he have known about the oracles?" asked Venus. "We didn't build them until after we fled from him."

Salvatore gazed at her for a moment.

"Perhaps he *didn't* know about them. I believe he boarded your vessel the first time to make sure he could take control. While he was there, he would have seen your oracle and wondered what it was. Disguised as you, he would have been able to access it—and he could have used it to find Vesta."

"And that means he knows where the others are now, too," Venus pointed out.

Chapter Sixteen: Malia

"Wait—how could Lucifer take control of your ship?" asked Vesta. "That's impossible!"

"He's developed holographic emitters," Venus explained. "Using those, he can disguise himself as someone else. He must have done a thorough scan of each of us when we entered his compound—he was able to fool my ship's security system and take control using his emitter. That would have given him access to my oracle."

"But the ship's security system does a DNA scan," said Vesta.

"Yes, and the system in his compound must have done so as well," Salvatore told them. "His holographic emitter could use that data to fool the scanner. I'll return to my ship. If Lucifer has your oracle, then we should be able to use mine to track him."

"Or I could go inside and grab mine if need be," said Vesta.

With a nod, Salvatore dropped through the floor and left the ship. Malia and Jaden followed Brian, Vesta, and Venus up to the cockpit. Several laser blasts hit Vesta's building as they sat down, blowing apart the upper stories in a fiery explosion.

"My tenants were in there!" Vesta screamed.

"Oh, no!" Malia yelled. She caught a glimpse of Lucifer's ship, high above them, as the final blast fired. "Look!" she added, pointing up through the dome.

"I see it," said Venus.

She fired two blasts from the ship's plasma cannon, but they flew into the sky—Lucifer's saucer was completely invisible again and must have moved away immediately after firing its last shot.

An instant later, the remains of Vesta's building collapsed, leaving only a giant heap of rubble. The initial blast had taken out portions of the adjoining buildings, and Malia wondered if they would collapse, too. She pointed this out to Venus.

"Emergency services are already on their way," Venus told her, pointing up the street. Malia saw police cars racing toward their position. Moments later, Venus added, "Salvatore's located Lucifer."

"Where?" asked Brian.

"Iowa."

"Who's in Iowa?" asked Jaden.

"That would be Vulcan," Vesta told him.

The ship streaked across the sky. They slowed to a standstill a few minutes later, and Malia could see agricultural fields stretching out in every direction. There was a barn not too far away but no other buildings in the vicinity.

"There's nothing here," she observed.

"Vulcan's here somewhere," said Venus. "At least, his oracle is."

"I don't see Lucifer, either," said Brian.

"He's here, too," Venus assured him.

"I'm not detecting any life signs," Salvatore's voice announced over the speakers. "Sensors can't penetrate the earth, so I suspect he must have an underground bunker here."

"Why can't the sensors find it?" asked Jaden.

"It must be shielded," said Venus.

"We'll have to do a ground search and see if we can find the entrance," said Salvatore.

"Agreed," Venus replied. "We should go in pairs. And make sure everyone is armed—don't forget, Lucifer's got two of our plasma cannons, now. And Salvatore, we'll need to secure our ships with passcodes—if we leave them unattended, Lucifer could march right in and retake control."

"Passcodes?" asked Brian, sounding incredulous. "All the technology you have available to you, and you're going to rely on a passcode?"

"What choice do we have?" said Salvatore. "Lucifer can mimic our DNA. The passcodes will be generated by our ships' computers and stored in our neural implants using gigabit encryption. It would take Lucifer's computer over a billion years to break the encryption in a brute-force attack."

"Oh, alright... I guess that should suffice," Brian conceded.

A holographic map appeared in the middle of the cockpit, showing the fields below and the barn, with a grid overlaid. Venus assigned everyone a partner and an area on the grid. She paired Malia with Vesta and gave them the area that included the barn.

They moved down to the main level. Jaden still had the plasma cannon he'd picked up in New York; Venus gave Malia one, too, and Vesta a pistol.

"Uh... can I get one of those instead?" Vesta asked with a frown.

"Not without some training," said Venus.

"Trust me, these work great," Brian told her, his pistol in hand.

They moved down to the ground; Malia spotted Sydney, Miguel, and Salvatore descending from the other ship. Malia and Vesta took to the air and moved to their search grid.

"So, did they give you the nanoparticles, then?" Vesta asked her when they landed.

"Huh? Oh—the flying, you mean. No, my brother and I can use our telekinesis to fly."

"Seriously? That's awesome—so, you can make other people fly, too?"

Malia reached out with her mind and lifted Vesta off the ground.

"Okay—cool!"

Malia returned her to the earth, and they began looking for the entry to the bunker. Nothing was growing in this field, giving them a clear view of the ground around them. They searched the area systematically but found nothing. Finally, they headed to the barn. The front doors were unlocked, so Vesta pulled one open, and they walked inside.

"Nothing but storage," she observed.

There were a couple of tractors, bales of hay stacked in one corner, and hand tools hanging from hooks. Malia didn't see any animals. They moved through the building, looking for any kind of trapdoor in the floor, but there was nothing here.

"Why do your people always live underground," Malia asked as they went back outside.

"Well, it was necessary back on our planet," said Vesta. "Millions of years of evolution ingrained that drive deep in our psyches, I guess."

"That makes sense," Malia said with a nod. "So, was Lucifer always evil? Like back when you all still lived on Mars?"

"I didn't know him very long before going into cryostasis," Vesta replied. "Thousands of our people entered a lottery for the Earth mission, so most of us didn't know each other beforehand. We trained together for several months, though. He did seem a little off, but I would never have predicted he'd do what he's doing now. I think he knows right from wrong, though—he's aware that murdering us is evil. Isis was different."

"How so?"

"She believed conquering the humans was right. And I think she would have believed the same thing about killing the rest of us."

"So, Lucifer chooses evil knowingly, but Isis actually *was* evil?" asked Malia.

"Yeah, that's a good way to sum it up. I think her views wore off on him over time—those two *did* know each other before the lottery. They'd been lovers for centuries."

"You seem like you've adjusted to life here pretty well," Malia observed.

"Yeah, I like it here. Humans are fun with all their craziness."

"So, what do you do—I know Venus is an arms dealer, and Salvatore is pretty much a hermit."

Vesta giggled.

"You're right; he is a hermit. I own real estate—I've got over thirty apartment buildings in New York alone—mostly in Queens and Brooklyn. That gives me plenty of passive income, so I can pretty much spend my time however I like."

"That sounds nice," said Malia.

They regrouped with Brian, Sydney, Miguel, Venus, and her soldiers—only Salvatore and Jaden were still out searching.

"Anything?" Brian asked.

"Nah," said Vesta. "It does look like someone's using the barn, but there's no underground entrance over there."

Salvatore and Jaden returned a few minutes later.

"We've found something," Salvatore reported. "It looks like the entrance, but we couldn't open it."

"Let's have a look," said Venus.

Salvatore led everyone to the area he'd searched. It was a grassy field, and in the middle was a slab of concrete. There was a layer of artificial turf he'd rolled off of it. Brian walked around its perimeter, examining it. Finally, he squatted down and dug some dirt away from the side of it.

"I don't see any openings or hinges or anything," he said. "Are we sure this is an opening—it could just be a solid slab of concrete."

"Unknown," said Salvatore. "My ship's scans can't penetrate it."

"One way to find out," said Venus, hoisting her plasma cannon onto her shoulder. Once the others had backed away, she shot a fireball at the center of the slab. It blew a clean hole through the concrete, and Malia could see that there was indeed an open area beneath—the floor was about eight feet down.

Venus ordered Miguel, Sydney, Flint, and one of the other soldiers to wait above ground, then moved inside, floating down to the floor. Brian and the other soldiers were able to hang from the edge of the opening and drop down. Malia, Jaden, and Vesta descended into the ground, and Salvatore came last.

"Hydraulic lifts," said Brian, examining the mechanism around the edges of the concrete slab.

"They're probably connected to his network," said Salvatore. "He must control them through his neural interface, the way we do with our ships."

"Vulcan's gonna be pissed at us for blowing a hole through his front door," Vesta opined.

"He'll live," said Venus. "Let's see if anyone's home."

Malia stuck with Vesta as they went exploring. There was an extensive cavern system, including living areas, a kitchen, and storage rooms. Everything was on one level, though. And it didn't look like anyone but Vulcan was living here. They met up with the others back by the opening.

"Nobody's here," Brian reported. "But it doesn't look like Vulcan's been gone very long."

"I couldn't find his oracle," said Salvatore, "but he's probably got it in a vault hidden in the floor or one of the walls somewhere."

"Well, let's go topside and wait for him to come home," Venus suggested.

Malia and Jaden used their powers to help Brian and the soldiers return to ground level before flying up themselves. They didn't have long to wait—Salvatore spotted a figure flying toward them at high speed. Malia noted his cat-like eyes and scaly skin when he landed and knew this must have been Vulcan.

"What the hell is going on?" he demanded. "Salvatore? Venus—what are you doing here?" he added, suddenly realizing it was them.

But at that moment, Salvatore shouted, "Everyone in the hole!" He grabbed the nearest two soldiers and leaped into the bunker with them.

Malia grabbed Brian and followed Salvatore, catching a glimpse of the sky as she moved—a flying saucer had appeared directly above them. Jaden took Miguel and Sydney inside the cavern and no sooner had Venus, Vesta, and Vulcan hit the ground beside them than the ship fired on them. The laser blast slammed into the concrete slab, blowing it apart and burying them beneath a pile of dirt and rubble.

For the next minute or so, Malia thought for sure she was going to die. She could feel blast after blast impacting the ground around them, completely sealing them off from the daylight. Malia lost contact with Brian and found herself being crushed by the surrounding earth.

Finally, the blasts stopped. Malia tried to call out to the others but regretted it immediately as dirt poured into her mouth.

"Jaden—are you alright?" she called out with her mind. There was no response. *"JADEN!"*

It was no use.

Malia tried to move her arms or legs but could do no more than wiggle her limbs against the dirt pressing against her entire body. She'd still had her plasma cannon hoisted over her shoulder, and that was now digging into her neck, causing extreme discomfort. Reaching out with her mind, she pushed the earth away from her. She kept this up for a few moments, finally clearing a hole through which she could see a faint light. Although she was tempted to hurl the entire pile of dirt away from her, she was afraid some of the others might be buried in there and get hurt if she tried it. So, she proceeded carefully, slowly moving more and more earth until she could climb to freedom.

Malia found herself standing in Vulcan's kitchen. Salvatore and one of the soldiers were lying on the floor, unconscious. Everyone else must have still been buried in the giant pile of earth.

Dropping beside him, Malia shook Salvatore by one shoulder. He moaned, then opened his eyes and sat up, taking in his surroundings.

"Lucifer hit us," he said to himself. "Is everyone else trapped in there?" he asked, pointing to the dirt.

"I think so," Malia confirmed.

She shook the soldier, but he wouldn't wake up. Reaching

out telepathically, she penetrated his mind and returned him to consciousness. He sat up, looked around, and said, "Oh, shit."

"Yeah," Malia agreed. "Can you use the gravity beam on your ship to remove the dirt?"

"Perhaps," Salvatore replied. "But that would enable Lucifer to target it with his weapons."

"Damn."

"We'd better start digging," Salvatore suggested, getting to his feet.

Malia and the soldier joined him, using their hands to shovel the dirt out of the way, searching for the others. They found one of the soldiers first. Malia used her telekinesis to pull him out of the earth and set him gently on the floor behind them. A few minutes later, they found a pair of feet but couldn't tell who it was. Malia managed to free them from the pile and realized it was Vesta. She set her down next to the soldier.

Malia set to work reviving Vesta and the soldier while the other two continued digging. It took only a few moments to awaken the soldier, shaking him by one shoulder. But Vesta wouldn't wake up that way. Malia penetrated her mind telepathically, unintentionally shocking her back to consciousness.

"Whoa!" said Vesta, scrambling to her feet, staring at Malia wide-eyed. "What the hell did you just do to me?"

"I'm sorry," Malia replied, "You wouldn't wake up, so I used my powers to go inside your mind."

"Holy shit—that was unsettling. Promise me you won't do that again, okay?"

"Even if you're buried alive, and it's the only way to wake you up?"

Vesta considered this for a moment.

"Alright, fine. You can do it again if it's a life-or-death situation. I had no idea you could do that!"

"I guess I forgot to mention it before," Malia said with a shrug.

They managed to free Brian, Venus, Vulcan, and the rest of the soldiers but couldn't find Jaden. Malia felt herself starting to panic—where could he be? Taking a deep breath, she reached out telepathically, trying to sense Jaden's mind somewhere in the earth.

Malia found him after a minute, but he seemed to be unconscious—his mind wasn't active, and he wasn't dreaming. He was buried far across the cavern—Malia believed it was somewhere on the other side of the entry. Using her powers, she began making a tunnel through the dirt to get to him. But then she hit the remains of the concrete slab. She explained the situation to Brian.

"I'm worried I'm going to bury *us* again if I pull it through the dirt," she concluded.

"Can you pulverize it and then bring out the rubble blocking your path?" he asked.

"I think so..."

Reaching out with her mind again, Malia focused on smashing the slab into gravel. It took significant effort, but she was able to do it. Once she'd removed the debris, she had a clear path to Jaden.

Carefully, she pulled him through the hole and set him down on the ground.

"Head wound," said Brian. "He must have hit the concrete—that's probably what knocked him out."

Jaden had a gash on his forehead, blood covering his face. Malia reached into his mind and focused on engaging his healing powers to mend the wound—but found that his body was already doing this all on its own. Instead, she concentrated on returning him to consciousness.

It worked. After a few moments, Jaden moaned, and his eyes fluttered open.

"What happened?" he asked, his voice barely more than a whisper.

As Malia told him the story, she could see his wound knitting itself back together, and Jaden grew stronger by the moment.

Venus and Salvatore brought Vulcan up to speed. He was angry with them at first for bringing Lucifer here but recognized that it wasn't their fault by the time they'd finished.

"What do we do now?" asked Brian.

"My ship's sensors aren't detecting Lucifer's saucer," said Venus. "But I have no doubt he's up there just waiting for us to emerge."

"And the moment we do, he'll fire on us again," Brian replied. "Malia, can you sense him up there?"

Malia focused, reaching out with her mind to the airspace above them. It took a few moments, but she finally sensed someone. As she concentrated on the person's thought patterns, she realized it was Lucifer. "He's there," she confirmed to the others.

"Vulcan, is there another way out of here?" Brian asked. "An escape tunnel, perhaps, that leads far enough away that our exit might escape Lucifer's notice?"

"No," he said with a sigh. "That was the only way out."

"I'll use one of the plasma cannons to blow a hole through the earth above us," Salvatore suggested, "and fly up to the surface. Lucifer's ship will become partially visible as he prepares to fire—I'll hit him with the plasma cannon when it does."

"These units don't pack enough power to destroy his vessel," Venus told him.

"But it will do some damage," Salvatore replied. "And I should be able to provide cover to give the rest of you time to get back to our ships."

"I'll join you with a second cannon," Venus replied with a nod. "He'll undoubtedly move his ship and try again, but together, we should be able to provide cover."

"Malia, Jaden, Vesta, and Vulcan—we'll need you to help move the humans to the surface quickly," Salvatore told them.

Salvatore chose a spot, and everyone else backed away, ready to move quickly. He fired his cannon, ripping open a hole in the ground above them, and flew up to the surface, Venus right behind him. Not a moment later, Malia spotted a section of Lucifer's ship directly overhead. One of the Martians fired at it, the fireball exploding against the hull. Suddenly, the entire vessel became visible for a moment before streaking across the sky away from them. A cheer went up from everyone waiting underground.

Malia and Jaden used their powers to move the soldiers up through the opening. Vesta and Vulcan grabbed Brian, Sydney, and Miguel and carried them to the surface. Malia and Jaden moved up last.

But as Malia landed in the field, Lucifer and one of the hybrids appeared out of nowhere only fifty feet away—each with a plasma cannon hoisted onto one shoulder. Lucifer fired his cannon at Vulcan; the fireball tore a hole through his chest. The hybrid aimed at Vesta and fired; she dove onto the ground, barely avoiding the shot.

In the next instant, Salvatore fired his cannon at Lucifer, and Vesta shot the hybrid. Lucifer hit the ground with a gaping hole in his torso; Vesta's shot had incapacitated the hybrid. Malia ran toward them—she knew Lucifer could still regenerate, but he had vanished.

"Can you heal Vulcan?" Venus asked Malia.

"I can try," she replied, not feeling too confident.

"Quickly—up to the ships first, then you can try it," said Salvatore.

He picked up Vulcan and floated up to his ship. Malia and Jaden went next, followed by Sydney, Miguel, Brian, and Vesta. Venus and her soldiers returned to her saucer.

Malia found Salvatore on the main level; he'd placed Vulcan in one of the medical pods.

"He's clinically dead," Salvatore told her. "His heart and lungs are gone. I don't know if you'll be able to do anything..."

Malia tried to access his thoughts, but Vulcan was either unconscious or brain-dead. Reaching out with her own mind, she was still able to enter his. But she found only minimal activity and no conscious thought. She tried to visualize his torso regenerating, but nothing happened. After a couple of minutes, his brain went completely dead. There was nothing more she could do.

"I'm sorry," she said, turning to find the others gathered behind her, frozen in anticipation.

"Well, shit," said Vesta, tears streaming down her cheeks.

"I don't get it," said Jaden. "Lucifer healed from this before—and he's probably healing again right now. How come you couldn't do it?"

"Lucifer's got our DNA," she told him. "Vulcan doesn't. This injury is way beyond my ability to heal in someone else. Maybe I could help the process along if it happened to you or me, but without our self-healing power?"

"It's alright, Malia," said Sydney, hugging her. "You did the best you could."

"I'm sorry—this is a profound loss," said Brian. "Not many of your people remain."

"No, not many at all," Salvatore agreed. "Let's see where Lucifer's going next, and hopefully, we can stop him this time."

Chapter Seventeen: Brian

Brian, Vesta, Malia, and Jaden followed Salvatore up to the cockpit. Salvatore reported to Venus that they'd been unable to save Vulcan.

"Hardly surprising," she replied over the speakers. "I would have been shocked if you had. But on the bright side, I believe we've damaged Lucifer's shields."

"Yes, his entire ship became visible after we hit him with the plasma cannon," said Salvatore.

"His ship returned a few moments ago, and it was still visible," Venus replied. "It was probably picking up the bastard—I fired on the vessel, but it took off again before impact. Where is he going now?"

"My oracle shows him heading due north."

"North? Well, that's odd—we don't have anyone north of here," said Venus. "What the hell is he up to?"

"One way to find out," suggested Brian.

"Yes," said Salvatore. "We should pursue him. His plans will become apparent in due time."

"Agreed," Venus replied.

The two ships took off to the north.

After several minutes, Salvatore said, "Lucifer has come to rest over northern Nunavut."

"Where's that?" asked Jaden.

"Northern Canada," Brian told him. "Very few people live there—much of it is inside the Arctic Circle."

"Why would he be there?" asked Malia.

"I can think of no reason," Salvatore told her. "But we'll know soon enough—we're only two minutes away."

Brian watched as the frozen landscape sped by below until finally, they came to rest above the coast of a snowy island. He gazed around the area but did not see Lucifer's ship anywhere.

"Where is he?" he asked.

"I don't know," Salvatore replied. "The oracle is here, but his ship is not showing up on sensors."

"The oracle is down on the surface, sitting in the snow," Venus's voice said over the speakers.

"Yes, I see it," Salvatore confirmed.

"What is it doing down there?" asked Malia.

"My best guess is that Lucifer wanted to mislead us," said Salvatore. "He will probably be on the way to his next target by now, and by leaving the oracle here, he has thrown us off his trail."

"But how can he find the other Martians without it?" asked Jaden.

"They don't move around very often," said Salvatore. "Lucifer will know their locations now, so he doesn't need the oracle anymore— unless they relocate."

"And now, we have no way of knowing who he's targeting next," said Vesta.

"I'll retrieve the oracle, and then we should split up," Venus suggested. "We'll improve our chances of saving the rest of our people that way—at least one of us is guaranteed to get to them before Lucifer does."

"I wonder..." said Salvatore.

"What is it, darling?" asked Venus.

"Lucifer had your oracle in his possession for quite some time. He could have tampered with it—modified it in some way."

"To do what?" asked Malia.

"Perhaps to relay its data to him somehow, even though he no longer possesses an oracle of his own," said Salvatore. "Or maybe he has turned it into a weapon. I think it would be best to destroy it without bringing it onto your vessel," he added to Venus.

"Hold on," said Brian. "Are we certain that Lucifer's not still in the area?"

"We'd see him, dear," Venus replied. "His shields are damaged."

"But he could have repaired them by now," said Brian. "When he's preparing to fire his weapons, his ship becomes partially visible—does the same hold true for these vessels?"

"Yes," Salvatore replied. "He may be waiting for us to fire on the oracle—at that moment, he would be able to lock his weapons on us."

"And if we just leave the oracle and go on our way, he could retrieve it and continue using it to track us," said Brian. "Malia, can you tell if he's nearby?"

"I'll try," she said.

Malia gazed out the window, her brow furrowed in concentration, and turned in a slow circle, searching in all directions.

"I don't sense anyone else out there," she told them.

"But we don't know for sure if his shields would block your telepathy," Salvatore pointed out. "His emitter doesn't, but we don't know about his vessel's shields."

"I sensed him when we were escaping Vulcan's," she told him, "and his shields were up then."

"Very well," Salvatore replied, nodding appreciatively.

"We've wasted enough time here," said Venus. "I believe leaving the oracle here is the entirety of the ruse. I'm going to destroy it just to be sure—but be ready to fire on his ship if I'm wrong."

"Confirmed," said Salvatore.

Moments later, Venus used her ship's plasma cannon to destroy the oracle. They waited with bated breath, but nothing else happened.

"That's it, then," said Brian. "How many of your people are left to warn?"

"Three," Salvatore replied. "Hathor, Anubis, and Bastet."

"I'll take care of Bastet," said Venus. "Where is she?"

"Northern China," Salvatore replied. "I'm sending you all the coordinates now. We'll find Anubis—he's in Turkey."

"Excellent," Vesta said with a smile. "Anubis is my favorite. We were besties back in the day."

Malia giggled.

"Understood," said Venus. "I'll be in touch—stay safe, darling."

Their ship accelerated into the distance. They passed over the Arctic Sea, Scandinavia, and Eastern Europe. But as they were flying over the Black Sea, Venus contacted them again.

"Salvatore—I just heard from Perry—Lucifer has infiltrated my compound! They're under attack!"

"How can that be?" asked Brian. "Your place is a fortress!"

"Perry says he thought Lucifer was me," Venus told him. "He used his emitter to fool the security system."

"We're over the Black Sea—I'll divert there now," Salvatore told her.

"I'll meet you there," Venus replied.

"How would he know where her compound is?" asked Vesta. "She just destroyed her oracle, and yours is here."

"Yes, but he had hers when we were at her compound," Salvatore told her.

"What does Lucifer want at Venus's place?" asked Jaden.

"Her weapons cache, most likely," said Salvatore.

"Oh... shit," Jaden replied.

"Yes," Salvatore agreed.

Thirty minutes later, they arrived at Venus's compound. The hangar bay doors were open, but there were no ships inside.

"Lucifer must have left already," said Brian.

"Assuming he has yet to repair his shields," Salvatore replied. "I'll take us inside."

Once they'd moved into the hangar bay, they dropped down to

the main level. Brian took a moment to bring Sydney and Miguel up to speed.

"Lucifer may still be here, or he might have left some of his hybrids behind," Salvatore told them. "We'll wait until Venus gets here before we disembark—she was only a few minutes farther away when we changed course.

"Once we do move in, have your weapons ready—we may be facing an ambush."

When Venus arrived, they moved out of the ship. They met up with her and her soldiers and then headed to the storage area. The door had been left open; Venus led them inside.

Lucifer and his people had thoroughly ransacked the room. They'd knocked over the storage shelves and destroyed entire crates of weapons. Many of the boxes were still smoldering, filling the chamber with smoke.

Brian heard someone moaning farther inside the room. Venus had heard it too and moved to investigate, her plasma cannon at the ready. Brian followed her. They found Lieutenant Perry lying on the floor with a hole in his abdomen by the back corner of the room.

"Perry!" Venus yelled, dropping to her knees by his side, taking his hand in hers.

"I'm sorry, ma'am," he said. "We thought he was you at first... there were too many of them... they overwhelmed us..."

"It's not your fault," Venus told him. "I should have taken measures to prevent this before I left. Where are the others?"

"Dead," Perry said, his voice barely audible. "They killed..."

His words trailed off with his last breath.

"Can you help him?" Venus asked.

Brian realized the others had gathered around them.

"I'll try," said Malia.

She turned her gaze to Perry and concentrated. Suddenly, the soldier gasped.

"He took weapons," he said. "Cannons... but he didn't find the nukes..."

"It's working," Venus said hopefully to Malia.

Malia shook her head.

"His organs won't regenerate. I restarted his heart, but..."

She closed her eyes, a tear sliding down her cheek.

"Perry—stay with me," said Venus.

But he was gone again.

"I'm sorry for your loss," said Brian, squeezing her shoulder.

"We should take inventory," Salvatore suggested. "Confirm what Lucifer has taken."

"Yes," Venus agreed, rising to her feet with a sniffle. "Please, see if you can find the rest of my men while I take care of that."

Salvatore nodded.

"How many were here?"

"Six, including Perry."

"The first time we were here, the soldier brought the fusion grenades from this room," said Malia. "Why wasn't Lucifer able to find them?"

"No, dear—the nuclear weapons are stored on the lower level,"

Venus replied. "I'm the only one with access to that area—it requires my command codes on top of the DNA scan. I retrieved the grenades the day you were here and took them up to the storage room while you were outside training with the plasma cannons.

"Actually... Flint, why don't you start on the inventory here, and I'll check on the nukes. Just to be sure."

"Yes, ma'am."

"You should take Malia with you," Salvatore suggested. "Have her use her powers to detect any unwelcome, invisible visitors."

"I can do that," said Malia. She went off with Venus.

"Jaden, could you accompany me, please?" said Salvatore.

"Sure."

"I'll join you, too," said Brian.

He and Jaden followed Salvatore as he searched the rest of the storage area. They found two soldiers lying near the opposite corner, each with a hole through his chest.

"Jaden, can you use your powers to see if Lucifer or any of his hybrids are here?" asked Salvatore.

"I'll try," he said. "I'm not as good at this as Malia, though."

Jaden concentrated in silence for a minute.

"There's nobody here that we can't see," he reported finally.

"Very well," said Salvatore. "Let's continue to the main part of the complex and see if we can find the other soldiers."

But suddenly, Jaden said, "Wait—Malia's down in the vault with Venus... something's wrong!"

"What is it?" Brian asked anxiously.

"Hold on... There are hybrids down there with them—they ambushed them getting on the elevator!"

"Let's go," said Salvatore, hurrying off to the rear of the room.

Brian and Jaden ran after him. He opened a door midway along the rear wall and led them through a short tunnel. At the end, they boarded a freight elevator and descended to the lower level.

"Be ready," Salvatore advised.

Brian had his pistol ready, and Jaden hoisted his plasma cannon onto his shoulder. The door opened, and they moved off the elevator. This room was smaller than the one above but also full of shelving units.

"Where are they?" Brian whispered.

Jaden pointed toward the rear corner of the room.

They moved cautiously down the nearest aisle. There were a few crates on the floor, their lids removed. One contained what appeared to be diamonds—Brian guessed they must have been worth several million dollars. The other two held microchips. At the end of the aisle, Brian peered around the edge of the shelves and spotted Malia and Venus. Six hybrids were standing behind them, pointing plasma cannons at them.

"Drop your weapons, gentlemen," one of the hybrids said with a smirk, "or we'll blow these ladies' heads off." She was much taller than her companions. There were three wooden crates on the floor next to her.

"You have no way out of here," Brian told her. "Even if you make it up to the surface with the nukes, we're thousands of miles away from civilization, in the middle of a barren wasteland. Surrender now, and we'll let you live."

The hybrid shook her head and scowled at him.

"Don't worry about us. Weapons on the floor—*now!*"

"Alright, take it easy," said Brian, squatting down and placing his pistol on the floor. "We'll cooperate—don't hurt them."

Salvatore and Jaden put their plasma cannons on the floor. One of the other hybrids hurried over and kicked the weapons down the rear aisle.

"You three—take these crates to the elevator," the tall one ordered.

Brian, Jaden, and Salvatore each picked up a crate and headed back across the room.

"*Uncle Brian,*" Malia said in his mind. "*Venus had me warn Sydney that we're coming. Her soldiers will be waiting for us upstairs.*"

"*We're carrying nuclear weapons! If they hit one of these crates...*"

"*Venus says to wait for her signal, then put the crate down and drop to the floor. That should give her snipers clear shots.*"

"*Understood—you'll need to let Jaden and Salvatore know, too.*"

"*I will.*"

They put the crates down inside the elevator. Two of the hybrids pushed Venus and Malia onto the elevator with their cannons, and then the hybrids boarded themselves. The door closed, and they began their ascent to the main level.

"Sabrina, the transport says they're two minutes out," one of the hybrids said.

"*Shut up*, you fool!" the tall hybrid replied.

"What transport?" asked Salvatore.

Sabrina hit him in the head with the butt end of her cannon. Salvatore stumbled forward a step, bracing himself against the elevator wall.

"Pick up the crates," Sabrina ordered.

Brian, Salvatore, and Jaden obeyed her command. One hybrid moved behind each of them as the doors opened, pushing them forward with their cannons. Salvatore went first, then Jaden. Moving into the storage room, Brian tried to locate Venus's soldiers, but the room appeared empty.

Venus yelled, "Now!"

Brian, Salvatore, and Jaden put their crates on the floor, dropping down next to them. Suddenly, a fireball hit Salvatore's hybrid, ripping a hole in his midsection. A moment later, another decapitated Jaden's. Brian turned, just in time to see a third fireball burn through his.

"Take cover!" Sabrina ordered.

The fireballs had come from above—looking up, Brian spotted one of the soldiers lying on the top of the nearest shelving unit, rolling out of the way as Sabrina fired on him. Three more soldiers emerged from the next aisle, and a firefight ensued, but it was over in seconds. They lost two soldiers but took out all of the hybrids.

"How did they get inside the lower level?" asked Salvatore.

"They ambushed us on the elevator," Venus told him.

"I searched the storage room and the hallway to the elevator with my telepathy," Malia explained, "but there was nobody there."

"They were waiting for us inside the ventilation shafts," said Venus. "Dropped out of the ceiling the moment we boarded the elevator."

"What transport were they talking about?" asked Brian.

"I'm not sure," said Venus. "We did pick up something on radar, approaching fast. But it's turned around."

"Headed where?" asked Salvatore.

"South America, at least until it moved out of range."

"Could that have been Lucifer?" asked Brian.

"Had to be," said Venus. "Although I cannot explain why he wouldn't have simply waited here."

"Why couldn't it have been someone else?" asked Brian.

"Because it was moving at Mach 22."

"So, if it *wasn't* Lucifer, then someone else out there has acquired your tech," Brian observed.

Venus had no answer for him.

Brian and Malia went with Salvatore to check the rest of the compound. They found the last three soldiers in the central tunnel. Malia was careful to check the ventilation system this time, but they didn't find any other hybrids. They found Venus's staff alive but bound and locked in a cooler behind the kitchen. Moving through the lower levels, they discovered that the hybrid children and their mothers were gone.

"They must have gone with Lucifer," said Salvatore.

Nothing else was missing, there was no damage to the compound, and Malia didn't find anyone who didn't belong there. They regrouped with the others in the hangar bay.

"Hey," said Sydney, handing Brian her phone. "Check this out."

Brian gazed down at the display. There was a message in the encrypted e-mail app Sydney had used previously to communicate with Babcock.

"Urgent—we need to talk ASAP. Tell me when you can meet, and I'll be there. Bring your whole entourage."

There was a set of coordinates at the end of the message. The timestamp was from several hours ago.

"Recognize these coordinates?" Brian asked.

"I don't think so," said Sydney. "Should I?"

"It's Carl's old bunker in the desert," he told her. "When did you get this?"

"I only noticed it just now," said Sydney. "There's no signal here, so it must have come in when we were in New York or Iowa."

"What is it?" asked Salvatore.

Brian read him the message and told him about the way Sydney's last meeting with Babcock had gone down.

"I don't understand," said Salvatore. "What could he want?"

"I don't know, but we should see what he has to say," said Sydney. "He told me Lucifer compromised him and that he's a double agent for his organization, now. It could be important."

"He did warn you last time that you'd be in danger if you continued to pursue Lucifer, and he was correct," Brian noted.

"Lucifer will be on his way to kill another of our brethren as we speak," said Salvatore. "And we have no way of knowing which one it will be. This diversion is going to be costly."

They took the message to Venus and explained what had happened before with Babcock.

"We don't have time for this," she said. "Take the humans, and go see what he wants. I'm going to find Bastet," she added to Salvatore.

"You could be walking into a trap," said Salvatore. "We should find out what this Babcock knows first."

"No," said Venus. "We've already lost too much time—we need to rescue the others. Find out what he's got and let me know—you'll get there before I arrive in China."

Salvatore nodded.

"And watch out—Lucifer took several dozen plasma cannons and laser pistols. Any hybrids you encounter will be well-armed."

"He didn't get any nukes?" asked Brian.

"No," Venus replied with a long sigh. "But he did access the computer system—he's got the plans and schematics for the nukes, the plasma cannons—everything."

"It will take time for him to build anything new," said Salvatore. "Let's stop him before he gets to that."

"I'll set a passcode to make sure nobody can get into the compound this time," Venus told them. "I'll send that to you, Salvatore—this can still be our safe house if we need it. I'm taking the rest of my troops, so only the staff will remain here. I'd like Malia to come with us, as well."

"Yes," said Salvatore. "We'll keep Jaden with us."

"Take good care of her, please," said Brian. "She's my only niece."

"Darling, she'll be the one taking care of *us*," Venus replied.

"I'll have to let Babcock know we're coming," said Sydney. "Can you get me on your network?"

Venus took her phone for a moment and gave her access. Sydney took it back and typed away on the screen.

"Alright," she said once she was done. "I let him know we're on our way. Let's go!"

Chapter Eighteen: Sydney

Once they'd said goodbye to Malia, she boarded the ship with Vesta, Venus, and her soldiers. Sydney, Brian, Miguel, and Jaden joined Salvatore on his vessel and moved up to the cockpit. Brian gave Salvatore the coordinates for Carl's compound, and they followed Venus's ship out of the hangar bay. Sydney looked back as the giant metal door closed behind them. Moments later, they flew off into the sky.

The ship slowed down when they reached the Nevada desert. Salvatore took them in low and moved into a giant gorge. They dropped down to the bottom level of the saucer and used the gravity beam to descend to the desert floor. Salvatore and Miguel took their plasma cannons and Brian his pistol.

"Lead the way," said Brian. "I've never been here before."

"I'll see if I can remember," Sydney replied. "I've only been here once."

Sydney led them to a fissure in the cliff face. Inside that, they found a metal door. It was unlocked; Sydney opened it wide, and they passed inside. There was a tunnel, but it was pitch dark. Sydney pulled out her phone and turned on the flashlight. At the end of the tunnel, they came to a large, open chamber.

"Hello?" Sydney called out, scanning the area with her flashlight. "Babcock, are you here?"

Her voice echoed ominously off the concrete walls; there was no reply.

"This could be a trap," said Salvatore. "You said yourselves that Lucifer compromised this person. He could have lured us here to turn us over to the enemy."

"That's possible," Brian agreed.

"Yeah, I'm with you—I don't trust this guy at all," said Jaden. "He's not as bad as Lucifer, but that's not saying much."

"I don't think so," said Sydney. "Not that I trust him any farther than I can throw him, but when he met with me last time, he risked his safety to warn me of the danger I was getting into. Let's give him some time."

"We should wait on the ship," Salvatore suggested. "Just in case."

They moved back toward the access tunnel, but at that moment, they heard the door opening, followed by footsteps. A man emerged into the chamber—it was Officer Babcock.

"We were worried you weren't coming," Brian told him, shaking his hand.

"You didn't give me much notice," Babcock replied. "I got here as quickly as I could. You're sure you weren't followed?"

"We no longer have any way to track our enemy, so no, we're not sure," said Salvatore. "But we have no evidence that we were."

"That'll have to do," Babcock muttered with a sigh.

"So, what's this urgent information you have for us?" asked Sydney.

"I heard about your little meeting with the president," Babcock told them, shaking his head. "And I know you're going after the man in black. But you need to listen to me—you people are in *way* over your heads. I tried to warn you last time—and I was right, wasn't I? The man in black tried to use you as leverage to get the Wonder Twins to work for him, didn't he?"

"You *knew* he had Malia and Jaden?" asked Brian.

"You bet your sweet ass, I did."

"How?" demanded Sydney. "And why didn't you tell me?"

"Honey, what difference would it have made?"

"*Don't* call me that!"

"Look, there's no way you could have gotten them out of there," said Babcock. "The best I could do was to warn you of the danger and try to keep *you* safe, at least. But you didn't want to listen. Well, you need to hear me this time. You got the kids back, and you *must* ensure he doesn't retake them. Now *leave it alone.*"

"We can't do that," said Brian. "Lucifer is hunting down the rest of the Martians, and after that, he's going to destroy humanity. We're the only ones who can stop him."

"You *can't* stop him! He's only the tip of the iceberg—you have no idea what you're up against."

"We will if you tell us," said Sydney.

"Oh, no. Not a chance—I told you, he'll kill my son and his family if he finds out I'm talking to you."

"How much do you know?" asked Brian. "Do you have information that would help us defeat him?"

Babcock chuckled.

"You just don't get it. There is no defeating him. I have information that would help you stay alive. Primarily because if you knew what I do, then you would walk away from this insanity!"

"Now, hold on," said Jaden. "You know Lucifer's gonna kill everyone, right? So why bother warning us about *anything*? What's the point—either we die trying to stop him, or we die because we failed."

"He's got a valid point," Brian said. "If you don't help us, then you're dooming your family along with everyone else. Tell us what you know, and then at least we've got a better shot at stopping him. You've got nothing to lose."

"There's no telling how long it will take them to execute their plan," said Babcock, shaking his head. "It could be another thirty years for all we know. You got the kids back—so, now the most important thing is to make sure they don't fall into his hands again."

"Help us, and we will protect your family," Salvatore told him.

Babcock scoffed at this.

"How? You can barely protect yourselves!"

"We'll take them to a secure location," Salvatore said. "Right now. Lucifer won't be able to touch them."

Sydney knew he must have been talking about Venus's compound, and she found herself questioning the veracity of his statement—Lucifer *had* managed to infiltrate her fortress. But then she reminded herself that Venus had added the passcode, which should prevent him from getting inside the same way again.

Babcock seemed to be struggling with Salvatore's proposal. He opened his mouth to speak a couple of times but changed his mind.

"Why did you kidnap Malia and Jaden?" Sydney asked him. "Why did you kill their parents and then bring them to your lab the first chance you had?"

"They were a government project," said Babcock. "Their powers would help us defend our country—look at what they did to those aliens. I told you last time I'd do it all again."

"Right, and you have an opportunity right now to help us *defend the country* and the whole world for that matter! We're going to do everything we can to take Lucifer down, with or without your help. If you're so convinced that we're going to lose, then *help us*!"

Babcock let out a long sigh.

"We move Steven and his family *first*," he said finally. "Before they realize I've betrayed them. I'm not telling you a thing until they're safe."

"Agreed," said Salvatore. "We can go right now. Where are they?"

"Steve and his wife live in Colesville, just north of D.C.," he told him. "The girls—my granddaughters are both at school. They're at Wesleyan up in Connecticut."

Salvatore nodded.

"Let's do it."

Chapter Nineteen: Malia

Venus's ship soared into the air, rising high above the clouds.

"Hey, do you think we could go get Anubis first?" asked Vesta. "Lucifer *hated* him—he'd probably go for him before Bastet."

"Oh, why not?" said Venus. "But I know it's only because you two became intimate."

"True, but Lucifer *did* hate him."

"He hates all of us, darling."

"Did you know Anubis before you joined the Earth mission?" asked Malia.

"No, we met during training," Vesta said with a smile. "Fell in love and thought we'd spend the rest of our lives together. And then Lucifer happened."

"Why couldn't you stay together after that?"

"Well, there aren't too many of us left," said Vesta. "We had to take measures to ensure our survival. Staying separate increased our chances—even if Lucifer found one of us, it wouldn't lead him to anyone else."

"Hmm. I guess that makes sense," said Malia. "What is he like?"

"Very laidback. Funny—for a Martian, anyway. Full of life. Our people tend to be... uh... well, like Salvatore. Dry and logical."

"You two aren't that way," Malia observed.

"We used to be, dear," said Venus.

"Living with humans has rubbed off on us, I guess," said Vesta. "But Anubis was different even before we got here."

Venus's ship came to a standstill over central Turkey; it was nighttime here. They dropped out of the sky before hovering above a small city.

"This is strange," said Venus. "These are the coordinates for Anubis's oracle, but there's only an empty field."

"You're not detecting the oracle down on the ground?" asked Vesta.

"No... but hang on."

A three-dimensional image of the city showed up in the center of the cockpit. There was a red dot in the middle of an empty lot.

"That's where the oracle was?" asked Malia. "That red dot?"

"Yes," Venus confirmed. "But according to your internet, there's an underground city here."

"So, Anubis must be below the surface," said Vesta.

"Underground city?" asked Malia. "Where are we?"

"It's called Derinkuyu," Venus told her.

"I've never heard of it," Malia replied.

"Apparently, there are over two hundred subterranean cities in this region of Turkey," Venus explained. "They were originally built in the seventh and eighth centuries B.C. but were abandoned in the 1920s. This one's a tourist attraction, now. I've found an entrance in the city center."

"Weird," Vesta observed. "I never knew humans ever built underground like this. They'd have felt right at home with our people!"

"I'm going to move us outside the city limits before we go down," Venus told them. "Should help us avoid being seen."

Malia descended to the ground with Vesta, Venus, and three of her soldiers.

"Be ready," said Venus, hoisting her plasma cannon onto her shoulder. "Lucifer might be here."

Malia and the soldiers lifted their weapons onto their shoulders, too; Vesta had her pistol in hand. They walked into the city. Near the center square, they found a small building that housed the Derinkuyu tour company.

"Oh, shit," said Vesta.

Malia spotted a guard lying near the entrance in a pool of blood. The door to the building was hanging by one hinge.

"We're too late!"

"Inside," said Venus.

Malia followed her into the building, Vesta and the soldiers right behind her. They found steps leading down into the city.

Venus led the way. There were lights in the ceiling illuminating their path. They found a tunnel at the bottom of the steps and headed west, weapons at the ready. But before long, they came to a dead end.

"The oracle is farther west than this," Venus whispered. "The city is eight levels deep—let's go deeper and see if we can find a way to keep going."

Backtracking, they came to a narrower tunnel leading north. They followed that and found a stairway down to the next level. But the central corridor still didn't go far enough to the west. After descending three more stories and still not finding the way, Venus changed her mind.

"This is going to take all night. Let's get back to the ship."

"We're giving up?" Vesta asked with a tone of disbelief.

"Of course not, darling."

They moved back up to the first level but froze at the top of the steps—voices were heading their way.

"What the hell is this?" Vesta whispered, pointing her gun toward the source of the noise.

"Hybrids?" asked one of the soldiers.

Suddenly, a man appeared in the tunnel, rounding the far corner.

"Police," said Malia.

The man spotted them—he pointed his gun at them and shouted at them in a language Malia didn't understand. She could hear more voices coming from somewhere behind him.

"Damn," Venus muttered. "Looks like we're shooting our way out."

"No, wait," said Malia.

Reaching out with her mind, she flung the officer's gun away from him; he started in surprise before running back the other way.

Looking above, Malia used her plasma cannon to blow a hole in the ceiling big enough for them to escape.

"That works," Vesta said before jumping up through the hole.

Malia used her powers to move the soldiers up, then flew up herself, Venus right behind her. They were standing in the middle of a street.

"Now what?" asked Vesta.

But at that moment, they floated up into the air and back into Venus's ship.

"Now, we stop wasting time," said Venus. "I'm taking us directly above the oracle."

They moved back to the ground, this time in the middle of the empty lot they'd spotted earlier. Venus fired her plasma cannon at the earth, blowing a hole in the ground. They jumped in, landing in an underground chamber.

"I don't see an oracle," said Vesta.

"Or a Martian," Malia added.

"Must be farther down," said Venus. "I don't know how stable the structure will be if we start blowing holes in it—we should find the steps again."

They found stairs at the end of an adjacent tunnel. Descending one level at a time, they found the target coordinates but no sign of Anubis or his oracle.

"I don't get it," said Vesta after they'd cleared all eight levels. "He must be here somewhere, right? Or at least his oracle."

Venus thought about it for a moment.

"He must have delved deeper. This area doesn't seem like it's open to the public, and we had enough trouble finding it, but the people in charge of this place would know about it."

"Good point," Vesta agreed. "He probably would have dug out his own separate space."

They moved back through that level, searching for any kind of access point to take them deeper. Inside one of the chambers, Malia found a square hole in the wall. Peering inside, she found it too dark to see. She called Venus over; she shone a light into the opening, and they discovered a shaft leading down into the darkness.

"This must be it," said Venus.

Vesta and the soldiers joined them.

"You stand guard up here," Venus told one of the soldiers. "The rest of us will head down."

Venus climbed into the hole and dropped through the shaft. Malia followed her down, taking the other two soldiers; Vesta brought up the rear. At the bottom, they emerged into an elliptical chamber, with Persian rugs covering the floor and a crystal chandelier hanging from the ceiling.

"This must be the place," said Venus.

"Great, now where's Anubis?" asked Vesta.

"This way," said Venus, leading them toward a tunnel at the far end of the room.

Malia felt a cold chill run down her spine—this place was dark and spooky. She worried about what they would find at the end of this tunnel.

The passage widened, and they found themselves in another chamber, smaller than the first. There was a bed in the middle and a figure with a hole in its chest lying in the bed.

"Oh, no," said Vesta, hurrying over and stroking the man's face with her hand.

"Anubis?" asked Malia, noting his scaly skin.

Venus only nodded, a tear sliding down her cheek.

"We're too late."

"Better late than never," said a voice behind them.

Turning, Malia saw a hybrid standing in the tunnel, pointing a plasma cannon at them.

Chapter Twenty: Jaden

Salvatore led the way outside. Brian and Babcock followed him out; Jaden brought up the rear with Sydney and Miguel, but they hung back a bit.

"I kinda can't believe we're going along with this," Jaden said quietly once they'd moved out into the gorge. "I don't trust him after what he did with Malia and me—he could've just given us his info already."

"I don't blame you," Sydney replied. "But the enemy of our enemy is our friend, I guess."

"This guy ain't our friend," said Miguel. "He's just oozing unfriendly vibes if you ask me. But hell, he's got info that we sure could use, so we do what we gotta do."

They reached Salvatore's ship. Babcock flew up into the saucer with Salvatore, shouting in surprise the whole way up. Jaden had to laugh as he followed with the others.

"We should get the kids, first," Babcock suggested once they'd moved up to the cockpit.

Salvatore nodded, and the ship sped into the sky.

"Holy shit, this thing is fast!" said Babcock. "Why don't we feel any acceleration?"

"Inertial dampeners," Salvatore told him.

"Oh... Well, the boys back at the Ranch would give their right arm to get access to this tech."

"The ranch?" asked Sydney.

"Area 51—people who work there just call it the Ranch," Babcock replied.

"Hey, do you want to shoot your grandkids a text to let them know you're coming?" asked Jaden.

"And tip our hand? Not a chance," said Babcock. "I can guarantee you their lines are monitored."

"Oh, right," said Jaden.

The ship came to rest high above the university minutes later, the Connecticut River glistening nearby.

"Why are we stopping," asked Babcock, looking out the windows. "Wait—this is it. How the hell did we get here so fast?!"

"We would have been here sooner, but we keep our speed down to Mach 22 to avoid detection," said Salvatore.

Babcock chuckled.

"I wouldn't have believed it if I weren't here to see it for myself. Anyway, listen—speaking of avoiding detection. This group your Lucifer character works for has eyes and ears *everywhere.* If we go down there with your lizard friend here, and those bazookas strapped over your shoulders, we'll attract attention—and that will go very badly for us."

"Jaden and I will go down with him," Brian said to Salvatore. "The rest of you should stay here."

"We'll need to find a discreet location for you to land," said Salvatore. It was late afternoon, and people were coming and going all around the campus.

"The cemetery at the top of the hill should work," said Babcock. "It's close to Nicole's dorm."

Salvatore moved them into position.

"I don't see anyone down there," said Brian. "Let's go."

Jaden and Babcock followed him down to the lower level, and they descended to the ground. Babcock led them out of the cemetery and down to the road. They turned onto a side street and came up behind a dormitory building.

"We'll go in the rear entrance," said Babcock, setting out up the steps. "Fewer eyes back here."

They followed him into the building. He led them down to the lower level and knocked on a doorway halfway down the corridor.

The door opened, and a young woman stared at them for a moment before saying, "Who are you guys?"

"I'm Nicole's grandfather," said Babcock. "Is she here?"

"No, she's got her astronomy class right now. But she'll be back in a half hour or so."

"I'm sorry, but this can't wait. Where would her class be?"

"Observatory," the woman said. "It's right out front, across the parking lot."

"Thank you," Babcock replied, setting off back down the hall.

They went out the front door and spotted the observatory immediately. Jaden found himself feeling nervous that Lucifer or his hybrids would show up—he eyed every passerby suspiciously. Babcock led them up the steps to the observatory and into the main corridor. The building wasn't very large; Jaden could hear a professor lecturing in the classroom adjacent to the entrance. Babcock knocked on the door. The professor's voice trailed off, and moments later, he answered the door.

"Yes?" he asked, seeming surprised to have visitors.

"I need to speak with Nicole Babcock."

"Oh," he said with a nod, turning back to the classroom. "Nicole, there's someone here to see you."

Jaden got a look inside the classroom—there were only about twenty desks and only twelve or thirteen students. A dark-haired woman in the back row came out to meet them; the professor went back into the room and closed the door.

"Grandpa!" the woman said, hugging Babcock. "What are you doing here?"

"It's a long story—but you're in grave danger, and I need to get you out of here immediately."

"What is it—should I warn the rest of the class?"

"No, no—*they're* not in danger. Only you. We need to find your sister—where would she be now?"

"Uh... probably at her house. Hang on—let me grab my stuff."

"There's no time!" Babcock insisted, but it was too late—she'd already ducked back inside the classroom. A moment later, she came out again, a backpack slung over her shoulder and her phone in hand.

"Julia's house isn't far," Nicole told them as they headed back outside.

"She's in college, and she has a *house*?" asked Jaden.

"What? No—she rents it with a few friends," said Nicole. "A lot of landlords around here rent to students."

"So, why don't *you* live in a house?"

"Because I'm only a sophomore," she said with a scowl. "Julia's a senior, and they only let juniors and seniors live off-campus."

They'd walked only a few blocks when Nicole trotted up the steps to the front porch of a two-story Victorian. She took them inside without bothering to knock. Dropping her backpack on the couch, she knocked on a door across the room.

"Jules—you home?" she called out.

The door opened, and Jaden saw a woman standing there in her underwear.

"Yeah, what's—"

She spotted the visitors, squealed, and slammed the door shut again. Moments later, she emerged fully clothed, closing the door behind her again.

"Grandpa! Why are *you* here—and who are these people?"

Before Babcock could answer, Julia's door opened again, and a man walked out wearing only his boxers.

"Jules, what the hell—why do I... oh. Hi!"

"We'll discuss *him* later," Babcock told his granddaughter. "Right now, you need to come with me—you're in extreme danger."

"What the hell are you talking about? Where are we going?"

"To pick up your parents and get you all to safety."

"But—what's the danger? Should Malcolm come with us?"

"*He's* not in any danger. Let's go!"

Jaden thought that Julia seemed much more reluctant to leave her friend than Nicole had been to skip the rest of her class, but they left the house with Babcock. As they headed back to the cemetery, Jaden's anxiety increased—he expected hybrids to appear around them at any moment. None showed up, but he noted a couple of people he felt sure were watching them.

"A *cemetery*?" said Julia. "What are you doing here? Gramps, can you *please* tell us what's going on?"

"I will in a minute," he told her as they headed to the top of the hill. "Okay, we're here," he said, stopping where they'd left Salvatore's ship.

"I don't understand—" Julia said before screaming as they floated up into the air.

Jaden chuckled as he gazed skyward, realizing that Salvatore's ship was still invisible. He'd become used to this but knew that Julia and Nicole must have been freaking out by now.

They moved into the main level of the ship. Julia gazed around the chamber, her eyes wide.

"Grandpa, what the *hell*?" said Nicole.

"Can you give us a minute?" Babcock said to Brian.

"Of course," he replied. "What's your son's address in Colesville?"

Babcock gave him the address, and then Brian and Jaden went up to the cockpit.

"Success?" asked Salvatore.

"We got them," Brian confirmed. He gave Salvatore Babcock's son's address.

"This must be quite the eye-opener for his grandkids," said Sydney.

"You can say that again," Brian agreed.

Minutes later, they arrived at their destination.

"This stop could be significantly more dangerous," said Salvatore. "Lucifer may well have had people monitoring the grandchildren. If so, we will meet resistance here."

"So we go down, guns blazing?" asked Miguel, patting his plasma cannon.

"Easy, now," Brian said with a chuckle. "But there doesn't seem to be much foot traffic here, so I think we can take the weapons and our scaly friend this time."

"And this is our last stop," Sydney added. "So, it's not as crucial to avoid being seen."

"Jaden and I will go this time," said Salvatore. "And take our weapons. I'll alert you if we need assistance."

"Good luck," Brian said with a nod.

Jaden moved down to the main level with Salvatore. There was some sort of argument taking place—Julia was crying now, and Nicole was yelling at Babcock.

"We're here," Salvatore said to Babcock.

"Where?" Nicole demanded.

"Your parents' house," said Babcock. "Now, stay here, please. We'll be right back."

Jaden dropped to the ground with Salvatore and Babcock. He hoisted his plasma cannon onto his shoulder the moment they landed. There was no sign of the hybrids, but he felt nervous anyway. They moved up to the front door, and Babcock knocked. There was no answer and no noise from inside the house.

"Odd... both cars are in the driveway," said Babcock. "Stevie—it's me, Pops," he called out, knocking louder.

"We should go inside," said Salvatore. "The hybrids could be here already."

"Yeah," Babcock agreed. He tried the door—it was unlocked. "Shit—that's not good. They always keep it locked."

They moved into the house, closing the door behind them.

"Stevie!" Babcock called out as they walked into the living room. But at that moment, Jaden noticed someone sitting at the dining room table. "Hey! Who the hell are you?"

The man rose to his feet, approaching them with a smirk. He had a plasma cannon hanging from his shoulder.

"You knew the consequences for disloyalty."

"What? Where's my son?!" Babcock demanded, his voice panicky.

The man raised his weapon, pointing it at Babcock. Salvatore fired his cannon, blowing a hole in the man's abdomen. He collapsed on the floor and didn't move.

"Stevie!" Babcock called out again, hurrying around the first floor, looking for his son.

Jaden felt his heart sink—he had a bad feeling about this.

They followed Babcock to the second floor. But when they moved into the master bedroom, Jaden froze. Lying face down on the floor were a man and a woman, gaping holes in their torsos.

"*STEVIE*!" Babcock screamed, dropping to his son's side.

Chapter Twenty-one: Malia

Malia tried using her telekinesis to hurl the plasma cannon out of the hybrid's hands, but it didn't work—he must have been wearing an emitter. Instead, she reached inside his mind. She forced him to release his grip on the weapon, but it was too late—he'd shot one of the soldiers. The hybrid's cannon fell to his side, hanging by its strap, and moments later, a fireball tore through his chest. He collapsed to the ground and didn't move. Turning, Malia saw that it was Venus who'd shot him.

"Let's move!" Venus said, stepping over the hybrid's corpse. "Back to the surface!"

Malia and Vesta followed her out, the remaining soldier right behind them. Venus and Vesta flew up the shaft out of Anubis's cavern. Malia used her powers to propel the soldier up after them before ascending herself. But as they moved through the bottom level of the ancient city, four more hybrids appeared out of nowhere.

"Shit!" yelled Vesta, shooting one of them in the chest; the hybrid crumpled against the wall.

Venus shot one of the other hybrids with her cannon, and Malia took out the third. But the last hybrid had backed herself into the corner, pointing her cannon at Venus.

"I have orders to take the human girl alive," the hybrid told her. "Give her to me, and I'll let you live."

"Horseshit," said Venus. "You'll shoot me no matter what I do."

Malia reached into the woman's mind and forced her to drop the cannon. Venus hoisted her weapon onto her shoulder, aiming at the hybrid.

"No—wait," Malia said out loud. *"How many more of you are there down here?"*

The hybrid gazed at her with a smirk.

"I'm the only one left—you've killed the rest."

"Where's your ship?"

"What ship?"

"I've had enough of your lies."

Malia dug deeper into her mind, surfacing recent memories— more than twenty hybrids dropping into the hole in the ground that Venus had created with her cannon, as well as their flying saucer hovering over the city.

"Okay, I've got what I wanted," Malia said to Venus, withdrawing from the hybrid's mind. "Shoot her."

"What? No—"

Venus shot her head off; the corpse dropped to the floor.

"We've got trouble," Malia told them, explaining what she'd seen in the hybrid's mind.

"Well, damn," said Vesta. "Now what?"

"With those numbers, they're sure to overwhelm us," said Venus. "We'll have to create another way out."

They made it to the far end of that level without encountering any more hybrids.

"Must be waiting for us farther up," Vesta said.

"That's what I'd do," Venus agreed. "Ambush us as we come up the steps somewhere."

Raising her cannon, she fired at the stone wall. The blast blew out a crater in the wall, spraying dirt and debris all over them.

"What was the point of that?" asked Vesta, spitting out a mouthful of dust.

"That area where we started should be on the other side of this wall," said Venus, raising her weapon to try again.

"Hang on," said Malia, pushing her cannon down. "Let me try."

Venus nodded and stood back with Vesta and the soldiers. Malia focused on the crater, reaching out with her mind and gathering her power. The wall was solid stone; it didn't feel like she'd be able to generate enough force. She focused inside of herself, activating her adrenal glands. Suddenly, she felt the Earth's magnetic field amplifying her power. With a scream, she released her energy, blasting a hole through the stone.

"Wow," said Vesta, eyeing her appreciatively.

It had worked—they now had a clear passage into the other section of the city. Venus led the way, and the others followed. But by the time they'd climbed two levels higher, they encountered police officers searching the area. The men pointed their guns and shouted at them. Malia reached out with her mind, flinging their weapons away from them. The officers retreated, running up the steps.

Malia stayed by Venus's side the rest of the way up to ground level. They encountered a few more police, but Malia disarmed them each time, and they fled. But when they made it back to the tour company building and emerged outside, they found themselves surrounded by a couple of dozen officers, all of them pointing their guns. Someone shouted orders at them over a bullhorn, but they weren't speaking English; Malia couldn't understand a single word.

With a burst of energy, Malia disarmed them all, lifting the officers into the air. She moved them to the roof of a nearby building. A moment later, Malia, Venus, Vesta, and the two soldiers floated into the air.

"I summoned my ship on the way up," Venus told them by way of explanation as they entered the airlock.

"Yeah, I figured," said Vesta.

Malia made her way up to the cockpit with the two Martians. But as they took their seats, sections of three other flying saucers became visible as they fired on Venus's ship.

"Whoa—*three* of them?" said Vesta.

"Not for long," Venus muttered.

Moments later, a massive fireball hit one of the other saucers, taking an enormous chunk out of the hull. Venus fired again; the second shot obliterated the rest of the ship. But the other two vessels kept firing on them.

"Shields are down to seventy percent," Venus reported as she fired on the second saucer. Once again, the second shot destroyed the vessel.

"Before you finish off the last one, we should try to abduct one of the hybrids," Malia told her.

"For what purpose?" asked Venus.

"These ships must come from that other compound I saw! If we can take one of the hybrids, I can access their memories—we could find their base!"

"Good thinking," said Venus.

But at that moment, the last vessel retreated, taking off into the night sky. Venus launched their ship in pursuit, but the saucer vanished.

"Damn, we lost them, said Malia.

"No, we didn't," Venus replied. "We're close enough to detect them with sensors. They're flying erratically, though—trying to lose us. But we're matching their course."

They were high in the sky with no frame of reference, and the ship's inertial dampeners prevented them from feeling their acceleration, so Malia had no sense of their changing direction. Suddenly the other ship fired on them, rendering it partially visible.

"Direct hit," said Venus. "Our shields are down to fifty percent."

Venus returned fire with the plasma cannon. The fireball blew a hole in the other ship's hull; suddenly, the entire vessel became visible.

"Their engines are failing," said Venus. "Can you use your powers to extract one of them through the hull breach?"

"Yes, I think so," Malia replied. "Can you get us in closer?"

Venus moved their ship into close range with the other saucer. Malia could see inside their main deck—there were at least a dozen hybrids in there. Reaching out with her mind, she focused on one of them and removed him from the ship. Venus fired another blast, destroying the ship. Malia brought the hybrid right up to the outside of their cockpit, slamming him against the window and pressing his face into the glass.

"Where is your compound?" Malia said in his mind.

"Go to hell!"

"Fine, we'll do this the hard way."

Malia reached into his mind; she sensed his fear at this intrusion. Searching his memories, she found images of their compound. She saw Lucifer addressing a group of hybrids inside their hangar.

But suddenly, something else caught her attention—the hybrid was clamping his jaw shut. Malia could feel a tooth shattering in his mouth, and then he inhaled sharply.

"What the hell did you do?" she demanded.

"You people cannot win," he told her, his face spreading in a smirk despite being pressed to the window.

Malia felt his heartbeat weaken and die. She tried retrieving any memory that might give her the compound's location, but his brain was dying too. There must have been some sort of toxin in his tooth, but before she could go any deeper to try purging it from his system, he died. She relinquished her control of his body; he slid off the cockpit window and down to the hull.

"What happened?" asked Venus.

"I'm not sure," said Malia. "I think he had a fake tooth—he crushed it and inhaled some sort of poison. It killed him in seconds."

"Cyanide, probably," Vesta told her. "I've heard of stuff like this—they must *really* not want us to find that compound!"

"Were you able to locate it before he died?" asked Venus.

"No," said Malia. "I did see inside their hangar bay, though. Venus... they have a whole *fleet* of flying saucers. The hangar is way bigger than Lucifer's was—there had to be a hundred ships in there."

"Terrific," she replied sardonically. "Well, let's check in with Salvatore and see what was so urgent."

Chapter Twenty-two: Jaden

Babcock collapsed on top of his son's body, sobbing uncontrollably. Despite everything this man had done to him, Jaden felt terrible for him. The scene reminded him of his father's death, and his eyes welled up. He couldn't watch this; he moved to the window and gazed outside.

"I'm sorry for your loss," said Salvatore. "But we should move. There may be more hybrids."

It took a couple more minutes, but Salvatore managed to coax Babcock to his feet. But as he was about to follow the other two downstairs, Jaden saw four hybrids appear out of nowhere on the front lawn.

"We have a problem," he called out to Salvatore. "I wouldn't go down there if I were you!"

Salvatore was already partway down the steps with Babcock, but he grabbed him by the arm and hauled him back into the bedroom. Jaden used the butt end of his plasma cannon to smash the window, then he aimed and fired at one of the hybrids; the fireball blew a hole in the man's chest, and he fell to the ground.

Salvatore smashed the next window and took out another hybrid. The other two returned fire with their own plasma cannons.

Jaden and Salvatore dove away from the windows, crashing to the floor as the fireballs took out the entire wall.

Jaden scrambled to his knees, aimed through the wreckage, and shot one of the hybrids. Salvatore eliminated the last one moments later.

"That was *way* too close!" said Jaden, getting back to his feet.

"Yes," Salvatore agreed. "We need to move. Can you take our friend?"

Jaden nodded.

"Whoa, hold on," said Babcock, cowering next to the bed. "What do you mean—"

Jaden reached out with his mind, lifting Babcock off the floor, and flew out of the house with him. Babcock screamed. Salvatore followed, and they moved back inside his ship. They ascended to the main level and found Babcock's granddaughters waiting for them with bated breath.

"Well?" Julia said impatiently. "Where are mom and dad?"

Babcock turned to Salvatore, tears in his eyes.

"Can we have a minute?"

Salvatore nodded; Jaden followed him up to the cockpit.

"What happened in there?" asked Brian; Sydney and Miguel were staring at Salvatore expectantly. "We saw the shootout with those hybrids..."

But before Salvatore or Jaden could answer, another saucer appeared and fired on them.

"Oh, shit!" said Jaden.

"Not to worry," Salvatore told him. "Venus upgraded our weapons."

A fireball erupted from somewhere below them and slammed into the enemy ship, blowing a hole in its hull. A second shot destroyed the vessel, and then Salvatore moved them high into the sky.

"Was that Lucifer's ship?" asked Jaden.

"There's no way to know for sure," said Salvatore, "but I have a feeling it wasn't."

"Who else could it have been?" asked Jaden.

"Someone from their new compound, perhaps," Salvatore suggested. "Lucifer replaced the saucer that we destroyed with the fusion grenade. I believe that ship probably came from that other compound as well."

They sat down, and Salvatore told the others what had happened inside the house.

"Oh, no," said Sydney. "That's horrible!"

"I know he's grieving, but we need to find out what Babcock knows," said Brian.

But before anyone could reply, Babcock rose through the floor.

"Chris, I'm so sorry for your loss," Brian told him, getting to his feet and patting him on the shoulder.

Babcock took a deep breath.

"You know... somehow, I always knew this would happen. I've dreaded it for years, and I did everything I could do to prevent it... but you people were right. It was inevitable."

He broke down, crying and sobbing.

"Sit down, Chris," said Brian, guiding him to one of the seats.

Babcock took a few moments to collect himself.

"I'll tell you everything I know—and I want to help you destroy that son of a bitch. But we need to get the girls to safety—they're all I have left."

"Yes," Salvatore agreed. "We'll go there now."

They flew to Venus's compound in silence. Babcock didn't cry anymore, but Jaden knew he had to be devastated. Quite familiar with what it felt like to lose a parent, he had no doubt losing a child would be even worse.

Once they'd reached Venus's compound, docked the ship inside the hangar, and secured the door, Salvatore disembarked with Babcock and his granddaughters. Jaden waited in the cockpit with the others. Sydney's cat jumped into her lap, and she scratched his head absentmindedly, lost in thought. Salvatore and Babcock returned several minutes later and retook their seats.

"We arranged lodging for Julia and Nicole and introduced them to the staff," Salvatore told them. "They'll be safe here."

"Alright," said Babcock with a long sigh. "I'm not sure where to begin... It started years ago, back when they first discovered the hidden chamber under the Great Pyramid."

"The one me and Malia came from?" asked Jaden.

"Yes. I didn't know at that point *what* they'd found, only that it was some sort of advanced technology that had been buried there for millennia. I'd worked on the Roswell Project at Area 51 for years, and they promoted me to director of the Giza Project. We would be in charge of testing and weaponizing the tech once it arrived at the Ranch.

"But only days into my new assignment, the man in black—Lucifer—infiltrated the base. You need to understand that this is one of the most secure military installations on the planet. I had no idea how he'd managed it. But when I tried to investigate, my superiors ordered me to let it go."

"With a breach that serious, they must have been conducting an internal investigation, I would think," said Brian.

"No. They weren't," Babcock replied. "The orders came down from the White House to drop it. So, I went rogue. I found out about these alien abductions that were happening and this man in black who kept showing up whenever someone tried looking into them, and I knew he was my guy.

"Well, I managed to track him down. And that was the worst mistake I've ever made. I *should* have followed orders and let it go."

"That's when Lucifer compromised you?" asked Sydney.

"Yeah," Babcock confirmed, taking a deep breath. "Basically, he told me that as long as I provided him regular updates about the Giza Project, he'd let my family live. I didn't see any way out, so I went along with it. And once I'd learned about you and your sister, I convinced him to let you two stay with your parents until your powers manifested," he added to Jaden. "And when they did, we executed our plan to bring you both to the Ranch."

"Yeah, that didn't work out so well," Jaden muttered.

"No. That's for sure," Babcock agreed. "But here's the thing. A lot of years have gone by since my initial contact with Lucifer. I agreed to his terms, but I vowed to myself that someday, I'd find a way to take him down. So, I kept digging. I had to be extremely careful to cover my tracks. If he found out what I was doing, I have no doubt he would have killed my son or one of my granddaughters just to remind me what I could lose."

"So, what did you find out?" asked Sydney.

"Lucifer works for an organization called Majestic. The UFO conspiracy theorists out there would have you believe that President Truman ordered the creation of Majestic in 1947 in response to the Roswell crash. It was supposed to be a group of scientists, military leaders, and government officials charged with recovering and investigating UFOs and other alien technology."

"That sounds familiar," said Sydney. "I seem to recall reading something about that..."

"Yeah, well, it's bullshit," Babcock told her. "I worked on the project at the Ranch that was responsible for alien tech, and trust me; we aren't Majestic.

"Majestic is real. But it operates *outside* of the U.S. government— or any world government, for that matter. When I first encountered Lucifer, the base commander at the Ranch told me that Majestic was more than a myth. He said they had established relations with the aliens responsible for sending the Roswell UFO here and that their true purpose was to establish a world government and prepare the people of Earth for an alien invasion."

"That sounds like bullshit, too," Brian said. "The Roswell crash was a Malor scout ship. They don't seem to have anything to do with Lucifer."

"Exactly," Babcock agreed. "Majestic *does* have people everywhere—they've infiltrated every major world government, world financial institutions, tech companies—you name it. They've got people in the CIA, the NSA—hell, even the White House. But make no mistake, they're *not* part of our legitimate government. Majestic is an independent organization that operates above the laws of any country."

"How do you know all of this?" Brian asked skeptically.

"Through careful investigation and collaboration with other concerned members of the intelligence community," said Babcock. "Believe me; information is difficult to come by. Majestic is elusive. Their people take great care in covering their tracks. But they're not perfect. They do leave behind traces—breadcrumbs if you like. Any one piece of evidence by itself doesn't amount to much. But taken together, the pieces add up to a greater puzzle."

"Can you give us an example?" asked Brian.

"World finance. When I was still tracking down Lucifer, I met an FBI agent who'd done some work on the alien abductions. He'd also worked alongside Saudi intelligence to crack a massive international money laundering scheme. They found evidence that top officials from the Central Bank of Russia, the People's Bank of China, the United States Treasury, and the Saudi Central Bank, among others, were siphoning money from their respective organizations into international shell companies."

"For what purpose?" asked Brian.

"To fund Majestic!" said Babcock. "Look, when the agent took the evidence to his superiors, the bureau *shut down* their investigation. The same day, the Saudi government closed *its* operation. Majestic has people embedded in both agencies to make sure none of their people dig too deep."

"I don't know," said Brian. "That seems a little circumstantial. It could have been any organized crime organization."

"Yeah, that's what I thought at first," Babcock replied. "But think about it—the U.S. and Russia are *adversaries*, for Christ's sake. Why would officials from our Treasury Department and the Central Bank of Russia be diverting funds to the *same* shell companies?

"But that's only one example. Take the alien abductions. You people aren't the only ones who have tried to investigate that over the years. Both the FBI and the CIA have looked into it. But every time someone gets too close, they're shut down."

"What is Majestic's objective?" asked Salvatore.

"It's impossible to know for sure," said Babcock. "But I believe they *are* working toward establishing a world government. It's the only thing that jibes with all the evidence."

"That would be in line with Lucifer's goal of world domination," said Salvatore.

"Except that *he* wants to exterminate most of humanity to achieve it," Brian noted.

"Lucifer works for Majestic, but I'm telling you he's not in charge," Babcock told them. "And a couple of my colleagues have uncovered evidence that points to research into biological weapons that could wipe out most of the planet—so, that may well be one of Majestic's objectives."

"Who *is* in charge of Majestic if it's not Lucifer?" asked Sydney. "I can't imagine him obeying anyone else."

"Unfortunately, I have no idea," said Babcock. "You need to understand—we don't have any *direct* evidence whatsoever about any Majestic activities. We can infer things based on orders, personnel assignments, financial transactions, and the like—circumstantial evidence, as you would call it. But there's nothing in the CIA database that explicitly references Majestic or any of its operatives. My colleagues have confirmed that no such information exists on the FBI, NSA, or DHS networks, either.

"But when I was at Langley to interview the two of you, I did find something. There's a protected server there that's only accessible from inside that building. It's not even visible from the network out at the Ranch."

"What's on it?" asked Sydney.

"Who knows? I didn't try accessing it—I'm sure that would have alerted someone in Majestic that I was snooping, and it would have gotten back to Lucifer. I couldn't take that risk. But chances are my credentials wouldn't have been sufficient anyway."

"Then how do you know it's got anything to do with Majestic?" asked Brian.

"An old buddy of mine works at headquarters—one of my collaborators looking into Majestic. We went out for drinks one night while I was out there, and I asked him if he knew anything about that server. He said that he didn't, but he'd look into it. Well, a few days later, he disappeared. His wife says he went to work one morning and never came home. The folks at Langley claim to have no idea what happened to him. His wife filed a missing person's report, but as you can guess, that's come up empty. I think he found something on that server, and Majestic killed him for it."

The others gazed at him in silence for a moment.

"Chris, I've gotta be honest with you," Brian said finally. "While that does sound suspicious, it hardly connects the dots."

"Yeah, I mean, the whole thing does seem fishy," Sydney added, "but I'm not sure I see how that server ties into Majestic."

Babcock opened his mouth to reply, but Salvatore cut him off.

"I think it bears investigating. Lucifer does have eyes and ears everywhere—it would not surprise me if he's got people inside the CIA."

"*He* doesn't—Majestic does," Babcock insisted.

"Either way," Salvatore replied. "It would be in our best interest to find out what's on that server."

"Alright," Brian said with a sigh. "Let's go to Langley."

"Yes," Salvatore agreed. "I will confer with Venus and let her know there's been a change of plans on our end."

Chapter Twenty-three: Malia

Venus contacted Salvatore and told him what had happened in Turkey.

"These new saucers must have come from that other compound that Malia saw," she concluded.

"I agree," said Salvatore. "We have reason to believe Lucifer is indeed working for a much larger organization. There is a computer at the CIA headquarters in Virginia that may hold more information about this group. We are diverting there now to investigate."

"Understood," Venus replied. "We are going to find Bastet. If you are not done by then, we will visit Hathor next."

"Very well," said Salvatore.

Malia gazed out the window but could see nothing but darkness—no city lights anywhere.

"Where are we?" she asked.

"Flying over the Taklamakan Desert," said Venus. "We're almost there."

They came to rest minutes later to find a flying saucer firing on an isolated structure down on the ground. Venus fired the ship's plasma cannon, but the other vessel fled before impact, streaking off across the night sky.

"The oracle is inside that building," Venus told them.

"What is this place?" asked Vesta.

"I don't know, but they're in trouble," Venus replied.

"Yeah, I'd say," Vesta agreed.

It looked to Malia like the building had been constructed from stone or adobe, but she could see flames through the windows, and parts of the roof had collapsed. The enemy ship had been firing at the courtyard in the middle of the structure when they arrived, but the damage suggested that it had fired on the building itself before that.

"I'm going to put out the fire, and then we'll go down," said Venus.

"How?" asked Malia.

"Sound waves, darling. Using the right frequency, you can push the oxygen away from the source of the flames."

The next moment, the fire went out; it looked like a great gust of wind had blown through.

"Wow," said Malia.

They gathered their weapons and then headed down to the surface with Venus's last four soldiers. It was warm here, and the wind was blowing sand around them, making it difficult to see. They found a heavy wooden door on the front of the building, but as they approached, a dozen figures surrounded them; Malia couldn't see where they'd come from. They were wearing earth-colored robes and headscarves and brandishing swords. Venus hoisted her plasma cannon onto her shoulder, aiming for the nearest one.

"Wait," said Malia.

Reaching out with her mind, she disarmed the entire group,

dropping the swords in a pile in front of her. She heard several of them gasp as they backed away from her.

One of them stepped forward, saying, "Who are you people?" The voice sounded female.

"My name is Venus. We're here looking for our associate, Bastet," said Venus, lowering her weapon.

"That is not a name that is known to us," the woman replied. "I am Li Meiling. Are you in league with the devil who came with the other two ships and attacked us? He killed our leader, <u>Zhang Yi</u>."

"*Two* ships?" asked Vesta.

"One departed moments before your arrival—the man who attacked our leader left on that one."

"What man?" asked Venus. "What did he look like?"

"He wore a suit and sunglasses—and used a weapon that looks like yours."

"We are not in league with him—he is our sworn enemy," Venus told her. "Where is your leader now?"

"Buried beneath the courtyard."

"We'll see about that," said Venus. "Make sure your people stay out of that area."

"What are you going to do?" Li asked.

Venus floated up to her ship without answering her. The woman opened the door; Malia, Vesta, and the soldiers followed her through the building to a terrace at the edge of the inner courtyard. Malia spotted several bodies lying on the ground with holes through their torsos.

"What is this place?" asked Vesta.

"The temple of Yao Mo," said Li.

"Oh, is this a martial arts place?" asked Vesta. "You do kung fu here, like the Shaolin Temple or something?"

"Wushu," Li replied, glaring at her. "We are independent—there is no affiliation with Shaolin. Only women train here."

"Oh, cool," said Vesta. "I'm sorry; I didn't mean to offend you."

The temple's other occupants gathered around them as Venus used her ship's gravity beam to excavate a giant hole in the courtyard center. When she was done, she descended back to the ground. Malia and Vesta joined her, staring down into the ground.

"There's a cavern complex down there," Vesta observed.

"Yes," said Venus. "Let's go. I believe their leader is probably Bastet."

They flew to the bottom of the pit, landing at the intersection of two tunnels that crisscrossed beneath the courtyard. The ceiling had collapsed in a pile of rubble in one direction, but the other tunnels were clear.

Much to Malia's surprise, Li Meiling jumped into the pit, too, landing beside them.

"That must be a forty-foot drop," Vesta commented, gazing at Li appreciatively. "I've never seen a human do that before."

"We possess many skills that would surprise you," Li replied.

"I'm betting Bastet is buried in there," said Venus, indicating the collapsed tunnel. "Malia? Can you sense anyone down there?"

Malia reached out with her mind, trying to discern if there was anyone in the rubble. At first, she couldn't find anyone. But as she was about to give up, she felt something—it was faint.

"Someone's in there," she reported, "but I think they're unconscious."

"That must be Zhang Yi!" said Li. "You're sure she's alive?"

"Yes," Malia replied. "But I don't think she will be for long."

"Can you get her out?" asked Venus.

Malia nodded. They backed into the adjacent tunnel. Using her powers, Malia moved the debris into the other end of the passage. After clearing about fifty feet of rubble, she found Zhang Yi. They hurried over to her. The woman was lying on the ground, covered in dust. Her clothing was torn, and there was a gash on her forehead. There was human skin grafted onto her face, but it had peeled back around her wound, revealing the scales underneath.

"This is Bastet," Venus told them.

Looking more closely, Malia realized that there were puncture wounds beneath the tears in her robes. She was losing a lot of blood.

"That devil tried to shoot her," Li told them, "but she sliced his weapon in half with her sword. He disarmed her, and they fought hand-to-hand. My sisters and I tried to help her, but he had claws like daggers—he killed some of the others. I followed them down here—Zhang and I were beating him. But he pulled out another weapon from his jacket and fired some sort of laser; he brought the ceiling down on top of her. It was all I could do to escape after that."

Li stroked Bastet's hair and seemed to notice the scales around her wound.

"I saw that she has razor claws, too. I've trained with her since I was a girl, and I never knew. She's not human, is she? Nor are you."

"No," Venus confirmed.

"We should get her to the surface," Vesta suggested.

"No," said Venus. "Moving her in this condition might only make matters worse. Malia, can you help her?"

"I think so."

Malia kneeled beside Bastet, taking one of her hands in both of hers. She reached out telepathically, entering Bastet's mind. The light of her consciousness had grown dim; she was near death. Malia wasted no time. She focused on moving coagulant to her wounds—stopping the bleeding was critical. It worked; Bastet's injuries healed as Malia watched, the skin regenerating.

Next, Malia concentrated on her mind, tapping into her power to increase the woman's strength. Slowly, the light of her mind grew brighter.

"Bastet, can you hear me? You've been injured—my name is Malia, and I'm trying to help you."

There was no reply, but Malia could tell the woman sensed her presence—she felt her thoughts trying to coalesce.

"Focus on my voice. You fought Lucifer—he buried you under the courtyard. I'm here with Venus and Vesta. We came to warn you but were too late."

Malia knew her words were getting through—she could feel Bastet's mind coming into focus now. Suddenly, the woman opened her eyes with a gasp. Looking around and seeing Venus and Vesta, she tried to sit up but fell back again. Malia withdrew from her mind.

"I recognize my ancient sisters, but who are you?" Bastet asked, sounding groggy. "And how did you get inside my head?"

"That's a long story," Malia said with a grin.

"Can you walk?" asked Venus. "We should get you out of here."

"Just a moment," said Bastet. "My chi is weak." Closing her eyes, she took several deep breaths, sharply exhaling each time. When she opened her eyes again, she seemed more focused. "Where is Lucifer?"

"He's left," said Venus.

Bastet got to her feet.

"That bastard murdered several of my sisters," she said. "He must pay. Do you know where he might have gone?"

"We can make an educated guess," Venus told her. "He's hunting us—he's killed Anubis and Vulcan. We managed to save Vesta and rescue you. Only Hathor remains—Lucifer has probably gone to find her."

"What about Salvatore?" Bastet asked.

"He's alive," Venus said. "But working on a separate objective at the moment."

They returned to the intersection and shot up to the surface. Malia was surprised again to see Li Meiling make the jump on her own.

"Yeah, so seriously," said Vesta, "how the hell are you doing that? I mean, I've seen humans do that in kung fu movies and what not, but never in real life. Did Bastet give you the nanoparticles?"

"What nanoparticles?" Li asked.

"Forget it," Vesta muttered.

"Can we depart now to find Lucifer?" asked Bastet.

"Yes, of course," said Venus.

"Li Meiling," said Bastet. "I must leave you now. As my successor, you will take up the mantle of leadership in my absence."

Li pressed her hands together in front of her chest and bowed her head.

"I will guard our sanctuary with my life."

"Hopefully, it won't come to that."

"Will you return?"

Bastet glanced at Venus for a moment.

"We shall see."

At that moment, something in the sky caught Malia's eye. Looking up, she realized a flying saucer had moved into position above the courtyard—and was about to fire.

"Look out!" she yelled, diving toward the shelter of the terrace.

The others followed her in the nick of time—a moment later, a laser blast hit the ground where they'd been standing, spraying dust and debris all over them.

"Dammit!" yelled Venus.

An instant later, her own ship became visible, firing a massive fireball at the enemy saucer. It smashed into the vessel, splitting it in two. The remaining sections fell to the ground in piles of fiery wreckage.

"You're going to pay for that!" a voice cried behind them.

Turning, Malia gasped as she spotted four hybrids pointing plasma cannons at them. She reached out with her mind to disarm them, but one of them fired before she could do it. The fireball hit Malia in the stomach. Looking down in a moment of shock, she realized there was now a giant hole in her abdomen. Everything went black, and she knew no more.

Malia opened her eyes, but everything was still dark. Sitting up and looking around, she realized she was in the middle of a construction zone. There was an enormous structure composed of steel beams. It was nighttime, but there were dozens of people laying bricks to build walls between the beams. They were moving incredibly fast—much faster than she'd ever seen someone move before; it was as if she were watching a movie in fast motion.

Getting to her feet, she approached one of the workers.

"Excuse me, but where are we?"

The worker ignored her, spreading mortar across the top of his section of the wall.

Suddenly, Malia heard a voice—it was faint, but it was calling her name. She thought she recognized that voice but couldn't place it.

"Hello?" she called out.

"Malia!" someone said again.

The voice was female, and Malia was sure she'd heard it before. She gazed out into the distance, trying to find its source, but there was only darkness in that direction. Turning back toward the building, she started in surprise—it was nearly finished already.

Somehow, these people had completed the walls in only the moments she'd looked away.

She realized this had to be a dream.

"Malia! Wake up!"

Malia gasped, opening her eyes for real this time. She was lying flat on her back—faces were staring down at her with expressions of astonishment and disbelief. Venus was there, along with Vesta and Bastet and her successor, Li Meiling.

"How did you recover from that—I've never seen anything like it!" said Li. "You should be dead!"

"She possesses many skills that would surprise you," Vesta told her.

Bastet fixed her with a shrewd gaze but didn't say anything.

Memories came flooding back—Malia remembered the hybrid shooting her. Looking down, she realized that her wound had healed—her abdomen had rebuilt itself, just as she'd seen Lucifer's do after the battle in Russia. But her top was now a half-shirt, leaving her midriff exposed.

Malia sat up, and Venus helped her get to her feet.

"What happened to the hybrids?" she asked.

"Bastet's people took care of them," Vesta told her, gazing pointedly behind Malia.

Turning, Malia spotted the four of them lying on the ground, bleeding out from multiple puncture wounds.

"We should go," said Venus. "Are you alright to move?" she asked Malia.

"I think so."

Malia rose into the ship with Venus, Vesta, Bastet, and the soldiers. The men remained on the main level while Malia moved up to the cockpit with the Martians.

"Now," said Bastet as they took their seats. "What the hell is going on?"

Venus told her the whole story as the ship sped into the night.

"We always knew this day would come," Bastet said with a sigh. "So, now we must destroy Lucifer before he kills the few of us who remain. Where is Hathor?"

"Mexico," Venus told her. "We're headed there now."

"Hey, if you don't mind my asking," said Vesta, reaching out to Bastet's forehead, "is that human skin?"

"It's synthetic," Bastet told her, snatching her hand and moving it away from her head. "I had it grafted onto my face and arms so I could move freely among the humans."

"Damn," said Vesta. "Wish I'd known about that..."

"So," said Bastet, turning to Malia. "What is your story?"

Chapter Twenty-four: Jaden

"How do we get inside Langley?" Brian asked once they'd left Venus's compound. "I don't imagine we're walking in the front door at this point."

"Hardly," Babcock agreed. "I'm sure by now my security clearance has been rescinded. We'll be going in by force. There's a rear entrance we can use. It's guarded, but there won't be many people back there. We can use one of the nearby offices to get computer access, but I'm not sure what good that'll do us. My credentials certainly won't get us on that server now."

"There are ways around that," Brian said.

They arrived at Langley, and Salvatore took them in low over a wooded area behind the building.

"Jaden, you should wait here," Sydney suggested. "The CIA will still want to recapture you."

"Oh, man—but I can help!"

"Jaden's powers would be helpful," said Salvatore. "It's unlikely Lucifer would have anticipated this move, so I doubt we'll encounter him here."

"I agree with Salvatore," said Brian. "Having Jaden along gives us a much better shot at overcoming any resistance."

"Alright," Sydney said with a sigh. "But your mother's going to kill us if anything happens to you in there."

"You worry too much," Jaden told her.

"We should take pistols as well as plasma cannons," said Salvatore. "Save the cannons for any hybrids we may encounter."

They dropped to the main level. Salvatore removed a floor panel and retrieved pistols for everyone. Then they moved down to the ground and through the trees toward the building. There were a few cars parked in a small parking lot directly behind the structure, but no people around.

Babcock led the way to the rear entrance. Only one guard was on duty. He didn't seem to recognize Babcock but spotted Salvatore and the weapons they were carrying and drew his gun as they walked inside.

"Hold it right there," he told them. "This is a secure building—you can't just walk in like this—"

The guard reached for the microphone clipped to his shoulder, but Jaden used his powers to stop him. He flung the man's gun to the ground and unplugged his microphone.

"I'm sorry about this," said Brian before shooting him in the chest with his pistol. The guard fell to the ground and didn't move.

"Let's go," said Babcock.

They moved down the corridor and into an empty office. Sydney closed the door behind them. Babcock sat down at the desk and tried logging into the computer.

"No good," he said. "I don't have access."

"Let me try," said Brian.

Babcock got up, and Brian sat down at the desk.

"My company upgraded the systems here a couple of years ago, and we left a backdoor." He typed in his credentials and added, "I'm in. Now what?"

Babcock took the mouse and showed Brian where he'd found the mysterious server. Brian went to work for a few minutes, typing away at the keyboard.

"Strange," he said with a frown. "I can't get access."

"*You* can't get access?" said Sydney. "That's a first."

"I don't recall hearing anything about this server when we did the work here, but I didn't work directly on this project. It probably predates the equipment we installed. Do you know where the server room is?"

"No idea," said Babcock.

"We should see if we can find it," Brian suggested. "If all else fails, we can physically take the server with us, and I can probably gain access at my lab."

"If we can get it to the ship, I can access it from there," said Salvatore.

They moved into the hallway to find a dozen guards pointing their guns at them. Standing in front of them was a man in a dark suit and tie. For an instant, Jaden thought it was Lucifer, and he raised his plasma cannon, but it was someone else.

"Whoa!" the man said, holding his hands up in the air. "Everyone, let's stand down—we're all on the same side here."

"Are we, Craig?" said Babcock.

The guards lowered their weapons but kept them drawn.

"Chris—Director Salazar wants to speak with you. He sent me to bring you and your colleagues directly to his office."

"What does he want with us?" Babcock asked. "And why the armed escort?"

"He has reason to believe a hostile organization has infiltrated the agency and that you might have some information about that."

"Well, how about that," said Babcock.

"Can we trust this guy?" asked Brian.

"I think so," said Babcock. "This is Craig Anderson. He and I worked together at the Ranch for over ten years before he transferred here. Craig, can we trust you?"

"The director sent *me* because he knew you could."

Babcock looked to Brian; he nodded.

"Lead the way," said Babcock.

They followed Anderson through the building, into an elevator, and up to the director's office on the top floor. There was a waiting area in front. The woman sitting there opened her eyes wide when she saw Salvatore.

"We're here to see Director Salazar, Jane," Anderson told her.

"Yes... he's expecting you," she said.

Jane picked up the phone and pressed two buttons.

"Officer Anderson is here with our guests." She listened for a moment. "Yes, sir," she said, hanging up the phone. "You can go right in," she said to Anderson.

234

Anderson opened the door for them; Jaden went inside with Salvatore, Brian, Sydney, and Miguel. Anderson followed them in, closing the door behind him. The guards waited outside.

"You must be Babcock," Salazar said, getting to his feet and shaking Babcock's hand.

"Yes, sir."

He introduced the others.

"So, this young man is half of the Giza Project, in the flesh," he said, shaking Jaden's hand. "Where is the girl?"

"She's safe," Brian told him.

"Director, why is it that you wanted to speak to us?" asked Babcock. "You couldn't have known we were coming..."

"No, we had no idea you were headed here," Salazar told him. "But we saw you on the cameras coming in the rear entry. I met with the president a little while ago. She told me about the warning the girl gave her—about spies in her administration. I'm sorry to say they've infiltrated the agency as well."

"Yes... about that," said Babcock.

He spent the next few minutes telling Salazar about Majestic, Lucifer, and the way he'd been compromised so many years ago.

"They killed my son and his wife today," he concluded, a tear sliding down his cheek. "We didn't get there in time."

"I'm sorry to hear that," said Salazar. "The president tells me these hybrids possess holographic technology that they can use to disguise themselves?"

"Yes," Brian confirmed. "They can appear as anyone they wish, right down to the DNA."

"That explains quite a bit," the director muttered. "Is there a way to detect them?"

"No," said Salvatore. "We found one potential exploit, but they've been made aware of that. Chances are they've corrected for it by now."

"Damn," Salazar replied, shaking his head. "I have reason to believe the Deputy Director is one of them."

"Carter?" said Anderson, sounding shocked.

Salazar nodded.

"And he's not the only one. We've had a spate of rogue operations recently—in every case, the officers involved have reported directly to Carter. But we only know that because we've begun surveilling him."

"A surveillance op targeting the *Deputy Director of the CIA*?" said Anderson. "I never thought I'd see the day..."

"Neither did I," said Salazar. "I've known Carter for over twenty years. But I don't think it's Carter anymore. One of these hybrids must have replaced him.

"In any event, the president tells me you people are trying to root out Majestic. You must have had a good reason for coming here—how can I assist?"

Babcock told him about the server.

"Show me," said Salazar, moving behind his desk and offering his chair to Babcock.

Babcock sat down at his computer. But after working for a minute, he said, "What the hell?"

"What is it?" asked Brian, moving behind the desk to see what he was doing.

"It's gone," said Babcock. "The server isn't showing up at all now."

"May I?" asked Brian.

Babcock got up, and Brian took his place at the computer.

"They know we're here," he said after a few moments. "We should go to the server room—access the machine directly."

"It's in the basement," said Salazar. "I'll go with you."

He strode across his office and opened the door. A woman was standing just outside, aiming a plasma cannon at him.

"Jane?!" Salazar said in shock.

Jane fired her weapon. A fireball ate through Salazar's chest and slammed into the far wall. Salazar's body fell to the floor.

"Shit!" yelled Babcock.

Jaden got a look outside the door—the guards who'd accompanied them were lying dead on the floor. Beyond them stood four more people holding plasma cannons. Jaden reached out with his mind, trying to disarm them, but it was no good. Nothing happened—they must have been wearing emitters.

One of them fired his weapon, barely missing Salvatore. Miguel raised his pistol and shot Jane. A moment later, Brian, Salvatore, and Sydney fired their pistols; they took out two of the other hybrids, but Brian's shot went wide. Miguel fired a second later, dropping the hybrid Brian had missed.

The last hybrid turned and ran down the hall. Sydney shot him in the back, and he collapsed.

"Let's go!" said Brian, hurrying out the door and stepping over Jane's body. The others followed him.

"It would be best to take the stairs," Babcock suggested as they ran down the hall. "They could lock us down in the elevator."

"Agreed!" Brian replied.

They found the nearest stairwell and raced down to the basement. Emerging into the corridor, they found an officer standing there, flanked by half a dozen guards pointing their guns at them.

"Show's over," the officer said. "Drop your weapons."

"Nope," Jaden replied. He used his powers to disarm the guards, tossing their guns across the floor. Next, he slammed the guards into the wall, then hurled them across the basement in the opposite direction.

"You were saying?" Babcock said to the officer.

The man turned to run, but Brian shot him with his pistol. The officer hit the ground and didn't move.

"Now we have to find the server room," said Babcock, but a moment later they spotted a guidepost on the wall.

"This way," said Brian, hurrying down the hall.

They located the server room without any trouble but found several racks of computers.

"How do we know which one is the mystery server?" asked Babcock.

"Hang on," said Brian, pulling out his phone. He tapped on the screen for a moment, then held the device up to his ear. "Andre! Hey, it's me. Listen—you remember when we did the project at Langley? I need you to check the files for something..."

A minute later, he had the server location. They found it in the rear corner of the room, on the bottom of one server rack.

"Looks exactly like the others," Babcock observed.

"Except for this," Brian replied, kneeling and holding a cable running out of the back of the machine.

"What is that?" asked Miguel.

"Fiber optic cable," Brian told him. He stood up and followed the cable up to the top of the rack and into the ceiling. "Very strange. None of the other servers have it."

"There's no terminal here," said Babcock.

"Let's take it to the ship—we should be able to gain access there," Salvatore suggested.

Brian nodded. He unplugged the various wires from the server and tucked it under one arm.

"Good to go," he told them.

They ran up to the main level and out the rear door. But they skidded to a halt in the parking lot—there was a helicopter hovering above them, a voice issuing commands over a loudspeaker.

"Drop your weapons and put your hands on your heads!"

Jaden reached out with his mind and hurled the helicopter up and over the top of the building.

"Nicely done," Brian told him.

Salvatore brought his ship into position directly above them.

Moments later, they rose into the air and boarded the saucer. They moved up to the main level, and Brian placed the server on the floor.

"All yours," he said.

Salvatore nodded. The lights on the server lit up.

"It's got power," Brian noted with a note of surprise. "How are you doing that?"

"Wireless power transfer," Salvatore told him. "But we have a problem—I cannot access the file system."

"Why not?" asked Sydney.

"It's encrypted."

"Oh, I'm sure with your advanced tech, you can crack a puny 256-bit encryption key," Brian opined.

"No—this machine has gigabit encryption. We're not breaking this."

"Well, you were right, Chris," Brian told him. "Majestic had to be behind this—that's Martian tech."

"This is strange, though," Salvatore said. "I can physically scan the storage device. It's very low capacity—whatever it is, they're not storing much on this."

Brian considered this for a moment.

"Perhaps it's nothing more than a gateway. Is there any way you can scan that fiber optic line we found and see where it goes?"

"Yes," Salvatore replied. "Just a minute."

"I don't get it," said Babcock. "What the hell is a gateway?"

"A computer used to route traffic somewhere else," said Brian. "They must have a server off-site somewhere. Majestic agents in this building could have connected to this machine and used it to access the true server—wherever that is."

"I've got it," said Salvatore. "That line runs all the way to Mount Rushmore. There are equipment huts every fifty miles or so."

"What is an equipment hut?" asked Jaden.

"The lasers that carry the signals over fiber-optic lines can travel up to about sixty miles or so," Brian explained. "The huts will have devices that receive and re-transmit the signals, allowing them to cover an unlimited distance."

"Why Mount Rushmore?" asked Sydney. "That's just a big carving in the side of a mountain—isn't it?"

"I read about this researching one of my books," Miguel replied. "The guy who sculpted the monument wanted to build a chamber inside the thing to house a bunch of documents that were historically relevant to our democracy—you know, the Constitution and Declaration of Independence—stuff like that."

"*Wanted to?*" asked Brian.

"Well, they cut his funding, so they dug out the chamber, but it was never completed in his lifetime. They finally put some stuff in there in the late nineties. But from what I read, it's just this one little chamber—like a vault. Doesn't sound like it'd be near big enough for these Majestic folks to use."

"Well, there's something there," said Brian, "and we need to go see what it is."

Chapter Twenty-five: Venus

Venus laid in the course for the location of Hathor's oracle. She listened intently to Malia's story as they soared into the sky. The girl went into more detail than Venus had heard before. It was remarkable how composed and astute she was for such a young human.

They crossed over the arctic and moved into daylight again as they flew over North America. Venus took them in low once they'd reached the Yucatan Peninsula.

"We're here," she told the others as they hovered over a stone pyramid. There were steps in the center of all four sides of the structure leading to the top.

"This is Chichen Itza," said Malia. "Hathor is *here*?"

"According to the data from Salvatore's ship, she is," Venus replied. "Or at least, her oracle is."

"Hey, we're not far from Cancun," said Vesta. "What do you say we let Hathor fend for herself and go have some margaritas on the beach?"

Bastet fixed her with an intense stare.

"I'm kidding," Vesta muttered.

"It wasn't funny," said Bastet.

"There's a temple at the top. Scans are showing secondary and tertiary nested structures inside the primary pyramid," Venus told them. "There are a couple of small chambers in there, but nothing significant."

"Nested structures—you mean like those Russian dolls?" asked Malia.

"Yes, exactly," said Venus. "There is a sinkhole in the limestone beneath the pyramid... but I can't scan below that."

"Why not?" asked Bastet.

"It's shielded."

"So, I'm going to guess that's where Hathor must be," said Vesta. "How do we get inside that thing?"

"There's an entrance on one side of the northern steps," Venus told her. "That seems to lead to the inner structures, but it's not clear from my scans if there's access to anything underground from there. We'll need to go down and have a look around."

"What about all the tourists?" asked Malia.

Venus was tempted to disregard them and simply go about their business, but some security guard was sure to try playing the hero, and then she'd have to shoot him. Things would get messy, and Salvatore would chastise her for harming civilians.

She had another idea. Making the ship visible, she fired the plasma cannon at an unoccupied patch of grass in front of the pyramid.

"What are you doing?!" Malia demanded.

"Clearing the area," Venus told her.

Sure enough, the humans on the ground fled the site, screaming their heads off—including the security personnel. Within minutes, the place had become a ghost town.

"We'll have to hurry—I'm sure they'll call in the troops," said Venus.

They dropped to the main level. Venus retrieved a laser pistol from the compartment in the floor and handed it to Bastet.

"It's been a while since I used one of these," she said.

"Nothing's changed," Venus told her, strapping her plasma cannon over her shoulder. "Point and shoot."

Using the gravity beam, they moved down to the surface. Venus ordered her four soldiers to stand guard as she explored the site with Vesta, Bastet, and Malia. They circled the pyramid, but the entrance on the northern face was the only one they could find. They arrived at the door to find that someone had blasted off the lock.

"This was done with a laser," Venus told them.

"Lucifer must have been here already," said Vesta.

"He may still be in there—be ready," Venus replied.

It was pitch dark inside; Venus shone a light to illuminate their way. They moved down a narrow tunnel and found a staircase going up.

"This must lead to the top of the inner pyramid," said Venus. "Let's see if we can find one leading down."

Farther along the central tunnel, they did find a few steps going down into the ground, but the shaft had been filled in with stone.

"There's no access here—the ship's sensors show it's blocked down to the sinkhole," Venus told the others.

Failing to find any other access point inside the pyramid, they moved back out of the structure. There was an area out in front of the pyramid where people had been excavating. Getting a closer look at that area, they found steps leading down to a tunnel that bored into the ground, but it was filled with stone and gravel.

"My scans do show a tunnel similar to this behind the pyramid," said Venus. "No entrance is apparent, but let's go back there and see what we can find."

The land in front of the pyramid was cleared, but the trees grew much closer behind it. They moved around to the steps that led up the center of the rear face.

"The tunnel passes beneath the rear wall here," said Venus.

"There's nothing but grass and dirt," Vesta replied.

"Stand back," Venus told the others. "We're going to try a little excavating of our own."

Hoisting her plasma cannon onto her shoulder, she fired a shot into the earth twenty feet behind the pyramid. It blew a hole in the ground, exposing some sort of concrete structure beneath.

"I'll be damned," said Vesta. "There's a portal."

Looking into the pit she'd created, Venus spotted a roughly circular seam in the concrete. She aimed her cannon, but Malia pushed her weapon down.

"This is a historic site," she said. "We shouldn't damage it. I can get us in."

Venus nodded.

Malia focused, and suddenly the round section of concrete floated into the air, landing on the grass next to the pit.

"Fascinating," Bastet muttered, staring at Malia with an expression of awe.

"You'll get used to it," Vesta told her. "But this can't exactly be the front door to Hathor's pad—it doesn't look like anyone's used this in centuries."

"No," Venus agreed. "But it's the only way inside we've got. Let's go."

She dropped into the pit and through the opening to find steps inside. Moving down those, she reached a tunnel at the bottom; the others followed close behind. The tunnel made a ninety-degree turn, beyond which they found another set of steps leading much farther into the earth. At the bottom, they emerged into a massive chamber with an underground lake in the middle.

"Looks like we found the sinkhole," said Vesta.

"The ship's sensors weren't able to scan any lower than this," Venus told them. "Let's get a look around and see if we can find a way to go farther down—the shielding would suggest there must be *something* down there."

Venus led the way around the lake. The ground here was solid limestone. At the far end, they found a small circular chamber. And in the center of that was a round metal plate.

"A manhole," said Malia.

Venus squatted down and ran her finger around the edge of the metal.

"There's no place to get a grip. This was meant to be an exit, not an entrance. Can you open it?"

Malia nodded. Venus backed away, and Malia used her powers to lift the metal out of the ground. It turned out to be a long cylinder; she placed it on the ground nearby. Shining her light into the shaft, Venus couldn't see the bottom.

"This must be what we're looking for," she told the others. "Let's see what's down there."

Venus dropped into the opening and descended into the earth. After moving at least a hundred meters, the shaft opened into a massive chamber. She landed, the others right behind her. Venus shone her light around the area.

"Yep, this must be Hathor's place," said Vesta.

They were in the middle of a living room—there were plush couches and chairs, thick rugs covering the floor, and wood paneling on the walls. Venus crossed the room and found a bedroom through a doorway at the far end. They also found a kitchen, bathroom, and storage areas. There was a table inside what looked like a closet, and they found Hathor's oracle sitting on that.

"There's a thick layer of dust covering everything," said Bastet. "It doesn't look like anyone's been here in quite some time."

"I wonder where she went," Venus muttered.

Moving back across the living room, they found another door that led to a long tunnel.

"This must be the main entrance," said Bastet.

"Yes," Venus agreed. "It looks like it leads far beyond the

pyramid's footprint. She must have a hatch somewhere out in the trees—I didn't scan that far out."

"Well, now what?" asked Vesta.

"Let's have a closer look around and see if Hathor left any indication of where she went," Venus suggested.

"She left her oracle here," said Bastet. "It doesn't seem like she wanted to be found."

"You're probably right," Venus agreed. "But let's be thorough."

They split up and searched the entire complex. Venus used her neural implants to access Hathor's computer system. The network had been wiped clean except for one file. Venus accessed it to discover a message from Hathor.

"I've got something," Venus told the others. "Hathor went to New York City five years ago."

"You never ran into her?" Malia asked Vesta.

"No, but that's hardly surprising—last I knew, the city's population was over eight million," Vesta replied. "Does it mention *why* she went there?"

"No. The message is one sentence: 'I'm relocating to New York City.' And the timestamp is five years old. That's it. Nothing else."

"Strange that she didn't contact any of us," Vesta noted.

"Yes," said Venus. "Although she did leave the network unprotected so that anyone with neural implants could access it."

"And she left her oracle here," said Bastet. "So, she wanted to make sure we would know where she was if we ever came looking for her."

"Yes," Venus agreed. "Let's get out of here. We can go out the way we came and close everything up behind us."

She was about to fly up to the shaft they'd used on the way down when she heard Malia scream. Turning, she saw her standing by the door to the entry tunnel. Standing next to her, holding a pistol to her head, was Lucifer.

Chapter Twenty-six: Jaden

They arrived at Mount Rushmore, and Salvatore hovered the ship directly in front of the monument. Looking closely, Jaden spotted an opening in the rock behind Lincoln's head. He pointed it out to the others.

"Yes, there's a chamber in there, behind that granite slab," Salvatore confirmed. "But Miguel was correct—there's nothing interesting inside."

"Is there anything beyond that?" asked Brian. "Any hidden chambers deeper inside the mountain?"

"Scanning now," said Salvatore. "Yes. There is a cavern complex. They've got some sort of data center in there. I'm detecting an entrance from that rock terrace farther back behind the vault."

He moved the saucer directly above the terrace. They gathered their weapons and prepared to head down.

"What about me?" said Babcock. "Do I get one of those fancy laser guns?"

"No," Salvatore replied.

They descended to the ground. There was a rock wall on one side of the terrace and a precipitous drop on the other.

"I don't see any openings," said Jaden.

"They've hidden it," Salvatore told him, nodding toward the rock wall. Lifting his pistol, he fired a shot. Part of the cliff face vanished, revealing a steel portal.

"They used a hologram to disguise the entrance?" asked Jaden.

Salvatore nodded, moving to the metal door. He gazed at it for a moment, then ran his fingers along its edges.

"I believe it uses a biometric scanner to provide access."

"We're not getting in that way, then," said Sydney.

"I beg to differ," Miguel replied, hoisting his plasma cannon onto his shoulder. The others backed away, and he fired at the door. The shot blew a hole in the steel, and the door creaked open. Peering inside, he said, "There's a shaft in there, but it's a long way down, and there's no ladder."

Salvatore moved in closer to get a look himself.

"Jaden, between the two of us, we'll have to help the others get down there."

"No problem," Jaden replied.

Brian climbed onto Salvatore's back, and they disappeared into the shaft. Using his telekinesis, Jaden lowered Sydney through the opening, followed her in, and took Babcock along behind him. It was dark, but Jaden could make out a light source far below them. He made a second trip to retrieve Miguel.

They found themselves inside what resembled the lobby of a corporate office building at the bottom of the shaft. Looking through the glass walls, Jaden could see rows and rows of server racks—far more than they'd had in Langley.

"I'll be damned," Miguel muttered.

"I'd say we hit the jackpot," said Brian.

Salvatore opened one of the doors, and they walked into the data center. It was warm in here, and a humming noise filled the air. There was a long table in the far corner that hosted several computer terminals. Jaden was about to remark that there were no people here when someone emerged from one of the aisles. The man stopped and gaped at them for a moment, then turned to run back up the aisle.

"Not so fast," said Brian, pointing his pistol at him. "Stop, or I'll shoot!"

The man froze, slowly putting his hands over his head and turning to face them again. Jaden got a good look at him—his pupils were round. His appearance was human, but he might have been wearing an emitter.

"What do you people want?"

"How many others are here?" asked Salvatore.

The man hesitated for a moment, then said, "None. I'm the only one on duty."

"Bullshit," said Miguel.

"Yes," Brian agreed. "I think that's bullshit, too. Jaden?"

Jaden nodded. Extending his thoughts, he reached into the man's mind.

"How many more are here?"

The man's jaw dropped.

"What—how can you be inside my head?"

"How many?" Jaden demanded more forcefully.

"I told you," the man said out loud. "It's only me."

But inside his mind, Jaden saw an image of a woman working in an equipment room somewhere behind the servers. He searched his memories and saw a few other people working here, too, but it didn't seem like they were here now.

"There's a woman in the back," Jaden told the others, "and they have other people that work here, but I don't think any of them are on duty right now."

The man turned to run again. Using his telepathy, Jaden could feel his legs moving and forced them to stop. The man fell flat on his face.

"*You're a hybrid*," Jaden told him. This wasn't a question—he could sense it somehow.

"Go to hell!"

"Miguel, can you guard him, please?" said Brian. Miguel nodded, lifting his plasma cannon onto his shoulder and pointing it at the hybrid. "Salvatore, you and I should see if we can access their systems. Sydney and Jaden—see if you can find his colleague."

"I'll, uh… hang with you guys," Babcock said.

"Yes," Brian agreed. "Good idea."

Brian and Salvatore hurried over to the computer terminals. Jaden relinquished control of the hybrid and followed Sydney down one of the aisles. They found a door at the far end of the room, but someone opened it from the other side as they approached. A woman walked out, starting at the sight of them, and rushed back through the door.

"Hey—get back here!" Sydney yelled.

They followed her through the door and found themselves in a long hallway with doors lining both sides. The woman was running toward the far end. Jaden reached out with his mind, trying to use his telekinesis to stop her, but it didn't work. This was definitely a hybrid using an emitter.

Sydney raised her pistol and hit the woman in the back with a laser blast. She collapsed on the floor and didn't move.

"Nice shooting!" said Jaden.

"Thanks," she replied with a grin. "Let's see what else they've got back here."

They checked inside each of the doors but found only offices, equipment rooms, and some storage. But when they opened the door at the far end of the hall, they found a massive hangar bay. And sitting in the middle of it was a cigar-shaped vessel that Jaden would recognize anywhere: an Othali shuttle.

"Whoa—what the hell?" said Jaden, walking toward it. "How did this get here?"

"I don't know," Sydney replied, coming up behind him. "Didn't you say the Othali were still orbiting Mars with a damaged engine?"

"Yeah, last I knew, that was the situation."

Moving around the far side of the shuttle, they found the main hatch to be open. Jaden climbed on board. From the inside, he could tell this vessel was different from the ones he'd seen before. The layout was unfamiliar—there were only the two seats in the cockpit and a bench along one wall in the cargo area. And the control console looked like a completely different design.

"This is very strange," Sydney said from outside the hatch. "We should go let Salvatore know this is here."

They ran back to the server room to tell Salvatore what they'd found. He and Brian followed them back to the hangar bay to get a look himself.

"I don't understand what this is doing here," he said. "I'm going to access my ship's systems and run a full scan." A moment later, he added, "Odd indeed. This shuttle is very old."

"*How* old?" asked Jaden.

"At least 40,000 years."

"That means this must be from Atlantis," said Jaden.

"How the hell did an ancient Othali shuttle find its way in here?" Brian said, his expression puzzled.

Nobody could answer him.

"Did you two have any luck accessing their computers?" asked Sydney.

"Not yet," Brian said with a sigh.

"The system is secure and encrypted," Salvatore told them.

"What about the hybrid?" asked Jaden. "He must know the password, right?"

"He claims that he doesn't," said Salvatore. "And I'm inclined to believe him. They'd only use these terminals as a backup. The hybrids have implants just like us—they must have direct neural access to the system."

"Jaden, why don't you search his memories and see if he does know the password," Brian suggested. "Just to be sure."

They returned to the server room. Jaden walked over to where Miguel was guarding the hybrid, the others right behind him. He reached out telepathically.

"What's the password for those computers over there?"

The man smirked at him.

"I have no idea. We don't use *passwords*. We have direct—"

"Yeah, yeah—I know. You're plugged in."

Jaden searched his memories, but not a single image surfaced of the man using the terminals.

"I think he's telling the truth," he told the others. "He doesn't know the password."

"Could Jaden go inside his mind and force him to access the system?" asked Sydney.

"Yeah, that might work!" said Jaden.

"Perhaps," said Salvatore, considering this for a moment. "But his lack of familiarity with Martian computer systems might present an obstacle. I have another idea."

Squatting down, Salvatore reached toward the hybrid's waist. He removed a small device from his belt.

"What's that?" asked Jaden.

"His emitter," Salvatore replied. "Get up—you're coming with us," he added to the hybrid.

"Go to hell," the man replied. Jaden noted that his eyes now looked cat-like. "I'm not going anywhere."

"Shoot him," Salvatore said to Miguel. "But use your pistol—we need him whole."

"Alright, alright!" said the hybrid, scrambling to his feet.

"Damn," Miguel muttered. "I was hoping you'd stay down—I really wanted to shoot you."

The whole group escorted the hybrid back toward the hangar bay, but Salvatore stopped them before going inside. Jaden heard an explosion beyond the door.

"What was that?"

Salvatore led them into the hangar. Jaden could see that he'd used his ship's weapons to blast open the bay doors—his saucer was now hovering inside the hangar.

"Into the ship," said Salvatore.

They followed him into the saucer; Miguel kept his cannon pointed at the hybrid the whole time. Once they'd reached the main level, Salvatore attached the emitter to his own belt.

"I can access the device through my implants," he told the others. "I'm using the ship's sensors to run a full biometric scan on our friend here."

"You're gonna do the same thing Lucifer did to access Venus's ship!" said Jaden.

Salvatore nodded. A moment later, his entire appearance changed until he looked identical to the hybrid.

"Now, my DNA and even my brainwaves match his precisely," said Salvatore. He focused for a moment, then added, "I've got access to their entire network."

Chapter Twenty-seven: Malia

Malia felt embarrassed for screaming in front of the three women, but Lucifer had startled her. He'd appeared out of thin air, already holding the weapon to her head. Malia reached out with her mind, trying to disarm Lucifer or throw him across the room, but predictably, due to his emitter, this had no effect. Instead, she tried to invade his mind, but he was ready, forcefully expelling her before she could access his thoughts.

"Let her go!" Venus shouted as she pointed her plasma cannon at him. Vesta and Bastet raised their pistols, aiming them at Lucifer.

Lucifer grabbed Malia by the hair, moving her between himself and the three women and pulling her partway into the tunnel, but keeping his weapon pointed at her head.

"I thought for sure I'd seen the end of you, Bastet," he drawled.

"Sorry to disappoint you," she replied.

"I owe you three a debt of gratitude for showing me the way down here," he said. "I managed to beat you here but couldn't find the way in. Now tell me—what is our dear sister, Hathor doing in New York?"

"Wish we knew," said Venus. "Now let the girl go."

"I don't think I will."

"What the hell do you want?" Venus demanded.

"You three dead, of course, but for now, I'll settle for this one."

Lucifer pointed his weapon at Bastet and fired. She shot into the air, barely avoiding the blast. Lucifer shot at Venus next, but she and Vesta both flew out of the way. He pulled Malia into the tunnel, walking backward to keep them facing toward the others. Malia spotted Venus sticking her head around the corner to the tunnel entry. Lucifer had seen her, too, and fired his pistol at her. She ducked out of the way in the nick of time, and the shot blasted a chunk of masonry out of the wall.

Lucifer backed them farther into the tunnel, then fired several shots into the ceiling over the tunnel entry, bringing down a giant pile of rubble. He did this three more times, creating a significant barrier. Malia figured Venus could probably still get through it with her plasma cannon, but it would take a few shots.

"Let me go!" Malia demanded, trying to squirm out of his viselike grip.

Lucifer said nothing, turning them to face the opposite direction. Malia could see the light coming from the far end of the tunnel. But before they'd gone that far, Lucifer stopped and threw her away from him. Malia landed on the ground hard and felt cuts and scrapes on her hands and knees. Scrambling to her feet, she rounded on Lucifer—but gasped when she saw him.

"What the hell are you doing?"

Lucifer could now pass for her identical twin.

"I need to be you for a little while," he told her, his voice sounding exactly like hers. "Fortunately, I have your full bioscans, so I can now pass for you down to my DNA and even my brainwaves. But for this to work, I'll need you to stay down here."

He turned, firing a laser blast into the ceiling between him and the exit. A pile of rubble fell to the floor.

"You're going to seal me in here?" said Malia. "Psh, go ahead—I can get through that."

"Not if you're unconscious, you can't," he said with a smirk, pointing the weapon at her.

"No—wait!" Malia yelled.

She tried to reach out with her thoughts to warn the others that he was taking on her identity. But it was too late. Lucifer fired the pistol, hitting her square in the chest. Everything went black before Malia had hit the ground.

Chapter Twenty-eight: Venus

Venus peered around the corner into the tunnel, but Lucifer saw her and fired his weapon. She pulled away just in time as the laser blast hit the edge of the wall, spraying dust and debris into the room. There was another blast, and she heard the sound of rubble hitting the floor. Looking into the tunnel again, she saw that part of the ceiling had collapsed. She heard two more blasts and knew that Lucifer was sealing off this end of the tunnel.

"Shit!"

"You can get through that with your cannon, can't you?" said Vesta.

"I'm sure I could, but the fireball might hit the girl, too," Venus pointed out. "Can't take that risk."

"We should go find where that tunnel comes out," said Bastet.

Venus nodded. She grabbed Hathor's oracle, and then the three of them flew up through the shaft and back into the chamber by the underground lake. Together, Venus and Bastet were able to move the cover back into the hole.

They hurried around the lake and back up to the surface. Once they'd replaced the concrete cover on the tunnel entrance in the ground, they did their best to cover it with dirt.

"It's pretty obvious someone's done some digging here," Vesta observed. "The people in charge of this place will probably investigate."

"It doesn't matter anymore," said Venus. "We recovered the oracle. There's nothing else down there that can compromise us in any way. Let's find Malia."

She was about to take to the air when a noise in the trees caught her attention.

"Someone's out there," Bastet whispered, pointing her pistol.

Venus lifted her plasma cannon onto her shoulders, aiming toward the sound. But at that moment, Malia stepped out of the trees.

"You nearly gave me a heart attack," Venus said with a sigh of relief, lowering her weapon. The girl had blood and dirt on her hands and forehead. "What the hell happened? We were just coming to find you."

"Lucifer dragged me out of the tunnel," Malia told them. "I tried to fight him, but my telekinesis doesn't work when he's wearing his emitter, and he kicked me out of his head when I tried telepathy.

"But then, all of a sudden, he let me go and flew away. It was weird—like something else distracted him. You haven't seen him?"

"No, we haven't," said Venus, looking around for any sign of him. "But we'd better get out of here before he does return."

They flew up to Venus's ship and moved into the cockpit.

"I'm not detecting any other ships," Venus told them. "Which means either that Lucifer has already left the area or that he's repaired his shields."

"What now?" asked Vesta.

"It's time to check in with Salvatore," said Venus.

Chapter Twenty-nine: Brian

"It's time for you to leave," Salvatore said to the hybrid. "Shoot him."

"My pleasure," said Miguel.

"Wait—what—," the hybrid shouted.

Miguel shot him with his laser pistol, and he fell to the floor. Salvatore activated the gravity beam and ejected him from the ship. They moved up to the cockpit, each taking a seat. Salvatore remained quiet for several minutes, deep in concentration. Finally, he said, "This is astounding."

"What is it?" asked Brian.

"This facility is the data center for the entire North American division of Majestic. They have records of operations and personnel dating back to the 1950s. The organization has a separate command hierarchy for every continent except Antarctica. There is a directory of every Majestic agent in the United States, Canada, Mexico, and Central America. They do indeed have people embedded in every major government agency, including the State Department, the CIA, and DHS."

"I knew it!" said Babcock.

"They have a command center in a complex beneath Grand Central Terminal in New York City."

"Could that be the place Malia saw in Lucifer's thoughts?" asked Sydney.

"Perhaps," said Salvatore. "At the top of the hierarchy is an entity called 'The Sphinx.' I believe that is their leader, but there is no indication of who that might be—or their location. There is very little information on this system about their operations on the other continents."

"Does the system contain anything about their plans to exterminate humanity?" asked Brian.

"There are references to that plan, but no details. It does appear that Lucifer's operation in Arizona was instrumental in that project. But he also seems to have had a great amount of autonomy from the command hierarchy—as if his complex was an island unto itself. The data from his experiments is not here."

"Could he have lost all of his work when we blew up his place?" asked Miguel.

"I don't think so," said Salvatore. "Lucifer was working in conjunction with the Sphinx on that project. It appears they have his data.

"From what I can gather, every Majestic operative is a hybrid—except Lucifer. There are no humans in the organization. And every hybrid came from either Lucifer's compound or another one in northern Africa. They were all created from genetic material taken from Lucifer or Isis that was then combined with human DNA."

"Then, that other compound must be abducting people, too," Sydney suggested.

"Yes," Salvatore agreed. "It would seem so."

"Can you transfer all this data to your ship?" asked Brian.

"I am doing that now," said Salvatore. "But I have nowhere near enough storage capacity to hold everything—I must be selective."

He focused in silence for a few moments.

"Majestic has been dismantling the Malor mother ship, trying to reverse-engineer some of its technology. They also retrieved one of their scout ships back in the nineties, fully intact, and had an entire team working on that vessel."

"We had one at the Ranch, but our boys weren't able to crack the tech," said Babcock.

"Majestic had somewhat better luck—there is data here that references a construction project based on the Malor technology, but there are no details. Whatever they're building, it's happening somewhere outside of North America."

"Can't wait to find out what that might be," Miguel said sarcastically.

"Vice President Roberts is a hybrid," Salvatore told them.

"*What*?!" said Babcock. "Not even I suspected that!"

"They have a plan to assassinate President Ferris," said Salvatore. "But they're waiting for orders from the Sphinx to carry out their plan."

"We have to warn her!" said Sydney.

"That'll have to wait—they know we're here," Salvatore told

them. "The staff alerted their command center when we arrived. It's time to leave."

At that moment, a shot from a plasma cannon hit Salvatore's ship. Turning, Brian spotted several hybrids moving into the hangar, all wielding plasma cannons. Salvatore fired the ship's weapons, taking out the hybrids. They flew out of the hangar bay, but several laser blasts slammed into the saucer moments later. Brian spotted three vessels bearing down on them.

"Shields are holding at sixty-five percent," Salvatore told them.

"I don't think they like us very much," Miguel opined.

Salvatore fired the ship's plasma cannon, hitting the closest saucer—it blew a hole in the fuselage. He fired a second shot, and the vessel went up in a massive explosion. The other two saucers retreated before he could fire on them. They took off, rising high into the sky.

"Now what?" said Jaden.

"Venus should have recovered Hathor by now," said Salvatore. "And she was the last one of my people. Lucifer may be operating out of their command center in New York now, or perhaps from the Sphinx's headquarters. As we do not know the location of the latter, the former should be our next target. At the very least, we can eliminate their command center, and possibly Lucifer along with it."

"But that's crazy," said Sydney. "We can't just bomb Grand Central—there are something like a million people per day traveling through there!"

"No," Brian agreed. "We'll need to find and infiltrate the

command center itself. Destroy it from the inside and take out their leaders. But there's also a good chance they'll have information there about the Sphinx. At the very least, I'd think their leaders must know where they're located."

"Perhaps," said Salvatore.

"We should also warn President Ferris!" said Jaden.

"It's too late for that," Salvatore replied. "The story is all over your internet—they've assassinated her."

"Oh, shit!" said Miguel. "So, now the President of the United States is a hybrid?"

"Yes," Salvatore confirmed. "Roberts was sworn in moments ago. He's scheduled a press briefing that's due to start in a half hour."

"We should head to New York," said Brian.

"Yes," Salvatore agreed. "And we need to confer with Venus—she's transmitting to us now."

Chapter Thirty: Jaden

Jaden listened as Venus told Salvatore what had happened in Mexico.

"I have no idea why Hathor went to New York," she concluded.

"That is strange, indeed," said Salvatore. "But it would seem that our paths have converged."

"How so?"

Salvatore told her what they'd found at Mount Rushmore.

"We believe the command center should be our next target. Retrieve whatever information we can, particularly regarding this Sphinx, and then destroy the facility."

"What about Hathor?" asked Venus.

"Do we have any idea where in New York she may be? Or what she might be doing?"

"No, none."

"Then I'm afraid that is a dead end. Unless she comes to us, I don't see any way forward in finding her. Do you?"

Venus was silent for a moment.

"No, you're right, of course. So, what's our plan?"

"I believe we need to infiltrate the command center with a small team. As Sydney pointed out, bombing the entire complex is not an option due to the sheer volume of humans moving through the terminal every day."

"And if you did that, you'd lose the opportunity to gather data."

"Yes. I should go in with Malia. Using the emitter we acquired, I can adjust my appearance to look human. We can scan the area when we arrive and find the entry point to the Majestic command center. I'm sending you everything we retrieved from the data center now. According to their records, there are only half a dozen hybrids stationed at headquarters. The leader of their North American operation is a woman named Cynthia. Once we find her, Malia can use her powers to find out what she knows about the Sphinx. I'll access their network and see if there's any new data there. We'll destroy their complex, take out the hybrids who work there, and get out. If we're lucky, we'll run into Lucifer, and we can eliminate him, too."

"They may anticipate this move," said Bastet. "If so, you could encounter much more resistance than you think. It might be better to go in with everyone."

"We should go to New York first and see what the situation is there," Brian suggested.

"Agreed," said Salvatore.

"We'll see you there," Venus replied.

Jaden watched out the window as the clouds streaked by. Suddenly, they came to rest high above New York City.

"Something's wrong," said Salvatore.

"What is it?" asked Brian.

"Hang on—I'm patching Venus in, too."

"Yes, darling," said Venus's voice over the speakers.

"There is an aircraft carrier group off the coast of New Jersey—they've got fighter jets running air patrols over the city. I'm also detecting tanks and armored vehicles on the streets of Manhattan. Hold on... your major news outlets are reporting that the president has declared martial law in New York City."

"Are you kidding me?" asked Sydney.

"President Roberts is holding his press conference. He's revealed to the public that there are beings from Mars here on Earth. And he's claiming that they are responsible for President Ferris's assassination."

"It would seem that Bastet was correct," said Venus. "They anticipated our arrival."

"Yes," said Salvatore. "But instead of fortifying their headquarters' defenses, they've locked down the entire city."

"They may have done both," Bastet suggested. "We should scan the facility and see what's waiting for us."

"No," said Salvatore. "They've also initiated a network of particle streams over the area." He brought up a holographic image of the city in the center of the cockpit. Jaden could see a translucent dome covering Manhattan. "Our scanning beam would disrupt the streams, alerting them to our presence."

"Our ships would disrupt those beams, too," said Venus. "The shields make us invisible, but only if we stay outside of that dome."

"So, how do we get to Grand Central?" asked Jaden.

"Easy," said a voice over the speaker—Jaden recognized it as Vesta's. "Subway. We drop at the corner of Vernon and Fiftieth in Queens and take the 7 Train right into Grand Central. Piece of cake."

"Yes," said Salvatore. "But this situation only increases the need to keep the team small. I should go with Malia."

"Salvatore, have you ever used the New York subway system?" said Vesta.

"No."

"Malia, have you?"

"No, never," Malia's voice said over the speaker.

"Right. Then, I'm going with you."

"Alright," Salvatore agreed. "Only the three of us. I will take a portable scanner—we'll need that to find the entry to their complex. It will also be useful to scan one of the hybrids on duty if the body I'm using now doesn't have access to this network. And we should take pistols only."

"Yeah, carrying the plasma cannons on the subway would probably attract unwanted attention," Miguel said.

"Unfortunately, so will using the gravity beam to drop into a busy intersection in Queens," Salvatore pointed out. "There is a cemetery a little to the east of the intersection you suggested, Vesta. Very few people are in there right now—we should be able to get down unseen."

"We'll have a bit of a walk, but that works," Vesta agreed.

"Very well. I will meet you and Malia down there."

Chapter Thirty-one: Salvatore

Salvatore transferred his ship's controls to Venus. Dropping to the main level, he checked that his emitter was still projecting the appearance of the hybrid from Mount Rushmore and that he had his pistol. Then he descended into the airlock.

He moved down to the ground, landing next to a mausoleum. Moments later, he spotted Vesta and Malia floating down nearby. He hurried over to meet them.

"Hey, Sal," said Vesta, grinning at him. "You look great as a human!"

"Thank you," he replied. "Which way?"

"Follow me!"

They followed her through the cemetery and onto a busy sidewalk. Several blocks away, they came to steps leading below ground. Vesta led them down those and up to a ticket counter. She paid for their fare and handed Salvatore and Malia each a card.

"One way," she told them. "I think we can fly back up to the ships once we're done here, yeah? Won't be much need for stealth at that point."

"Correct," said Salvatore.

They followed Vesta to the turnstiles, inserting their cards on the way through. Minutes later, the train pulled into the station, and they boarded. The odor of too many bodies packed into too small a space assaulted Salvatore's nasal passages. Seldom had he spent much time in Earth's cities, and he wasn't used to the smell.

"Is it always this crowded?" he asked.

"I mean, not in the middle of the night... usually," Vesta replied.

They disembarked at the stop for Grand Central. There were military personnel stationed here, rifles in hand, but they took no notice of them. Vesta led them through the passage to the main concourse.

"Well, here we are," she announced. "Now, what?"

Salvatore scanned the structure.

"I'm detecting another public level below this, and many subbasements beneath that... including a massive area ten levels down. It appears the electrical converters for the rail lines are housed there. But the area below that is shielded."

"So, headquarters must be down there?" asked Vesta.

"Yes."

Salvatore searched for any pits or shafts leading beyond the subbasements. Finally, he found one.

"The passage delves deep below the building. We'll need to move to the lower level to access it."

"Alright, let's go," said Vesta.

She led them down a ramp to the dining concourse.

"Now, where?"

Salvatore pointed.

"In the Oyster Bar? Okay!"

A hostess greeted them as they went inside the restaurant.

"Table for three?" she said.

"Uh... yes," Vesta replied. "Of course, yeah, three, please."

Salvatore gave her a questioning glance; Vesta shrugged.

"Right this way!" said the hostess.

They followed her to a table and sat down. The hostess cleared one place setting and hurried off.

"Where to, now?" Vesta asked.

"That corridor," said Salvatore, pointing across the dining area.

"By the restrooms, then?"

"Yes."

They got up again and walked toward the corridor. There was a door between the entries to the men's and ladies' rooms, but it was locked. Salvatore checked both ways along the corridor to make sure nobody was coming, then pulled out his pistol and fired at the lock. Opening the door, he gazed inside to find a tunnel running behind the restaurant.

Salvatore led them inside, and they closed the door behind them. The area was not lit; he shone a light to illuminate their way. They followed the tunnel for a few dozen meters—it didn't look like anyone had been in here for a very long time. Dirt and debris covered the floor, and there was graffiti on the brick walls.

The tunnel came to a right angle, and they found a concrete stairway around the corner. They hurried down the steps and through a short corridor, emerging inside a large open area. It looked like it may have served as storage space long ago but was empty now.

"Over there," said Salvatore, leading them across the chamber.

"There's nothing here," said Vesta. "Just a brick wall. You sure your scanner's working properly?"

"It's here," Salvatore replied. He ran his hand along the bricks for several feet until his arm passed through the wall. "This is it." He poked his head through, and sure enough, found the shaft leading far into the ground. "Be ready," he told them, drawing his weapon. "They may be expecting us."

Malia and Vesta drew their pistols as well, and they dropped into the shaft. This passage delved far deeper than the one at Lucifer's compound in Arizona. Salvatore stuck his head through the wall when they reached the bottom—there was an empty hallway beyond. The walls were stone, and there were a few metallic-looking doors on each side—this was much like Lucifer's complex in the desert, only smaller.

"Coast is clear," he told the others.

They moved into the tunnel, but before they'd taken ten steps, three hybrids appeared in front of them, pointing plasma cannons at them.

"Drop your weapons," one of them ordered with a smirk. Salvatore placed his pistol on the floor, as did Malia and Vesta. "Kick them over here." Salvatore pushed them toward the hybrids with one foot. One of them squatted down to pick them up. "Cynthia's been waiting for you. This way—move!"

The hybrids directed them toward the opposite end of the corridor. Just then, Salvatore heard a voice in his head.

"Salvatore? It's me, Jaden—can you hear me?"

"Yes—what's wrong?"

"Nothing—we were just worried that it was taking a long time. I tried reaching Malia, but I couldn't find her. Is she okay?"

Salvatore peered at the girl, suddenly growing suspicious.

"Yes. I'll be in contact soon."

The hybrids led them through the last door on the right. Beyond that was an office; there was an older, fierce-looking woman sitting behind a desk.

"Thank you," the woman said to the hybrids. "Leave us."

"Yes, ma'am."

"Took you long enough," the woman said once the hybrids had left. "I knew you'd show up here next when I got word that you'd destroyed the data center."

The woman got to her feet and transformed—this was no hybrid.

"Hathor!" said Vesta, stunned.

Sure enough, this was their missing comrade. But Salvatore couldn't help but feel uneasy—they hadn't had contact with Hathor in decades. Her unexpected and unexplained absence from her compound beneath Chichen Itza could mean many things.

"We tried to find you in Mexico, but you weren't there anymore," said Vesta. "We've been warning everyone—Lucifer got his hands on an oracle, and he's hunting us down!"

"How did you come to be here, in this role?" Salvatore asked.

"This is a long story, and we don't have much time," said Hathor. "The hybrids will be expecting me to execute you two and apprehend the girl. We have orders from the Sphinx."

"You're masquerading as the leader of Majestic's North American operations—we deserve some sort of explanation," said Salvatore. "How do we know you're not a traitor?"

"Listen—if I were, I would have given them your locations ages ago. Hell, I would have ordered the kills myself. But I didn't do that—Vesta's been living right here in Brooklyn this whole time, and nobody ever came knocking, did they?"

"That's a fair point," Vesta said with a frown.

Salvatore had to agree. If Hathor *were* a traitor, it would have been a simple matter for her to eliminate the rest of their people.

"Briefly then, how did you come to occupy this position?"

"A hybrid showed up in Mexico—he assassinated someone I cared about very deeply. I captured him, but he killed himself before I could interrogate him—a fake tooth hiding a cyanide capsule. Standard equipment for Majestic agents, as it turns out. A couple of others showed up looking for him. They came up emptyhanded, but I tracked them back to the States. They were stationed in San Antonio. I studied them for a few weeks—that's how I found out about Majestic. Eventually, I killed one of them and confiscated his emitter. Using that, I took on his identity.

"From there, I worked my way up the chain of command, killing and replacing one hybrid after another. It took several years, but I finally managed to find this place and assume the director's identity."

"Who is the Sphinx?" asked Salvatore.

"I don't know. I've been trying very hard to determine that, but whoever it is, they are maniacal about concealing their identity. They send me orders without betraying any glimmer of who—or where—they are."

"There's no information on the network here to indicate who they might be?" asked Salvatore.

"No, none," said Hathor. "There's little here you wouldn't have already found at the data center."

"We downloaded as much as we could but haven't had time to analyze much of it yet."

"Do you know about the chariot?"

"No—what is that?"

Hathor let out a long sigh.

"We have to get out of here. I'll download the data and fill you in on the way back up to the terminal." She opened a closet, and Salvatore could see half a dozen plasma cannons inside. "Take these," she said, handing them each one of the weapons. "Majestic distributed them to key facilities after removing them from Venus's compound."

"Thank you," said Salvatore. "We intended to destroy this place once we'd interrogated your predecessor."

"Yes, but I'm sorry to say there's been a change in plans," said Malia, mounting the cannon on her shoulder and firing at Salvatore. He dodged, barely evading the shot; the fireball hit Vesta—she'd been standing behind him.

"What the hell?!" said Hathor, staring at Malia in shock.

Vesta stared down at the hole in her abdomen, then looked up at Malia with an expression of disbelief. But at that moment, Malia transformed, confirming Salvatore's suspicion—it was Lucifer pointing the cannon at them.

"Put the weapons back in the closet," he ordered them as Vesta collapsed on the floor.

"You're an evil bastard," Hathor told him, taking the cannon back from Salvatore and returning it to the closet.

"One good turn deserves another, wouldn't you say, Hathor?" Lucifer said with a smirk.

"What have you done with Malia?" Salvatore demanded.

"She's safe and sound," Lucifer replied. "I'll be retrieving her once I've finished with you fine people."

"You replaced her in Mexico," said Salvatore. "When they lost track of Malia, that's when you made the substitution. Why?"

"We've long suspected that someone had infiltrated our organization," said Lucifer. "Whoever it was left a path of missing hybrids in their wake... like a trail of breadcrumbs. But that trail went cold long ago. When Hathor turned up missing in Mexico— having left her oracle behind—it occurred to me that *she* was probably the culprit.

"We believed our mole was in New York and made an educated guess that you'd be coming here next as well. It stood to reason that she would reveal herself to you when you did—and I needed to make sure I was there for it. In hindsight, I'm a little surprised she didn't do it when you found Vesta. But this works out for the best—now you're *all* accounted for. And I'm afraid it's time to say goodbye."

Lucifer fired his cannon at Salvatore again; he'd anticipated this and dropped to the ground at the same time. Hathor launched herself at Lucifer, grabbing the weapon as he fired a second shot at Salvatore—that hit the wall instead.

Getting to his feet, Salvatore opened the closet and grabbed another cannon; hoisting it onto his shoulder, he aimed Lucifer—but at that moment, Lucifer disappeared. Hathor's expression showed surprise as she gained complete control of his cannon. The office door shimmered for a moment—Salvatore guessed that must have been Lucifer exiting. He fired a shot that rendered the door translucent long enough for him to see the fireball hit the opposite wall.

"Shit!" yelled Hathor. "We need to get out of here! Lucifer will have alerted the entire organization by now—he can access the communication system with his implants."

"Yes," Salvatore agreed. Kneeling next to Vesta, he checked her pulse; she was dead. "We should do as much damage as we can on the way out."

"The only thing worth destroying down here is the equipment room. Taking out the servers will sever communications with the Sphinx—temporarily, at least."

"Understood. We should eliminate the hybrids, too."

They moved into the hallway. Three hybrids were running toward them—Salvatore shot one of them, and Hathor took out the other two. Turning back toward the director's office, Salvatore fired a shot at the closet. It hit the weapons, generating an explosion that destroyed the room. The force of the blast threw him and Hathor to the floor.

Regaining their feet, they continued along the corridor. Suddenly, a fireball slammed into the wall next to Salvatore. Hathor fired her weapon into the empty passage—suddenly, a hybrid appeared out of nowhere with a hole in her chest, collapsing on the floor.

"There are two more down here," said Hathor.

"Plus Lucifer," Salvatore pointed out.

They checked the other rooms as they moved but found them empty.

"Last door on the right is the equipment room," said Hathor. "They must be in there."

Salvatore moved through the door, ready to fire, but there was nobody here.

"They must have fled," said Hathor. "We need to hurry."

They fired their cannons at the servers, then moved back into the corridor.

"The others could be waiting for us in the shaft," said Hathor.

"We should make ourselves invisible," Salvatore suggested.

Hathor nodded, then vanished. Salvatore moved into the shaft and only knew Hathor had followed because she bumped into him. They flew back up to the subbasement but encountered no resistance along the way.

"What is this chariot you mentioned before?" Salvatore asked as they both made themselves visible and headed across the empty storage area.

"It's a new warship—they're calling it 'The Chariot of the Gods.' Majestic recovered a Malor scout ship years ago and correctly guessed that the mother ship would turn up one day. They had only limited success reverse-engineering the scout's weapon systems, but using that, they began work on the chariot. They completed production right after the Malor invasion. It's got advanced weaponry and shields. After your little show at the data center, they've decided to skip trials and send it to New York."

"So, it's here now?"

"Yes. Patrolling the airspace over the city—on the lookout for you."

"But they cannot detect us through our shields—can they?"

"No, but I'm sure you noted the particle beams above Manhattan?"

"Yes—we kept the ships across the river to avoid them."

"That's good, but the chariot can carry a dozen saucers in its hangar bay. They're using those ships to patrol the other boroughs—and they're sweeping those areas with the same beams."

"I need to warn Venus."

Salvatore and Hathor continued back up to the Oyster Bar. They used the emitters to take on human appearances before returning to the main terminal—moving through the press of people invisible would have created issues if they bumped into someone. Salvatore contacted Venus to tell her about the chariot and its saucers.

"We know, darling. I've had to move our ships farther away to avoid detection. You'll need to refrain from flying, I think."

"Yes. We'll take the subway and return to the cemetery."

"Let me know when you arrive, and we'll come to fetch you."

"Also—if Malia shows up there without me, do *not* allow her on board."

"Why would she?"

"I'll explain when we get there."

Salvatore led them through the passage to the subway terminal. Neither of them had cash, so they became invisible again long enough to fly over the turnstiles. Then they caught the train back to Queens. Once they'd reached their stop, Salvatore led the way up to street level and back to the cemetery.

Chapter Thirty-two: Jaden

Jaden waited in the cockpit with Brian, Sydney, and Miguel while Salvatore went off with Malia and Vesta. Babcock stayed on the main level; Jaden suspected that he must have felt unwanted—an accurate assessment as far as he was concerned.

They chatted about the day's events for a while but eventually grew quiet. Sydney's cat, Charlie, went to sleep in her lap. Jaden felt himself growing bored and anxious—he kept staring off in the direction where he'd last seen the others, looking out for their return. But suddenly, he heard Venus's voice over the speakers.

"We've got trouble," she told them. Their ship shot into the air and away from the city. "There was a particle beam moving toward us. They must have ships patrolling the airspace around Manhattan. Their shields are keeping them invisible, but they can't hide those beams."

"Any word from Salvatore?" asked Brian.

"No—I can't reach him."

"Should that worry us?" asked Sydney.

"No, dear. I'm sure Majestic has shielding protecting their facility, so we won't be able to communicate with Salvatore until he exits that area."

"Jaden, can you see if you can reach your sister telepathically?" Brian suggested.

Jaden nodded. Reaching out with his mind, he tried to locate Malia but couldn't find her. He did manage to contact Salvatore.

"Salvatore? It's me, Jaden—can you hear me?"

"Yes—what's wrong?"

"Nothing—we were just worried that it was taking a long time. I tried reaching Malia, but I couldn't find her. Is she okay?"

"Yes. I'll be in contact soon."

"They're alright," he told the others but worried now why he couldn't locate Malia.

Jaden continued staring out the cockpit windows as the minutes dragged by. He didn't know where they were now—but it was somewhere high above the clouds. Finally, Venus contacted them again.

"Salvatore is on his way back. We'll be meeting him in the cemetery—stand by."

Several minutes later, the ship plummeted toward the ground, coming to rest again back where they'd started. Jaden spotted two people down on the ground—a man and a woman. He didn't recognize either of them but figured the man had to be Salvatore using his emitter to appear human.

Jaden dropped down to the main level with the others. Sure enough, Salvatore moved up from the airlock, looking like himself now. His companion's scaly skin revealed her to be Martian, but Jaden didn't recognize her.

"What happened out there?" asked Sydney.

"And where's Malia and Vesta?" added Jaden.

But before Salvatore could answer them, something hit the ship. Jaden knew immediately that this was catastrophic—whatever hit them had taken out one edge of the saucer. He now found himself staring out at the sky. The ship lurched, tossing them into the remaining wall.

"We're going down!" Salvatore yelled. "Jaden—we need your help. We need to get everyone off the ship *now*!"

The next moment, Salvatore grabbed Sydney and her cat and flew through the hole in the hull. The Martian woman hoisted Miguel over one shoulder and followed him out. Jaden wasted no time— reaching out with his mind, he took hold of his uncle and Babcock and flew them out of the vessel. Landing on the ground next to Salvatore and the others, he watched as the saucer crashed into the ground on the other side of the cemetery and went up in flames.

"What the hell just happened?" Brian demanded. "And where is my niece?"

"That must have been the chariot," said Salvatore. "No time to explain—Jaden, we need to fly. Follow me, and *stay low*!"

He picked up Sydney and Charlie again as his appearance returned to human form and flew out of the cemetery. The Martian woman also looked human now; she grabbed Miguel and took off after Salvatore. Jaden used his powers and took Brian and Babcock along as he took to the air once more.

Salvatore led them through Queens, taking a winding course

up one street and across another, flying around the buildings and keeping them only about ten feet above the sidewalks. People cried out and pointed as they passed—but Salvatore made no attempt to avoid being seen. Finally, he landed on the sidewalk by a busy intersection.

"They're tracking us—how?" said Salvatore.

The Martian woman stared at him for a moment before suddenly showing a look of dawning comprehension.

"The emitters!"

She reached to remove the device from her belt.

"Wait—we may need them later. Keep it but deactivate it—if they're using the same exploit I used to track Lucifer, then it won't work when it's dormant."

A moment later, they both took on their usual appearances.

"Fly!" Salvatore shouted.

They took off again, and Jaden felt the shockwave of an explosion directly behind them. Looking back, he spotted a fiery crater in the sidewalk where they'd been standing only moments earlier.

Jaden followed Salvatore and his companion for several more minutes, flying a seemingly random and winding route through Queens before they finally landed again in front of an apartment building. A man was sitting on the front steps—his jaw dropped at the sight of them.

Salvatore stared into the sky for several moments but finally said, "I think we lost them. I figured they would have eliminated the exploit by now, but it would seem otherwise."

"What the hell is going on?" Sydney demanded.

"Hang on—Venus is on her way. Once we're safe aboard her ship, I'll explain everything."

They didn't have long to wait—only moments later, Jaden found himself floating up into the air with the others. Once on board, they moved up to the main level, where they met Venus and Bastet.

"I'm moving us out of the city," Venus told them. "We should be safe now."

"Now, tell me—where the hell is Malia?!" Brian demanded.

"Mexico, I believe," said Salvatore.

"*What*?" said Venus and Sydney at the same time.

"I'm not certain, but I believe he must have incapacitated her and assumed her identity when you lost track of her at Chichen Itza."

"He must have left her in the tunnel," said Venus. "I'm laying in the course now—we'll be there in a few minutes."

"What about Vesta?" asked Jaden.

"I'm sorry," said Salvatore. "Lucifer killed her."

Jaden felt his eyes welling up with tears. He'd only met Vesta today but had liked her immediately. She was, in his mind, the "cool" Martian.

But a moment later, something distracted him from the bad news—it was Malia.

"Jaden? Can you hear me?"

"Yeah—where the hell are you?!"

"I'm still in Mexico—outside Chichen Itza; Lucifer trapped me

in a tunnel, but I escaped. Jaden, he's back—and the Sphinx is on his way! Tell Salvatore and Venus—I need help!"

"They already know—we're headed there now!"

He told the others that Malia had contacted them.

"She said that Lucifer's there, and the Sphinx is coming!"

Salvatore fixed Venus with a grave stare.

"We need to increase speed."

Venus nodded.

"Maximum velocity. They'll be able to detect us now."

"I know."

Chapter Thirty-three: Malia

Malia woke with a start. She gasped, inhaling a mouthful of dirt before coughing and spitting it back out again. Sitting up, she found she was surrounded by total darkness. Memories came flooding in— Lucifer had taken on her appearance and trapped her in the tunnel to Hathor's underground complex. She had to get out of here and warn the others.

Getting to her knees and then to her feet, she realized her entire body ached. Her head was still a little foggy, too. Reaching out with both hands, she could feel a pile of rocks and debris in front of her. The tunnel walls and ceiling were made of brick. She thought of going back the way she'd come and escaping through Hathor's compound but then recalled that Lucifer had brought down the ceiling at the other end of the tunnel, too. And she was worried that if she tried blasting her way up to the surface, she'd only bring down a giant pile of dirt on top of herself. One way or another, she was going to have to dig her way out.

This was going to be difficult, though—she couldn't see a thing. She could *feel* the rubble, so she was pretty sure she could visualize it well enough to use her powers to move it. But the tunnel was narrow, and getting the rubble behind her without covering herself with it would be problematic. And she didn't know how much there was—Lucifer had knocked her out before finishing the job.

Well, she decided, the longer she thought about it, the longer it would take her to escape. She pressed herself against one wall and focused on hurling the rubble from the pile into the open end of the tunnel. In the end, it took only a few minutes, and she was able to continue toward the exit.

Malia walked with her arms extended in front of her—she still couldn't see a thing and didn't want to walk into a wall. She remembered seeing the light in the distance before Lucifer had knocked her out, but that was gone. Had he left another rubble pile in her way? No—she realized it had probably been daylight she saw earlier, and it must have been nighttime by now.

She kept going and felt a brick wall in front of her a few minutes later. Looking up, she spotted pinpricks of light far above and realized she must have been seeing the night sky. Flying up toward the lights, she found she was moving through a shaft in the ground. There was a grate at the top. She tried opening it with her hands, but it was either latched or locked and wouldn't budge. Instead, she reached out with her mind, and with a bit of effort, was able to blow the grate off the opening. Rising through it and landing on the ground, there was enough light for her to see that she was out in the trees.

"Lovely," a voice said. "You've saved me the trouble of digging you out."

Suddenly, the figure of a man appeared in front of her, maybe twenty feet away. She couldn't see his face, but she'd recognize that voice anywhere.

"Lucifer," she said, her heart jumping into her throat.

"It's time to go home."

Though she couldn't see it, she knew he'd be smirking. Malia took off into the sky. High above Chichen Itza, she turned, realizing that Lucifer had followed her. There was much more light up here, and she could see that he was pointing a pistol at her.

"I truly don't want to shoot you again, but I will if you don't come quietly."

Malia reached out with her mind and tried to fling the weapon from his hand, but it was no use. His emitter was shielding him from her telekinesis. Instead, she tried moving inside his mind. But like before, Lucifer ejected her with ease.

Flying away from him as fast as she could, Malia focused internally, trying to force an adrenaline dump. This turned out not to be difficult—her heart was already beating a mile a minute from fear. She felt the power surging through her as her body tapped into the Earth's magnetic field.

A laser blast flew past her, missing her by inches. Malia came to rest, rounding on Lucifer hundreds of feet above the ground. Reaching out with her thoughts again, she slammed her consciousness into Lucifer's mind, easily overcoming his attempt to expel her this time. Feeling the weapon in his hand, she forced his fingers to release their grip. Lucifer cried out in surprise as he dropped the pistol. Malia felt him trying to fly away and overrode his will, forcing him to stay where he was.

"*I've got you, you evil bastard,*" she told him telepathically. "*I'm going to stop your heart, knock you out, and drop you out of the sky.*"

"*I will heal.*"

"*Yeah, but I'll be long gone by then—and it's going to hurt like hell.*"

Malia could feel his heartbeat. But as she focused on stilling it, she sensed his thoughts.

"*I require assistance.*"

She was about to reply when she realized he wasn't talking to her. Of course—he had neural implants just like Salvatore and Venus. He was communicating with someone else—but whom? An image surfaced in his mind—an enormous flying saucer, ten times larger than Lucifer's ship. There was a hooded figure on board the vessel— Lucifer thought of this person as the Sphinx.

"*We are on our way,*" came the reply.

The voice sounded male in Lucifer's mind, but Malia could not make out their face—the hood kept it in shadow. It didn't sound like anyone Malia knew.

Suddenly, Lucifer ejected her from his mind—she'd been distracted by the image of the Sphinx, and he caught her by surprise. She tried to get back inside his head, but he vanished, and she couldn't find him telepathically.

"Shit!" Malia said out loud.

Racing back to the ground, she dropped into the middle of the forest, hoping she could hide among the trees. She could feel the power still coursing through her veins and had an idea. Reaching out with her mind, she tried to contact her brother.

"Jaden? Can you hear me?"

Chapter Thirty-four: Jaden

Everyone still had many questions for Salvatore, but suddenly, none of that seemed to matter. Jaden was thinking only of Malia, and he could tell the same was true for the others. He moved up to the cockpit with Salvatore, Venus, and Brian and watched out the window as the world went by below.

It was nighttime now, so the only things visible below were the pools and streams of city lights as they raced to Mexico. They arrived very quickly.

"Let Malia know we're here," said Salvatore as they came to rest.

"Malia, can you hear me? We're here—where are you?"

There was no reply for a moment. Jaden became worried but then heard Malia's thoughts in his head.

"I'm in the woods to the east of Chichen Itza."

Jaden relayed the information to the others.

"I'm going to light up the airlock," said Venus. "Tell her to watch for that and to fly up to us as quickly as she can."

Jaden let Malia know.

"She's ready," he said to Venus.

"I see you! Coming up now."

Jaden hurried down to the main level with the others. Only

a moment later, Malia came up from the airlock. Much to his embarrassment, Malia grabbed him in a hug. He wriggled away, and then she hugged Brian and Sydney, tears streaming down her cheeks.

"Get us out of here," Salvatore said to Venus. "But... not *too* fast this time."

"Yes, darling."

"The Sphinx is coming—in a giant saucer," Malia told them.

"They call that ship the Chariot of the Gods—and it has already arrived at our previous location," said Venus. "We are now high above the Atlantic. They're sweeping the area back there with particle beams—we got out just in time."

"What do we do now?" asked Brian.

"We must contact the Othali," said Salvatore. "Their weapons are stronger than ours, and they may be able to overpower the chariot."

"It would be close, but yes," Hathor told them. "I've got the specs for the chariot, and Majestic analyzed the Othali's capabilities after their battle with the Malor."

"It's the best chance we have," Salvatore replied.

"We can try using the Bermuda power station to contact the warship," Brian suggested. "The Malor destroyed the Miami station during the attack, but the Bermuda one may still have power."

"Why can't we just send a radio signal or something to reach the Othali?" asked Sydney.

"We have no way of knowing what frequencies they use," said Salvatore. "But even if we did, there's a good chance Majestic would be able to intercept our transmission. The signals we use between our vessels are encrypted and scrambled to look like background noise. But anything we transmit to the Othali would be in the open."

"The communication system at the power station probably uses similar tech, so we should be able to reach the Othali without Majestic knowing about it," said Brian. "The problem is going to be figuring out how to access the Othali systems."

"That won't be too hard—we have him," Venus told them, pointing to Bomani, unconscious in one of her medical pods. "I'm sure he won't want to cooperate, but we have ways of persuading him, I would say."

"Let me see if I can reach our mom telepathically," said Malia. "I used the Earth's magnetic field to augment my powers when I was fighting Lucifer, and I was able to reach Jaden from Chichen Itza."

"Try it!" said Sydney. "It would save us the trouble of waking his sorry ass!" she added, nodding toward Bomani.

Malia giggled, then focused. She closed her eyes and furrowed her brow, and remained silent for a couple of minutes.

"No luck," she told the others finally. "I couldn't sense anyone. Guess we're going to have to wake Bomani's sorry ass after all."

"I'll bring him around," said Venus, hoisting her plasma cannon onto her shoulder.

"What's that for?" asked Bastet.

"Persuasion," she told him.

Moments later, Bomani began to stir. He moaned, opened his eyes, took in his surroundings, and saw everyone staring back at him.

"We need your help," Brian told him.

"With what?" asked Bomani, his voice groggy as he eyed Venus's weapon.

"The Bermuda power station. We need to contact the Othali."

"They're not going to be too happy to see me... What benefit do I get from this?"

"You stay alive a little longer," Venus told him.

Bomani sighed.

"Looks like I don't have much choice, then. Alright. I'll see what I can do—but the Malor hit the place pretty hard. The reactor went into meltdown. The communication system could run on reserve power, but there's no guarantee anything's gonna work down there anymore."

"One way to find out," said Brian.

Jaden and Malia joined Brian, Salvatore, Bomani, and Venus up in the cockpit. Venus kept her weapon pointed at Bomani as she took them back down toward the surface. Only minutes later, they arrived above an island surrounded by a sea of blackness.

"Bermuda," Venus told them. "Now, how do we get to this power station?"

"Can this thing go underwater?" asked Bomani. Venus nodded. "Alright, the power station is beneath the eastern end of the island. The entrance to the docking port is down by the ocean floor, underneath a ridge."

Venus took the ship into the water near the eastern end of the island. It didn't take long to find what looked like a cavern.

"Yeah, that's it," said Bomani.

Venus took them in, spotlights illuminating the way. After a couple of turns, they reached a wall of solid rock. Venus moved the ship up, and they emerged from the water inside of a cavity only a little larger than the saucer.

Malia and Jaden accompanied Brian, Salvatore, and Bomani down to the airlock. Malia and Jaden used their powers to fly Bomani and Brian from the airlock to the rock ledge at the water's edge; Salvatore came behind, keeping his plasma cannon pointed at Bomani the whole time.

"This way," said Bomani.

He led them up some steps into a tunnel. This delved far beneath the island, finally turning a corner and opening into a giant chasm. A black pyramid took up more than half the space, its edges like polished stone or glass. But unlike the pyramid Jaden had seen at the Miami station, this one had no electricity visible on its surface.

Bomani walked over to the pyramid and tapped its surface a few times. Nothing happened; he tried placing his entire palm flat against it.

"Not a chance," he told the others. "The system's down."

"Bring it back up," said Salvatore.

"I don't know how, man!"

"Why not?" asked Malia. "Back on the Othali ship, you told us that you learned systems engineering on the trip to Earth."

"I learned how to *use* them, but I'm no engineer. It would take someone with a lot more knowledge to figure out what's wrong with this."

"You'll forgive us if we don't take your word for it," said Brian. "Malia?"

Malia nodded, then turned her gaze to Bomani, focusing intently.

"Oh, no," said Bomani, raising his hands toward her as if to ward her off. "Not again—hey, wait—get out of my head!"

Malia concentrated for a minute, then her expression relaxed, and she said, "I think he's telling the truth—he doesn't know how to fix this thing. Who were those people I saw?" she added to Bomani.

"The Nooranis—Ervin and Suri. Husband and wife. They were our chief engineers—they're the ones who designed the stations. Now, *they* would probably be able to get this thing running, but unfortunately, they've been dead for several millennia, so... I wouldn't hold your breath."

"There are three power stations, right?" said Brian. "This one and Miami are disabled, but what about Puerto Rico? Is there any reason we couldn't use that one?"

"I don't think so," Bomani replied. "As far as I know, nobody's been there since Atlantis fell."

Brian looked to Salvatore; he nodded. They returned to the docking port and made their way back inside Venus's ship.

"We'll have to try Puerto Rico," Salvatore told her, explaining what they'd found.

Venus took them underwater and back out to the open ocean. Once they'd surfaced, she took them higher, and they took off into the night. Minutes later, they came to rest high above another island.

"Where to?" Venus asked Bomani.

"Northwest corner of the island. I've never been to this one, though, so we'll have to find the docking port."

"Hopefully, this one hasn't collapsed like the one in Miami," Brian added.

Venus took them in low and took the ship into the water.

"I'm detecting a large cavity inside the bedrock... and a cavern leading to it."

They sped above the ocean floor, arriving at a cavern moments later. Venus took them inside, once again illuminating the way with the ship's spotlights. They reached the end and rose into another docking port.

Jaden and Malia joined Salvatore, Brian, and Bomani again. They disembarked and made their way through a tunnel to a large chasm. There was another black pyramid here, and Jaden could see filaments of electricity flickering along its surface.

"Uh... what the hell is that?" said Bomani.

Next to the pyramid was a cube, its surface black and shiny—it looked like it was constructed from the same material. Electricity danced along its surface as well.

"If you don't know, then we certainly don't," Brian replied.

"Scans indicate that the cube is only about fifty years old," said Salvatore. "It's connected to the pyramid and transmitting power somewhere above ground."

Bomani moved to the pyramid and tapped on its surface. Jaden could see symbols and what looked like lines of computer code appear on the face of the structure. Bomani tapped some more, then swore in frustration.

"What is it?" asked Brian.

"Someone's reprogrammed this interface. I can't access it."

"Malia?" said Brian.

"Oh, come on, man!" said Bomani, backing away from Malia. "I'm telling the truth—I swear!"

Malia furrowed her brow in concentration as she started at Bomani. But moments later, she nodded to Brian.

"Who could have reprogrammed it?" asked Brian.

"No one, as far as I know," said Bomani. "I sure couldn't."

"The Malor gained control of the Miami station at one point," Brian pointed out. "Could they have come here?"

Nobody could provide an answer.

"They didn't come here during the invasion, did they?" asked Malia. "Could a rogue group have found this place after that—like the ones that made that camp out in Arizona?"

"Maybe," said Brian. "Although I fail to understand what purpose this would have served for them."

"It's a power station," Bomani pointed out. "If they've got a settlement around here, they could be using this place to generate their electricity."

"The age of the cube makes that unlikely, but this is a moot point," said Salvatore. "What matters for us is that we will not be able to contact the Othali this way."

They returned to the ship and found Venus on the main level; they updated everyone.

"We are left with only one choice," Salvatore concluded.

"We're going to Mars," said Venus. "Never thought I'd be going *there* again. But the trouble is that Majestic will be able to detect our engine output if we achieve escape velocity."

"Get us into space, and I can provide the acceleration," said Malia. "You'll just need to steer us—I don't know which way Mars is right now."

"Fair enough," Venus agreed.

"Now hold on a minute," said Babcock. "I'm not going to Mars. Forget it. Drop me off at your hideout in Antarctica, and I'll stay there with my granddaughters."

"That's not a wise idea," Venus replied. "I can guarantee you that Majestic has a ship down there watching out for my return. Not the chariot, I'm sure, and I can blow anything else they've got out of the sky. But if we do go there, it won't take long for that monster to show up. And with their armaments, they could destroy my compound."

"Then we need to get my grandkids out of there!" said Babcock.

"They're safe as long as *we* don't show up," Venus countered. "Our next stop is Mars. If you don't like it, you can get off here."

"I don't even know where the hell we are right now!"

"In a cave underneath Puerto Rico," Venus told him. "You'd have a bit of a swim to get back up to land."

Babcock glared at her for a moment.

"Fine. I'll go to Mars. Jesus Christ."

Chapter Thirty-five: Malia

"Keep your eye on this one, please," Venus said to Miguel, indicating Bomani.

"You got it," Miguel said, pointing his pistol at him.

Malia and Jaden returned to the cockpit with Venus, Salvatore, and Brian. Venus took them out of the cavern, through the water, and high into the sky.

"I'll take us out of the atmosphere, point us in the right direction, and bring our velocity as high as I dare," she said to Malia. "And then she's all yours."

Malia nodded. They rose through the stratosphere and into the darkness of space. When Venus gave her the signal, Malia went to work. She focused on pumping adrenaline into her system and then reached out with her mind. Imagining that she was somewhere outside the spacecraft, she concentrated on propelling the ship forward, channeling all of her power into the effort. Malia kept this up for several minutes until she felt completely drained.

"That's all I've got," she told Venus. "Was it enough?"

"Darling, we are now traveling at twelve percent the speed of light," Venus replied. "We'll arrive at Mars in a little over an hour.

Well, we *would*, but I'll need to start slowing us down before that to keep the engine output low enough to avoid detection."

"I doubt Majestic would detect us out here," said Brian.

"But they *could*, if they're looking this way," Venus told him. "And I'd rather not take any chances."

The rest of the trip was uneventful. When they reached Mars, Venus took them into orbit and began scanning for the Othali warship. They found it in a geosynchronous orbit, high above the Martian city where Venus and her comrades had lain in cryostasis for all those eons.

"Something's wrong," Venus told the others. "I'm detecting almost no power output from their ship."

"Take us closer," said Salvatore.

Malia couldn't see the ship at all at first but spotted it as they drew nearer. Indeed, the ship was dark, as if they'd shut off all the lights.

"This is strange," said Brian. "I wonder what's happened here."

Malia reached out to the ship with her thoughts.

"Mom? It's me, Malia—are you here?"

There was no reply.

"Mom? Can you hear me?"

"Malia?! What's happening—where are you?"

Malia felt herself smiling from ear to ear, tears of joy streaming down her cheeks.

"What is it?" asked Jaden.

"We're here at your ship," she told Melissa. *"What's going on— why is the ship so dark?"*

"That will take some explaining—how did you get here?"

"I'm with Salvatore and Uncle Brian and the other Martians— we're in Venus's saucer... wait, you don't even know about them..."

"You can come on board—they've still got power running to the hangar bay. Just give me a minute, and I'll let Commander Anhur know!"

Malia told the others that she'd contacted her mother.

"She says we can dock in the hangar bay! She's going to tell the commander that we're here."

"Sounds like a plan," Venus muttered.

She took them around to the other side of the ship. Sure enough, they found the energy field protecting the hangar bay to be operational. They waited until Malia had received the go-ahead from Melissa, and then they entered the docking port.

As they moved past the first couple of shuttles, Malia spotted her mother and several Othali soldiers waiting for them by one of the empty berths. She felt pure joy fill her heart for the first time in what felt like ages. Malia and Jaden moved down to the main level with the others.

"Time to rejoin your people, kid," Venus said to Bomani.

Malia thought it ironic that she was calling a 40,000-year-old man "kid" but then reminded herself that Venus was vastly older.

"Oh, no, now wait a minute—I helped you," said Bomani. "I can't go back to them—can't I stay here?"

"No," said Salvatore.

"Alright, everyone off my ship," said Venus.

"We need *everyone*?" asked Salvatore.

"Yes, I think we do. We've been jumping out of the frying pan and into the fire all day. It's time to take a breath and figure out how to proceed. Everyone here has information relevant to our current situation, not to mention a stake in the outcome. So, yes. All of us. Let's go."

Malia and Jaden moved out of the ship with Venus, Salvatore, Hathor, Bastet, Brian, Sydney and her cat, Miguel, Bomani, and Babcock—each Martian carried one of the humans, Malia took care of transporting Bomani, and they landed on the docking platform. Melissa greeted Malia and Jaden with tears streaming down her cheeks and gathered them both into a hug.

"I was *so worried* about you two!"

"We're alright, Mom," Malia assured her.

"We've brought you a present," Venus said to the Othali, pointing to Bomani.

"You," one of the Othali said with a scowl, drawing his weapon. "You're going to the brig." He left with Bomani.

"Commander Anhur is eager to meet all of you," one of the other Othali told the rest of the group. "If you'll come with us?"

The Othali led them through the ship. Unlike the last time Malia was here, the corridors were only dimly lit, with small emergency lights embedded in the floor providing the only light. Malia hadn't spent enough time here yet to be sure of where they were going at first but recognized the route to the bridge before too long. The Othali led them into Anhur's conference room, where they found the commander seated at the head of the table and a couple of his officers sitting in the adjacent seats. This room was also quite dark. Anhur got to his feet and shook Brian's hand; Brian introduced the Martians and Babcock.

"This is Lieutenant Bukhari and Ensign Shurani," Anhur told them, indicating the Othali woman and man. "I'm going to take an educated guess that you folks are the ones who survived the cryostasis and left this planet several decades ago?" he added to the Martians as everyone took seats around the table.

"That's correct," Salvatore told him.

Salvatore and Brian spent a few minutes giving the Othali a brief history of the Martians and a summary of recent developments with Lucifer and Majestic.

"We need your help," Salvatore concluded. "The chariot is vastly more powerful than our vessel, but we have reason to believe your armaments may be a match for theirs. If we can destroy that ship, then we will eliminate both Lucifer and the Sphinx."

Anhur considered this for a moment.

"Yet from what you've told us, this Majestic organization has agents embedded in every major government on your world. Taking out that ship would strike a blow, to be sure, but it would not end your problems, correct?"

"No, but it would cut the head off the snake," Venus told him. "And we can take care of the rest."

Anhur let out a long sigh.

"Well, I'll have to discuss this with my senior staff. Now that you've brought the twins back to us, we have no further interest in the affairs of Earth—this is not our fight. But as I'm sure you've noticed, we're not exactly operating at full capacity at the moment."

"Indeed—what's happening?" asked Brian. "Malia and Jaden told us that Bomani sabotaged your engines, but it looks things have worsened since then."

"We lack a critical component for our engine rebuild. Our teams down on the planet's surface are mining the material we need, but it exists only in trace amounts, and we're still at least a few weeks away from amassing a sufficient amount. In the meantime, our power reserves were running out, so we've had to power down all non-critical systems."

"What material do you require?" asked Salvatore.

"Diamond," said Anhur.

"Darling, I've got diamonds coming out my ass back in my compound on Earth," Venus told him. "How much do you need?"

"That's right—I remember seeing diamonds there," said Brian. "I forgot to ask why you have those?"

"To focus the laser triggers in my fusion grenades, of course," she said.

"I'll have you consult with engineering—they can tell you the precise quantity we need," said Anhur. "You would be willing to provide us with a supply?"

"Perhaps we could make a deal," Venus suggested. "I'll give you what you need to repair your ship if you agree to help us with our little problem back on Earth."

Anhur took a deep breath.

"I'll have someone escort you to engineering so you can confirm that your supply is sufficient for our needs. Meanwhile, I will discuss this with my senior staff, and then we can reconvene here and discuss the matter further."

Anhur and his officers left the room with Venus while the rest of the group remained at the table. Malia and Jaden took turns telling Melissa everything that had happened since they'd parted ways. But when Malia told her about all the things she could do with her healing powers now, Melissa's eyes went wide.

"Come with me," she said excitedly, getting to her feet. "I've got a patient who could use your help."

They followed her through the ship and down to the medical bay. Someone was lying in one of the exam rooms, and Malia recognized the man holding their hand—it was Nadia's husband, Awan. Suddenly, Malia realized who was lying in the bed.

"She's alive?!"

"Yes—her spacesuit took the brunt of the laser blast, but she still suffered massive internal damage. Her body has completely healed— physically, at least. But her mind has yet to recover.

"Awan, you remember my children, Malia and Jaden?"

He nodded to them with a smile.

"If it's alright with you, I think Malia might be able to help bring Nadia back to us," Melissa told him.

"With her telepathy, you mean?" asked Awan. Melissa nodded. "Yeah, go for it—we have nothing to lose at this point."

"Alright, I'll try," said Malia, taking a deep breath.

She reached out to Nadia telepathically. Although she could sense her thoughts, they were buried deep inside her subconscious mind. It felt like walking into a house with the electricity turned off.

"Nadia, can you hear me?"

Malia couldn't sense any awareness of her presence on Nadia's part. She pressed farther into her mind as if diving into deep water. There were flickers of light now; Malia tried to focus on these. Suddenly, she found herself walking around a barren landscape that had a fuzzy, dreamlike quality to it. The area looked like a desert, possibly the surface of Mars. But it was nighttime, and she couldn't make out many details.

She heard a noise somewhere behind her; turning, she tried to find its source. It sounded like someone moaning.

"Hello? Nadia—is that you?"

Walking half-blind, Malia stumbled upon something lying on the ground—it was a person wearing an Othali spacesuit. Kneeling down, Malia realized it was Nadia; she was on her side, curled up in the fetal position.

"Nadia, you have to wake up!"

Malia shook her by one shoulder. Nadia moaned again and rolled onto her back.

"Can you hear me?"

"He's a traitor... Bomani... he took them..."

"It's okay—Jaden and I are safe. I'm here with you now."

"Malia..."

"Yes—it's me. You were injured, and you're in a coma. But it's time to wake up."

Nadia moaned some more. Malia shook her by one shoulder again.

"Nadia—focus on my voice. You're healed, and it's time to come back."

The woman's eyes fluttered open. She gazed at Malia for a moment, then sat up and took in her surroundings.

"Where are we? Is this Mars?"

"I think so, but this is only a dream—we're actually in the medical bay on your ship. Awan's here, and Jaden and my mom."

"How do we get back to them?"

"You just have to wake up—we're already there."

Nadia stared at her in confusion for a moment, but then the landscape around them dissolved. Malia found herself inside the woman's mind again, and now it was brighter, as if someone were turning on the lights. Malia withdrew from her mind.

"I think it's working," she told Melissa.

"She's squeezing my hand!" said Awan.

"Nadia, can you hear me?" asked Melissa.

Nadia moaned, and her arm twitched. A moment later, her eyes fluttered open.

"Awan?" she said, her voice barely more than a whisper.

"I'm here—I'm right here, Nadia," he said, smiling and crying at the same time.

Melissa guided Malia and Jaden out of the room.

"Thank you," said Melissa, hugging Malia.

"I'm so glad she's alive—this whole time, we thought Bomani killed her."

They headed back to the conference room. Anhur and his officers returned a few minutes later, and Venus joined them not long after that.

"I've got more than enough diamond to fix your engines," she told them. "Do we have a deal?"

Anhur took a deep breath.

"We do. As much as I'd like to disentangle us from Earth's affairs, we cannot in good conscience ignore such a threat to humanity's very existence."

"Very well," said Venus. "I'll take my ship back to Earth and retrieve the diamonds. Malia will need to accompany me—that's the only way we'll be able to get back here without our Majestic friends detecting us."

"They will almost certainly have someone monitoring your compound," Salvatore told her.

"No doubt," Venus agreed. "But I'm sure it won't be the chariot—they'll want to keep her in New York to protect their puppet president. And we can handle anyone else."

"Perhaps, but it wouldn't take long for the chariot to get there."

"Do you think you could bring my granddaughters back with you?" asked Babcock.

"That would be wise," said Salvatore. "They may not be safe there anymore. And Venus, we should evacuate your staff, too."

"Yes."

"While you're off doing that, I'd like to get a look at this ship's specs," said Hathor. "Majestic analyzed your interactions with the Malor, and I believe your armaments are at least a match for the chariot. But it would be good to confirm the actual numbers."

"I'm afraid that information is classified," said Anhur. "But if you can provide details about the enemy ship to our engineering crew, we can run the analysis."

"Fair enough," Hathor replied with a nod. "Venus, I've got the chariot's specs, but can we upload the rest of the Majestic data to the Othali before you leave?"

"Of course, darling."

"My people have arranged quarters for the rest of you," Anhur said to Bastet, Sydney, Miguel, and Babcock. "I'll have someone show you there now if you'd like."

"Yes, please!" said Sydney.

"Alright," said Venus, getting to her feet. "Let's get this show on the road."

Chapter Thirty-six: Malia

Venus went to the bridge to set up the data transfer, returning to the conference room a few minutes later. Malia hugged her mom, then joined Venus, Salvatore, and an Othali, who guided them back to the hangar bay. They flew back into Venus's ship, and once on board, moved up to the cockpit. Venus steered them out of the docking port and set their course for Earth.

"Care to give us a boost again?" she asked Malia.

Malia nodded. She used her telekinesis to accelerate the ship; without the Earth's magnetic field, she wasn't able to provide as much power. But this meant that Venus didn't need to start slowing them down nearly so soon. Upon reaching Earth, she took them down to Antarctica, hovering high above her compound.

"Well, I'm not reading any signs of enemy presence," Venus told the others. "But, of course, I wouldn't if they've got their shields engaged. Let's open the hangar bay doors and see what happens..."

Malia watched through the windows as the giant doors opened far below.

"Aha," said Venus.

"What is it?" asked Salvatore.

"There's someone here, alright. They're using their particle beams to scan for us. I'm targeting the source of the beam with the plasma cannon."

A moment later, a fireball erupted from the saucer, slamming into an unseen object halfway down to the ground. The ship became visible, and Malia could see that the shot had torn a gaping hole right through the middle. Venus incinerated the vessel with a second shot. Taking them in low, she guided the ship into the hangar bay, closing the doors behind them.

"We need to hurry," said Salvatore. "The chariot could arrive in a matter of minutes."

Once they'd left the ship, Salvatore went to collect the humans, while Malia accompanied Venus to retrieve the diamonds. She led them down to the lower level, where they stored the fusion grenades. Venus hurried to the back of the room and opened a chamber that reminded Malia of a bank vault. Inside, Venus removed the lid from a metal box in the back corner. Peering inside, Malia saw that it was loaded with diamonds of all shapes and sizes.

"Wow... this must be worth millions of dollars!"

"*Hundreds* of millions, darling. It's way more than those Othali need, but we've got one shot at this, so we'll take them all. And while we're here, we might as well take some weapons, too, in case we need those."

Venus replaced the lid on the box, grabbed a crate of plasma cannons and several boxes of fusion grenades.

"Think you could levitate these up to the ship for us? Save us the trouble of carrying it?"

Malia nodded. She reached out with her mind and lifted the boxes off the floor. They hurried back to the elevator and took everything up to Venus's ship. By the time they'd returned to the hangar bay, Salvatore was hurrying over to them with Babcock's granddaughters and Venus's staff. Once everyone was on board, Malia joined Venus and Salvatore up in the cockpit. Venus opened the bay doors, and they moved outside, rising into the sky, but then came to rest high above the compound.

"Why are we stopping?" asked Malia.

"I want to give it a minute and see if anyone else shows up," said Venus. "Ah, and here they are. Someone's down there flooding the area with particle beams."

Malia stared out the window but couldn't see anything at first. Suddenly, a laser blast slammed into the compound, and there was a massive explosion, forming a giant mushroom cloud.

"Well, that would be the rest of the nukes," Venus noted. "Looks like I'm homeless, now."

"It's a good thing we got everyone out of there!" said Malia.

"Only the chariot could have penetrated your defenses," Salvatore told her. "We need to get out of here."

"Yes," Venus agreed. The ship sped off into the sky. "I'm going to drop my people off in New Zealand—we have a waystation there."

They dropped out of the sky only minutes later and hovered over a parking lot by a large brick building. Venus went down to the main level to say farewell to her staff. Once they'd disembarked, she returned, and they took off again, this time leaving the atmosphere.

Venus set their course for Mars, and Malia used her powers to accelerate them.

When they reached the Othali ship, Malia contacted her mother to let her know they'd arrived, and they docked in the hangar bay. Malia brought Babcock's granddaughters to the platform, Venus and Salvatore right behind her. Malia went back for the diamonds and weapons and took them over to the platform as well.

Three Othali met them there; two took care of the supplies, while the third escorted them back to the conference room. Babcock greeted his granddaughters, crying tears of relief, then they continued with the officer so he could show them to their quarters. Malia and Jaden sat down next to Melissa. Anhur arrived several minutes later with his officers, and they took their seats at the head of the table.

"Engineering has the diamonds, and we've recalled our crews from the surface. Once they finish the rebuild, we'll be fully operational. Now, we need a plan.

"Our people have finished the tactical analysis. The chariot is much faster and more maneuverable, but we outgun them. The energy output of our weapons is roughly fifty percent greater than theirs. And we have the antimatter warheads.

"However, defensive shielding is roughly equivalent for both ships. So, we'd have to wear down their defenses with blasters, and then we could finish them off with the missiles—if we can catch them.

"They'll be able to detect us using their particle beams, but we've analyzed the tech, and our people believe we can duplicate it with existing equipment—on both the warship and your saucer. And that will level the playing field when it comes to stealth."

"But we have one distinct advantage. Unlike the Malor, Majestic will *not* want to destroy this ship."

"Why not?" asked Brian.

"They want the twins," said Hathor. "That's been their top priority since the invasion, and I can tell you, they are *not* happy with Lucifer for losing them."

"And that means we've got a completely different dynamic, this time," said Anhur.

"So, what's their play?" asked Venus. "Their aim will be to reacquire the twins first, then destroy this ship—but how will they go about that?"

"They have more saucers in addition to the chariot," said Hathor. "We believe they will probably try to disable the shields protecting the docking port and board the ship with one or more of their smaller vessels. Once inside, they could send landing parties to find the twins.

"But I've got a proposal that would upend their plans. We'll move into the zone with the warship and take out the particle beam generators blanketing New York—the Othali weapons can get through their shielding. At that point, they'll be able to target us by tracking the source of the blasts. We've seen that they can generate the particle beams from their ships, so they'll have no problem tracking us and targeting the docking port. At that point, we'll use Venus's saucer to remove the twins from the warship."

"But then they'll be able to use their particle beams to track her saucer, as well," Bastet pointed out. "They'll send ships to pursue them."

"Yes, and we're counting on that," said Hathor. "I believe Lucifer will go after them himself so he can be the one to recapture the twins."

"How will they know the twins are on the saucer?" asked Sydney.

"They're sure to suspect it," said Hathor. "But if Malia uses her powers during the pursuit, then they'll know for sure."

"I can't get through their shields with my telekinesis," Malia pointed out.

"But you can get through them with your telepathy," said Hathor. "You take over the mind of one of the hybrids commanding the pursuing saucers and make them drop their shields. We take them out with the plasma cannon. Now Lucifer knows for sure that you're on Venus's ship. And when he engages us, we destroy him. I'll take on his identity, and we use his ship to take you to the chariot."

"Couldn't you just turn into Lucifer and waltz onto that chariot with the twins at any time?" asked Miguel. "Why do you need to draw him out first?"

"They'll know I'm an imposter if the real Lucifer is still on the field," said Hathor. "The saucers are sure to be networked with the chariot during the battle—including Lucifer's."

"And this plan eliminates Lucifer as well as the chariot," Salvatore added.

"You'll need Lucifer's full bioscan to emulate him," Venus pointed out.

"We've already got it," Hathor told her with a smile. "I scanned him at headquarters—you downloaded it from the data center. Once we're on board their ship, we plant a fusion grenade and get the hell out of there. Bye-bye, chariot."

"You'll destroy most of Manhattan that way, too," Sydney pointed out. "We'd be talking at least a million dead on the ground."

"We'll use the warship to lure the chariot away from the city while the saucers pursue the twins," said Anhur.

"And how do you know they won't use the chariot to pursue the saucer?" asked Venus.

"We don't know that at all," said Hathor. "But the warship will engage the chariot before the saucer departs and hopefully keep them busy. But the saucers can outrun the chariot, anyway. It's unlikely they'd pursue with their slowest ship."

"It's also possible we'll have taken out the chariot with the antimatter warheads before Hathor returns with the twins," Anhur pointed out. "We ran battle simulations while you were gone—if they go head-to-head with us, we win every time."

"They will figure that out pretty quickly themselves," said Salvatore. "And then adjust their tactics to utilize their greater speed and agility."

"Yes, and that's why we believe getting on board their ship will be essential for victory," Hathor replied.

"Can we get on board without using Malia and Jaden as bait?"

asked Brian. "This plan sounds pretty solid, but they may anticipate it and overwhelm you when you board the chariot. Then we lose the twins."

"I agree," said Melissa. "My children have risked everything over and over again—when will it be enough? I was worried I'd lost them for good when Bomani kidnapped them. I can't go through this again..."

"Mom, we *have* to help," said Jaden. "Those people want to kill everyone on Earth!"

"None of us can get on board that ship as ourselves," Hathor told them. "The only way through their security is to masquerade as someone who has clearance. And the chariot is a fortress—I'm not sure even Lucifer has a free pass. But again, if he's got the twins with him, they'll let him board. I don't see any other way in."

"Nor do I," said Salvatore. "I am also reluctant to put Malia and Jaden at such risk yet again. But it's the only way we're getting aboard that vessel."

"Well, now hang on," said Miguel. "How about this... Their shields don't stop Malia from using her telepathy, right? So, why not have her get inside the mind of the Sphinx and force him to drop their shields? That way, there ain't no need to get on board that thing—just hit it with your missiles and call it a day... right?"

"Maybe," Hathor replied. "And it would make sense to try that, first. But that ship has a structure on the bridge with the same shielding they used in the hangar bay of Lucifer's complex and the testing chambers at Area 51. And while we don't know for certain, we believe that area would protect anyone inside of it from the twins' telepathy."

"Well, I'm sure that's *exactly* what it would do," said Babcock. "When we prepared that area at the Ranch, the key was the material used in the chamber walls. We needed something that could absorb *every* frequency because their telepathy is all over the place. Those fancy emitters use electromagnetic radiation to dampen the signals coming from the kids' brains—but that's only going to be effective against their telekinesis because that uses a much narrower band. There's no way to block *every* frequency that way—and even if there were, it would stop the emitter from generating its holographic output, too."

"So, that's why their ships' shields can't block the twins' telepathy, either," Brian pointed out. "They're generated electromagnetically, too."

"Correct," said Salvatore.

"How exactly are we supposed to destroy Lucifer?" asked Jaden. "He's got our healing powers—Malia hit him with a plasma cannon, and he regenerated in seconds."

"Easy," said Hathor with a grim smile. "Blow his head off. Without a brain, he can't regenerate."

"That makes sense," said Malia. "Bomani told us that our powers reside in our cerebellums."

"Right," Hathor replied. "So, you take control of his mind and force him to stay still—and visible—while one of us obliterates his head."

"Well, that's the other problem," said Malia. "When I fought him at Chichen Itza, he was still able to communicate with the Sphinx when I was inside his head."

"Hathor can jam the signal from Venus's saucer," Salvatore told her. "But to be safe, it would be best to render him unconscious the moment you enter his mind. If he's able to warn the Sphinx, then the plan goes out the window."

Malia took a deep breath.

"I don't know if I'll be able to do it that fast..."

"You and I will practice first," Salvatore replied. "Commander Anhur, how long will it take to make the repairs to your ship?"

"Ten to twelve hours."

"Plenty of time," Salvatore said to Malia.

"I've got one request," said Brian. "I'd like Salvatore to be the one who goes with the twins. No offense to you, Hathor, but we barely know you. Salvatore has risked his life more than once to protect Malia and Jaden, so..."

"You have an established trust," Hathor replied with a nod. "I understand—no offense taken."

"You people are taking a pretty ballsy approach to this, and I appreciate that—I do," said Babcock. "But there are about a million different things that could go wrong with this plan. This is *Majestic* we're talking about here—and while I'll grant you that some of you have more experience with this organization than I do," he added with a nod to Hathor, "their whole thing is secrecy and running schemes inside of schemes. I spent the last decade and a half trying to crack this nut, and I'm telling you, no matter how well prepared you think you are, they'll have some surprises in store for you. I guarantee it."

"Do you suggest we just give up and go back to Mars with our tails between our legs?" asked Hathor.

"That's not where I'm coming from at all," Babcock retorted. "I'm just saying that you need to be ready for anything, and you're probably going to end up improvising your way through most of this. That's all."

"Well, listen, folks," said Miguel. "I don't know about you non-Earthlings, but the rest of us need some shuteye soon. We've been slogging this out for about twenty hours now."

"Yeah, I'm definitely going to need some sleep before we do this," Malia agreed. "Tapping into the magnetic field is exhausting..."

"Understood," said Anhur. "We're stuck here till engineering is done, anyway. Everyone, get some rest, and we'll reconvene in the morning."

Chapter Thirty-seven: Malia

Malia and Jaden returned to their quarters with Melissa; Malia fell asleep almost the moment her head hit the pillow. When she woke up, she realized that she was famished—she couldn't recall the last time she'd eaten. Melissa was gone already—Malia figured she'd probably gone to work—but Jaden was sound asleep in his room, so she woke him up and dragged him out of bed.

"What the hell—let me sleep!"

"Come on; I'm starving—let's go eat."

"Yeah, alright," he said through a yawn. "You're right—I could eat a horse."

They ran into Carl in the corridor, and he accompanied them to the mess hall. Malia and Jaden caught up with him while they ate, telling him everything that had happened back on Earth.

As they were finishing their food, Salvatore came to collect Malia and Jaden. They said farewell to Carl and followed Salvatore to the hangar bay. There, they found Venus waiting for them on the docking platform.

"Are you feeling refreshed, I hope?" Venus asked them.

"Yes," Malia replied.

"Uh... I dunno," said Jaden. "I mean, I probably could have slept a few more hours..."

Malia gave him a little shove.

"Don't listen to him. We're ready."

"Good," said Salvatore. "Here's the plan. Venus will be on her ship. You're going to enter my mind and try to render me unconscious immediately. When I sense your presence, I will send Venus a signal. She will alert you when she receives my signal."

"Alert us how?" asked Malia.

"Like this," said Venus.

Suddenly, a noise emanated from her ship that sounded almost like an air horn, startling Malia and Jaden.

"Okay... but without the Earth's magnetic field, I may not be able to do this," Malia told him.

"My understanding is that you've only needed that to overcome our resistance to your telepathy?" asked Salvatore.

"Right."

"When we practiced in Antarctica, you didn't use the magnetic field, and it still took me several seconds to eject you from my mind. That should give you enough time to knock me out."

Malia nodded; Venus boarded her ship.

"Whenever you're ready," said Salvatore.

Malia concentrated for a moment, then reached out with her powers and penetrated Salvatore's mind. She felt him trying to expel her but held on and focused on extinguishing his consciousness.

And though he resisted, it worked—Salvatore's eyes closed, and he fell to the floor. No sound came from Venus's ship.

"That looked easy," Jaden commented.

Malia restored Salvatore to consciousness, and they tried again. This time, he was able to alert Venus before Malia managed to knock him out. Once again, the noise startled Malia, even though she knew it was coming—she'd been able to sense Salvatore's message to Venus.

The next time, Malia put Salvatore under before he could reach Venus. The time after that, she was too late. After twenty tries, she'd succeeded only ten.

"I don't know about this," said Malia. "Fifty percent isn't so good…"

"Yes, but if you've tapped into the Earth's magnetic field, your powers will be exponentially stronger than they are now," Salvatore reminded her. "I believe in you."

Malia only wished she shared his confidence. But there was nothing more they could do—no matter how much she practiced, there was going to be an element of luck involved. Whoever was quicker to work would win every time. Malia had to hope that her increased power on Earth would give her the advantage—and that Salvatore would be able to jam Lucifer's signal if she failed.

They made their way up to the conference room, where they met Melissa, Sydney, and Miguel, as well as Hathor and Bastet. Babcock arrived a few minutes later, and then Commander Anhur and his officers joined them from the bridge.

"Good morning, everyone," said Anhur as he took his seat.

"Engineering reports that the repairs are completed—ahead of schedule, in fact. They've run their tests and confirmed we are fully operational. We are ready to commence our mission."

"So are we," said Venus.

The others voiced their agreement.

"Very well," said Anhur, getting to his feet. "We'll set course for Earth. It'll take several hours to get there, and then we'll proceed."

"Commander, I can get us there faster," said Malia.

"Oh?"

"Using my telepathy," she added, embarrassed to find the whole room looking at her now. "It won't be as fast as it was coming here with Venus—there's no magnetic field to use here. But it'll make a difference."

"I can help, too," Jaden added.

Anhur nodded.

"Let's go."

Malia and Jaden followed him to the bridge. Anhur ordered his crew to bring up the viewscreen and set a course for Earth. Malia could see the planet on the display—it looked like a star in the night sky.

"Take us out, Lieutenant," Anhur commanded. "Malia and Jaden will be giving us a little boost this morning."

"Yes, sir."

Malia imagined herself moving outside the spacecraft, looking back at it. Reaching out with her mind, she focused on propelling the vessel toward Earth. Moments later, she felt Jaden's power adding to her own.

"Sir, we're accelerating much faster than anticipated," the lieutenant reported.

Malia concentrated with all her might. It didn't feel like much compared to the thrust she'd given Venus's ship on the way here, but it was the best she could do. After a couple of minutes, she was spent and had to give up the effort.

"Damn, that's tiring," said Jaden.

"We are now traveling at four percent the speed of light," the lieutenant said, glancing at Malia. "At this velocity, we'll need to engage the engines at full reverse about halfway there to slow us down sufficiently for orbital insertion. But we'll arrive in under three hours."

"Thank you," said Anhur. "Malia and Jaden, please update the others with our ETA—and, well done."

Malia and Jaden returned to the conference room to inform the others. After that, they went to visit their mother in the medical bay. She gave them each a hug, wishing them luck, and then they joined Salvatore to pass the rest of the time on Venus's ship.

"How are you both feeling?" asked Salvatore.

"Ready to kick some Majestic ass," Jaden said.

"I'm nervous," Malia told him.

"Don't worry," said Salvatore. "You've never let us down before."

Sitting in the cockpit, staring out into the Othali docking port, Malia felt her anxiety increasing. She chatted intermittently with

Jaden and Salvatore, but the impending mission weighed heavily on her mind. Much of their success was riding on her—both in taking out Lucifer and destroying the chariot. She hoped she could rise to the occasion.

Hathor had worked with the Othali engineers to patch the saucer into the Othali communication system, so when the time came, the bridge notified Salvatore that they were entering Earth's atmosphere. Moments later, Salvatore brought up a holographic image in the cockpit center that showed only flames.

"Oh, damn—I forgot about this," said Jaden. "They're gonna know we're here because we're basically a fireball streaking across the sky! I got used to your flying saucers not doing that!"

"There is no reason for concern," Salvatore replied. "We *want* them to know we're here—if they've moved the chariot away from New York in our absence, they'll return it now that they know that's our destination."

Minutes later, the flames cleared from the image, and they spotted New York City in the distance. As they drew closer, the hologram showed the particle beams forming the dome over Manhattan, but there was no sign of any Majestic vessels in the area.

"I don't see their ships," Jaden observed.

"Hold on, you will," Salvatore assured him.

The Othali weapons fired at several points on the ground around the outer edges of Manhattan. Suddenly, the particle beams disappeared. Moments later, laser blasts exploded against their hull; Malia could feel nothing from inside Venus's saucer but noted through the windows that the rest of the docking port seemed to be shaking relative to their position.

Next, Malia spotted particle beams emanating from the Othali ship, flooding the area around the source of the weapons fire. They exposed a giant saucer bearing down on their position. The Othali fired on the vessel, hitting it with several laser blasts. But Malia noticed something else that sent a chill down her spine—there was an entire fleet of flying saucers beyond the chariot.

"Salvatore, we've got a little problem," said a voice over the speakers; Malia recognized it as Hathor's. "They have more saucers than we knew about—I'm counting fifty."

"Yes, we see it," he replied. "I do not believe this alters our plan."

"No, I don't think so either, for the most part. But you may want to depart a little sooner than we discussed—the air is going to be thick with those things once they engage."

"Malia, see if you can find the chariot's commander with your telepathy," said Salvatore.

Malia nodded. Reaching out with her mind, she searched but couldn't find anyone telepathically.

"They've shielded the *entire* chariot from our powers," she told Salvatore. "I'm sorry."

Salvatore relayed the information to Hathor.

"Understood," she replied. "It would seem my schematics are out of date."

As Malia watched the hologram, she saw the saucers suddenly surround the Othali warship, firing on it from all angles. The Othali blasters returned fire, creating a chaotic maelstrom of laser blasts around the ship. With a direct hit, they took out a saucer in one shot. But the saucers moved so fast that there weren't many direct hits.

"Time to leave," said Salvatore.

Malia noticed that a dozen saucers had converged on the entry to the docking port, firing at close range. A moment later, they shot out of the hangar bay and high into the sky. Malia could see six or seven saucers give chase, but only seconds later, they moved beyond the particle beams, and the ships were no longer visible.

"They may suspect we're a decoy," said Salvatore. "Most of the ships are still back there firing at the docking port."

At that moment, one of the pursuing ships hit them with a laser blast. Salvatore fired the plasma cannon at its source, and there was a giant explosion.

"Malia, this would be a good time for you to act against one of the commanders."

Malia nodded, focusing through the windows to their rear. Reaching out with her powers, she could sense the minds of dozens of hybrids aboard the enemy ships. Choosing the nearest vessel, she found its commander in the cockpit. Penetrating his mind, she planted a single command with the full force of her will: "*Lower the shields.*"

Suddenly, a saucer became visible behind them. Salvatore fired the plasma cannon, destroying the ship in one shot.

"One more saucer just took off in your direction," Hathor's voice reported over the speakers moments later.

"*That* will be Lucifer," said Salvatore. "He truly believed we were a decoy, then. The others must have alerted him to your presence here."

Malia found another saucer with her telepathy and entered the mind of its commander. She forced her to lower the shields; Salvatore fired the plasma cannon when it became visible, blasting it out of the sky. But after that, Malia realized that she couldn't find any hybrids pursuing them anymore.

"The other ships must have given up the chase," she told Salvatore. "I can't sense anyone else out there anymore."

"Lucifer must have ordered them to clear the field," said Salvatore. "Be ready. I'll bring us to rest and make us visible to make sure Lucifer can find us. The moment you sense his presence, go ahead and enter his mind. Once he's unconscious, we'll use the particle emitter to locate his ship."

Malia took a deep breath. Focusing inside of herself, she flooded her body with adrenaline. Within moments, she felt incredible power coursing through her system.

"I'm ready."

Salvatore stopped the ship. They were hovering high above a vast mountain range—Malia guessed it must have been the Rockies. Reaching out with her mind, she tried to find Lucifer, but there was no one out there.

"I don't sense him," she told Salvatore and Jaden.

"He'll be here," Salvatore replied. "Give it a little more time."

Malia continued searching, trying to sense anyone else sharing the sky with them. But the minutes dragged by, and still, there was nobody. Finally, Salvatore used the ship's particle emitter to scan the area. This didn't show any other ships nearby, either.

"What the hell is he doing?" asked Jaden.

"He must not be coming in too close because he knows we can detect him with the particle beams," said Malia. "And his ship is no match for this one because we've got the plasma cannon..."

Suddenly, Salvatore fixed her with a keen gaze.

"Someone's boarded the ship."

"What? Who—and how?" demanded Jaden.

"It must be Lucifer disguised as Venus," Salvatore told them. "Quickly—we need to retrieve the weapons!"

They dropped to the main level. Salvatore grabbed the fusion grenades and two plasma cannons from the storage compartment, handing one of the cannons to Jaden.

"Lucifer must be here somewhere—see if you can find him," Salvatore said to Malia.

But an instant later, a plasma blast slammed into the interior wall of the ship; an explosion threw the three of them into the opposite wall. There was a giant hole in the hull, and Malia had a clear view of the blue sky beyond. She knew that Lucifer must have fired the cannon that caused this.

"Fly!" yelled Salvatore.

Malia didn't need to be told twice; she shot out through the opening, Salvatore and Jaden right behind her.

Chapter Thirty-eight: Hathor

Anhur had asked the rest of the humans and Martians to wait in the conference room—he made sure their holographic viewscreen was active so they could follow the course of the battle. But he'd invited Hathor to join him on the bridge due to her involvement in planning the operation and assigned her a workstation. Salvatore had taken off with the twins moments before, but only a handful of the enemy saucers pursued them.

"Commander, Majestic must believe Salvatore's ship is a decoy," said Hathor.

The remaining saucers continued firing on them non-stop, with a large contingent targeting the docking port. They had entire blaster banks programmed to target the saucers and return fire automatically.

"Fire!" shouted Anhur.

Hathor watched a massive laser blast hit the chariot, but the ship disappeared from view before the Othali could fire a second shot.

"Direct hit, sir," said the lieutenant, "but they moved away immediately."

The viewscreen changed, showing the chariot's new location.

They returned fire, and Hathor felt her console shake as the blast hit the warship.

"Fire!" yelled Anhur.

But this time, the chariot had moved off before the Othali could react. This continued for a few minutes—the enemy hit them with every shot, but the warship managed to find its target only half the time.

"Sir, shields are holding, but it's only a matter of time before they fail," said the lieutenant. "We're weakening their defenses, too, but more slowly."

"Understood," the commander replied. "Stick to the plan—we knew this would be a battle of attrition."

"Commander, at this rate, our shields will fail before theirs weaken sufficiently for the antimatter weapons to be effective," Hathor told him.

"How close is it?" asked Anhur.

"Very," Hathor replied. "A ten percent increase in our hit rate or our power output would make up the difference."

"Lieutenant, enable automatic targeting for the primary blasters—we've got to hit them faster."

"Yes, sir."

"Engineering—we need to increase power output to the main weapons."

"Sir, we're already at maximum," said a voice over the intercom. "We could fry the circuits if we go any higher."

"They designed the system with a safety margin," said Anhur. "Override the protocol—we only need ten percent more."

"Yes, sir."

"Commander, the saucers are moving off," said an ensign at one of the rear consoles.

"Where are they going?"

"Not far—they're gathering off our port flank, about a kilometer away."

"Hathor—any idea what they're up to?"

"I'm sorry, but no."

"Sir, one saucer has broken away—it's following the same trajectory as Salvatore's ship."

"That must be Lucifer," said Hathor. "They've realized that our saucer wasn't a decoy."

She notified Salvatore, but a moment later, felt the warship shake much more forcefully than before.

"Ensign, what was that?" Anhur demanded.

"Something hit us... Sir, they crashed one of the saucers into the docking port."

"They're using their ships as missiles!" said Hathor.

"A few more hits like that, and they'll breach the hangar bay," said the ensign.

"Lieutenant, set a course out over the ocean—maximum velocity," said the commander.

"Yes, sir."

"Ensign, evacuate the docking port and close the blast doors—we need to seal it off from the rest of the ship."

"Yes, sir."

"We're in trouble if they board us," said Hathor. "Using their emitters, the hybrids can replicate any member of your crew and infiltrate your command structure."

"The docking port was designed to contain this kind of threat," Anhur replied. "The walls and blast doors to that area have the same shielding as the hull."

The warship shimmied again moments later.

"Another saucer hit the docking port, sir," said the ensign.

"Commander, the chariot is giving chase," the lieutenant announced. "They've moved away from the city, and we're both over open water now."

Hathor watched the viewscreen as the two vessels exchanged another round of blaster fire. Her analysis showed the Othali closing the gap in the rate of shield reduction. The next moment, the ship began shaking again, and this time didn't stop.

"Ensign?" said Anhur.

"Multiple sequential saucer strikes, sir... They've breached the docking port!"

The shaking let up for a minute, but then the ship shook so violently that Hathor fell out of her seat.

"Massive detonation inside the hangar bay," the ensign reported. "Interior blast shields are holding, but it looks like we've lost every shuttle."

"Damn," Anhur muttered.

Hathor retook her seat in time to see another blaster exchange between the warship and the chariot. She rechecked her console.

"A few more direct hits and the chariot's shields will be weak enough for an antimatter strike."

"Lieutenant, ready missiles," Anhur ordered.

"Yes, sir... Commander, missile systems are offline."

"What? Explain!"

"It looks like the blast in the hangar bay damaged the relays... I can't reroute."

"Damn! Engineering—we've got a problem. I need antimatter missiles back online immediately!"

"The hardline has been severed, sir," a voice responded. "Sending crews now."

"Understood. Hathor, any word from Salvatore?"

"Not yet."

"He'd better hurry," Anhur muttered.

Chapter Thirty-nine: Malia

Malia flew into the sky, turning just in time to see a second plasma shot slam into their saucer. This time, the ship exploded into a million pieces. Reaching out telepathically, Malia focused on the source of cannon fire and briefly sensed Lucifer's presence before she lost him again. She scanned the airspace around them but couldn't find him.

Searching the terrain below, she spotted a river flowing through a canyon, with a meadow on one side. Malia flew down to the ground, landing in the field up close to the cliff face, Salvatore and Jaden following close behind.

"What the hell was that?" Jaden demanded. "I thought he wanted to capture us, not kill us!"

"He won't kill us," said Malia, scanning the sky.

"Sure seems like he tried to just now!"

"Lucifer wants *me* dead," said Salvatore, "but he knows the two of you would recover quickly from cannon fire."

"Yeah, I guess that's true..."

"Be ready," Salvatore warned Malia. "He'll try to take us by surprise."

Malia could feel enormous power flowing through her body—

she remained alert, reaching out telepathically to search for Lucifer. Salvatore and Jaden had their plasma cannons in position, ready to fire.

A few minutes went by with no sign of their pursuer. Malia felt the tension starting to drain her energy and gave her adrenal glands a kick. Suddenly, she sensed a presence at the edge of her awareness. As she focused on it, something caught her eye—cannon fire at the top of the ridge. Malia found Lucifer telepathically and blasted her way into his mind. She felt him trying to expel her, but she overwhelmed him, using her full power to extinguish his consciousness. It worked—Lucifer was out.

Turning, she saw Salvatore kneeling by Jaden's side—he was lying unconscious on the ground with a hole through his chest.

"Jaden!" she screamed, dropping to her knees beside him.

"Did you find Lucifer?" Salvatore asked.

"Yes—I got him. He's unconscious up on top of the ridge."

"Let's go," he replied, getting to his feet.

"What about Jaden?"

"We'll come back for him—we have to hurry before Lucifer wakes up."

With one last glance at her brother, Malia took to the air. Climbing high above the canyon, she spotted Lucifer lying flat on his back near the canyon edge. She dropped out of the sky, landing nearby. Salvatore joined her a moment later. Raising his cannon onto his shoulder, he fired. The fireball slammed into Lucifer's head, incinerating it along with his upper torso. Malia had to turn away—the gruesome sight repulsed her, and she felt nauseated.

"It's done," said Salvatore. "I will assume his form and summon his saucer."

As Malia watched, Salvatore used his emitter to transform. In moments, his appearance was identical to Lucifer's, including the dark sunglasses.

"How do I look?"

Malia was stunned—even his voice was the same as his foe's.

"Scary," she told him.

They returned to the canyon floor. Malia kneeled next to Jaden; she could see his wound regenerating already. Within a couple of minutes, it had healed completely, new skin forming over the area.

"Jaden," said Malia, shaking him by one shoulder. "Jaden, wake up!"

There was no response. Malia was about to penetrate his mind, but suddenly, he stirred.

"Jaden!"

He groaned, his eyes slowly fluttering open.

"What happened?" he said. "I feel like I got run over by a bus…"

"Lucifer hit you with his plasma cannon. Right in the chest—but you've healed."

"Did you get him?"

"Yeah. He's gone."

Jaden heaved a sigh of relief.

It took a few minutes before he was strong enough to stand. By the time he did, Salvatore had brought Lucifer's saucer to them—it was hovering directly above the canyon. The three of them flew up to the ship and moved into the cockpit.

"I'm laying in a course back to New York," Salvatore told them. "Malia, can you let your mother know that we're on our way?"

Malia nodded—she could still feel the magnetic field augmenting her powers. Reaching out with her thoughts, she called out for Melissa.

"Mom—can you hear me?"

"Yes! Are you alright?"

"We're fine—can you let Commander Anhur know that we got Lucifer, and we're on our way to the chariot now?"

"I will. Be careful!"

"Okay, she knows," Malia told Salvatore.

"We'll dock with the chariot when we arrive," he told them, "drop a fusion grenade and then get out. This should be the easy part."

"You're sure we'll be able to get into their hangar bay?" asked Malia.

"I don't see why not," said Salvatore. "I'll let them know that I've got you—my signal will appear identical to Lucifer's. They'll scan the ship to confirm, and when they detect the two of you, they should allow us to dock."

Malia nodded, but she couldn't shake the ominous feeling she had that something would go wrong.

They slowed down a few minutes later, and Malia could see the New York skyline to the northwest. Directly ahead, the chariot was exchanging fire with the Othali warship. There was significant damage where the Othali docking port used to be—the edges of the area were scorched as if by fire.

"What happened there?" asked Jaden.

"I'm not sure," said Salvatore. "I've signaled the chariot. They've cleared us for docking."

Malia felt herself holding her breath as the saucer approached the enemy ship. But they passed inside the docking port without issue. There were no other saucers here.

"We have a couple of problems," Salvatore reported.

"What is it?" asked Malia, her heart jumping into her throat.

"They have shielding inside the hangar bay that was not present in Hathor's intelligence. It's strong enough to protect the rest of the ship from a fusion explosion."

"Meaning we're completely screwed?" asked Jaden.

"Meaning we're going to have to go farther inside the ship to plant the grenade," Salvatore replied.

"Shit," Jaden said with a sigh. "Why is it never easy?"

"What's the other problem?" asked Malia.

"They've taken control of the saucer," Salvatore told them.

"Meaning we won't be able to leave?" said Jaden. "You've *got* to be kidding me..."

"Malia will have to move us off the ship when the time comes," said Salvatore. "The Sphinx is summoning Lucifer. I'll go—you two stay here. I'm going to tell them that you're unconscious aboard my ship. Malia, use your telepathy to stay inside my mind and observe how this unfolds. If I give the order, you must use your powers to take this saucer out of the docking port and far from the chariot. Do you understand?"

"Why—what are you going to do?"

"I'm going to plant the grenade."

"You're going on a suicide mission?!" said Jaden.

"Hopefully not—I will try to return to you. But I'm going to set a short timer. If I give the order, or if they incapacitate me, you *must* leave—promise me!"

Malia nodded.

"I promise." She grabbed Salvatore in a hug, a tear streaming down her cheek. "Make sure you come back."

They dropped down to the lower level with him. Salvatore removed one grenade from the box, placing it in his jacket pocket, and handed the rest to Jaden. With a final nod, he dropped down to the airlock.

Malia and Jaden sat down on the floor, leaning against the wall. Malia reached out with her telepathy, entering Salvatore's mind, and watched as he left the hangar bay. Two hybrids met him in the corridor, plasma cannons strapped over their shoulders, and escorted him up to the main level.

Unlike the smaller saucers, this area was broken up into separate compartments. The bridge occupied the rear section of the ship. Several hybrids were sitting at consoles along the front of this area. It looked like there were windows on the wall above them, but Malia knew they must have been viewscreens.

The two hybrids led Salvatore to a chamber at the rear of the bridge, taking up positions on either side of a metal door—this reminded Malia of the openings inside Lucifer's compound in the desert. Sure enough, Salvatore walked right through the door. Inside, it was dark. Lights came up, revealing an enclosure in the center of the chamber. In the center was what looked like a golden throne. Malia was sure she recognized the man sitting there, but she couldn't place it; he looked human. He was wearing a golden headdress that made him look like an Egyptian pharaoh. In the center of that, just above his forehead, was a figure of a cobra poised to strike.

"You have done well, Lucifer," the man said with a smirk. "The twins are unharmed?"

"Unconscious but in good health."

"Excellent. Why did you not send the signal?"

Malia could feel Salvatore's anxiety rising—they were in trouble.

"I'm sorry?"

"We agreed you would contact us with your passcode once you had them to confirm you hadn't been replaced."

"Oh, no," Malia said out loud.

"What?" Jaden demanded.

Malia shushed him.

Salvatore said nothing.

"Remove your emitter," the Sphinx commanded.

Slowly, Salvatore reached down toward his belt. But at the same time, he slipped his other hand into his jacket pocket. Then in a flurry of motion, he armed the grenade, slapped it on the floor, and, turning, flew back out the door into the bridge.

Six hybrids were waiting for him, pointing plasma cannons at him. One of them fired but missed as he flew by them, slamming into one of the other hybrids. Extending his claws, he stabbed the man in the heart and ripped the plasma cannon off his shoulder.

He rolled across the floor as another hybrid fired his cannon; the shot just missed him. Salvatore returned fire, blowing a hole in the woman's chest, then ducked behind a console.

"Malia—you must leave NOW!"

"No! You can make it—run!"

"There's no time—you promised me!"

Reaching out with her mind, she tried snapping the nearest hybrid's cannon in half, but nothing happened—they were wearing emitters. Instead, she penetrated his mind and forced him to shoot his companions and then drop his weapon. Salvatore got to his feet and shot him.

"Now you have time!" Malia told Salvatore.

"You are incorrigible. Be ready to move the ship off the chariot the moment I'm on board!"

Malia and Jaden moved up to the cockpit. She could already feel the adrenaline coursing through her veins, but she boosted it anyway. The power flowing through her now was more than she'd ever felt before.

Salvatore ran down the corridor and hurried into the hangar bay. Watching from inside his mind, she saw him move into the saucer's airlock. Malia focused with all her might and flung the saucer out of the chariot's docking port and far across the sky.

Looking back through the cockpit windows, she saw the top section of the chariot lift away and launch high into the atmosphere—a moment later, a massive explosion annihilated the rest of the ship. The shockwave hit the top section and tossed it farther into the air.

"What is that?" asked Jaden as Salvatore rose into the cockpit.

Malia realized that the top section of the chariot had been a saucer.

"It must be an escape vessel for the Sphinx," said Salvatore. "Malia, see if you can penetrate his mind—make him lock his ship in place!"

Reaching out telepathically, Malia could sense only one person aboard that craft. She entered his mind with ease, forcing him to keep his saucer hovering in place. He tried to resist, but she overwhelmed him.

But suddenly, he sent a signal that said only, "We lost."

"*Who did you send that message to?*" Malia demanded.

An image formed in his mind of a hooded figure with its face hidden in shadow.

"*Who is that?*"

"*The Sphinx.*"

"*I thought you were the Sphinx?!*"

"*I am, but not I alone,*" he replied. "*You may have won this battle, little girl, but we will win the war.*"

Malia sensed the man biting down on a fake tooth, then inhaling deeply.

"*NO!*" she screamed. But it was too late—she withdrew from his mind as the man died. A moment later, his ship exploded.

"What happened?" asked Salvatore.

"He killed himself. And I think he must have set his ship to self-destruct."

"We still don't know the location of his command center," said Salvatore. "By taking his own life, he protected the rest of Majestic."

"We still won, though," said Jaden. "We killed the Sphinx."

"No," Malia replied. "The Sphinx wasn't just him."

"*What?*" said Jaden.

"Who else is it?" asked Salvatore.

"I don't know—I saw someone, but I couldn't make out their face. But I recognized this one, and I just realized where from."

Chapter Forty: Malia

The hangar bay on the Othali warship had been destroyed in the battle, so they had to board the ship through a starboard portal. Salvatore retook control of the saucer and took them in close, and then they had to fly from the airlock into the warship.

Once on board, they met an officer who escorted them up to Anhur's conference room. Melissa greeted Malia and Jaden with a big hug, tears of relief slipping down her face. Sydney hugged them, too, while Salvatore enjoyed a somewhat less emotional reunion with his comrades. Anhur and his officers arrived a few minutes later, and everyone sat down around the table.

"Well done, everyone," he said, gazing around at them all.

"Indeed," Venus agreed. "We've eliminated Majestic's greatest champion and cut the head off of the snake."

"Actually, we didn't—cut off the head, that is," Malia told them. She felt highly self-conscious as all eyes turned to her. "I made contact with their leader right at the end. The Sphinx wasn't just one person—there's someone else, too, and they're still out there."

"*What*?" said Hathor, as the others expressed surprise and disbelief.

"Malia established the identity of the one we eliminated today," Salvatore told them.

"Who was it?" asked Sydney.

Malia took a deep breath.

"Ervin Noorani."

The Othali at the table gasped.

"I'm sorry, who the hell is that?" asked Miguel.

"The Atlantis colonist?" asked Anhur.

Malia nodded.

"He and his wife, Suri, were our chief engineers," said Melissa. "They designed the power stations. But Malia, they died ten thousand years ago when Atlantis sunk into the sea..."

"No, they didn't," Malia replied. "Or at least, *he* didn't. I saw them in Bomani's head when we were at one of the power stations. He told us that he didn't know how to repair the system, and I penetrated his mind to confirm he was telling the truth. When I did, he was thinking of them. And the man on the chariot was Ervin. I'm certain of it."

"So, we have a two-headed snake, and we cut off only one head," Venus noted.

"Could the other one also be a former colonist?" asked Anhur.

"No idea," Malia said with a shrug. "I saw the other one in Ervin's head, but they were wearing a hood, and I couldn't make out the face."

The room fell silent for a few moments, the celebratory mood evaporating.

"We need to finish the job," Salvatore said finally.

"Yes, but not today," Hathor replied. "We don't know who the other leader might be, nor do we know where they're located. It's going to take some work to find them."

"We shouldn't wait too long," Salvatore insisted. "They still have plans to exterminate humanity, and we have not yet removed that threat."

"Yes, and at this point, I don't know what they're waiting for—but there's no more we can do right now," said Venus. "We have one saucer and no other way to move about. My compound is gone, and we have no base of operations. Hell, we don't have a place to sleep at this point. And we lost our supply of weapons. We need time, and we need to rebuild."

Anhur took a deep breath.

"We're going to need some time to repair the damage to our hangar bay. And we'll need to build at least a couple of new shuttles—I'm not willing to undertake an interstellar voyage without them. You are welcome to stay on board and use our fabrication facilities while we do this."

"Thank you," said Salvatore. "And meanwhile, we should explore our options for establishing a permanent base somewhere."

"I have some ideas about that," Brian told him.

"Me and Malia were talking," said Jaden, glancing at her for a moment before continuing, "and we were wondering if maybe we could stay here. You know, on Earth, instead of going to some planet hundreds of years away."

"You two and your mother are free to stay or go as you please," said Anhur.

"We'll talk," Melissa added, fixing Jaden with a curious look.

"Right, no, but I mean *all of us*—the Othali," Jaden added.

"I don't think so," said Anhur. "Humanity is not ready."

"We've lived among them for decades," Bastet pointed out. "Granted, it's been in hiding, one way or another. But we've proven it's doable."

"I have some ideas about this, too," Brian told them. "But it appears the decision doesn't need to be made today, right? I think, for now, we could all use a little R and R."

"Agreed," said Anhur, getting to his feet. "We'll adjourn for now. Lieutenant Bukhari, please take care of our guests—set up a workspace for them in engineering and... see to whatever other needs they may have."

"Yes, sir."

"Before we go," said Salvatore, all eyes turning to him, "we should verify that everyone in this room is who they appear to be."

"Yes," Venus agreed. "Using an emitter, a hybrid could have replaced any one of us."

"How do we go about doing that?" asked Anhur.

"It's going to take some work," said Hathor. "The emitter simulacrums were designed to be undetectable."

"Right before we destroyed Lucifer's compound, Malia was able to tell that Lucifer was masquerading as Venus," Salvatore told them.

"We should develop another means of detection, but for now, this will have to do."

"Very well," Anhur agreed. "Proceed."

Salvatore nodded to Malia. She penetrated their minds one at a time and confirmed that there were no imposters among them. Once she'd finished, the meeting broke up, and everyone went their separate ways. Malia and Jaden were heading to the mess hall with Melissa when they ran into Salvatore in the corridor.

"Salvatore," said Melissa. "I haven't had a chance to thank you for everything you did for my children—I owe you a debt of gratitude."

"It was my pleasure," Salvatore replied.

"We're going to get some food—would you care to join us? I'm hoping to hear more about the adventures you three have had!"

"I would enjoy that, but I'm afraid I have one more thing to handle down on Earth."

"What would that be?" asked Malia.

"I'll tell you all about it once I'm done," he said. "I promise."

Epilogue: Speaker Mendoza

Carla Mendoza was sitting back in her chair, exhausted and stressed beyond belief. Gazing around her office, she recalled the struggles and battles she'd won to get here—only the second woman in United States history to serve as the Speaker of the House of Representatives. And after the batshit crazy things she'd witnessed these last couple of months, she was no longer sure that she wanted to occupy this office.

The invasion had been bad enough—Miami and Washington D.C. gone. Half a million dead. The economy in turmoil. And humanity facing an existential crisis as a result of the realization that we aren't alone.

But this... At least the invasion had united humanity, pitting the citizens of the world against a common threat.

When President Ferris had requested a private, one-on-one meeting, Mendoza hadn't known what to expect. She'd thrown her full support behind Ferris in the primaries. And for the most part, they'd been able to agree on the legislative agenda since the election. But since the invasion, things had grown rocky between them. Ferris had adopted a hardline stance regarding planetary defense, pushing massive new projects that would weaponize outer space and provide the executive branch with sweeping new powers.

But what Ferris told her that day had rocked Mendoza to her core. She believed agents from some sort of clandestine, deep-state organization had infiltrated the very highest levels of government. Ferris told her that they had people in the CIA, NSA, DHS—and she'd even begun to suspect her vice president. Worse, she told Mendoza that she had evidence that the organization could be conspiring with an alien race.

Before the invasion, this would have been enough for Mendoza to consult her legal staff about invoking the Twenty-fifth Amendment and removing Ferris from office. But, now...

Mendoza recognized immediately that this threat could prove far more devastating than the invasion. Instead of uniting the people against a common foe, this had the potential to tear the country apart from the inside.

Only days after their meeting, Ferris had been assassinated. They'd apprehended the shooter, but then he'd mysteriously disappeared right out of police custody. No sooner had Roberts been sworn in than he'd declared martial law in the new capital. Mendoza had spotted the tanks rolling up the street right outside her office in midtown Manhattan—a sight she'd never expected to see in her lifetime.

Roberts had appointed a new vice president—a former Deputy Secretary of State, whom the Senate had unanimously confirmed. But Mendoza wasn't sure if she could trust her, either.

And now, some sort of battle had taken place in the airspace above New York. It had included flying saucers, laser weapons, and a final fusion explosion over the North Atlantic. She needed to coin a new term—"batshit crazy" hardly fit the bill anymore.

A knock at the door snapped Mendoza out of her reverie.

"Come in," she called out.

Gerald Simpson walked in, closing the door behind him. Only a second-term representative from California, he was a relative newcomer to Congress but had used his social media savvy to become something of a national superstar. He was an ally who'd been instrumental in securing the speakership for Mendoza.

"What can I do for you Gerald," she said with a sigh. Strangely, Simpson remained standing—stiffly, at that. Though they'd become close since his first election, he typically had a casual disregard for decorum that made her uncomfortable.

"Madam President, I don't have much time..."

"I'm sorry, what—"

"I have terminated Roberts and his vice president. According to the line of succession outlined by your laws, you are now the President of the United States."

Mendoza stared at him with her mouth wide open.

"You... what..? Gerald, what the hell are you saying?"

"I'm not Gerald," he said. Suddenly, a hooded sweatshirt and jeans replaced his suit and tie, and his face transformed. His skin was scaly, and the pupils of his eyes were slits like a cat's. When he spoke again, his voice was different. "My name is Salvatore; I am from Mars. A Martian-human hybrid replaced Nick Roberts several months after his election to the vice presidency. He was an agent for an organization called Majestic."

"He... you're saying he wasn't even human..?"

"That's correct. Neither was the new vice president. Majestic is plotting to take over the world and kill off the vast majority of human beings. My people and I are working to stop them. But we will need your help. I will be in touch again soon."

Mendoza opened her mouth to speak, but this stranger vanished into thin air. Seconds later, her door burst open, and several Secret Service agents rushed into the room.

"Ma'am, the president and vice president have both been assassinated. You're next in the line of succession—if you'll come with us, we need to escort you to a secure area of the building for your swearing-in ceremony."

To be continued...